Bolan dangled by his left arm

Tires squealing, the tanker careened into a turn. The Executioner was thrown to the right, his hand losing some of its purchase, the weight of his body working against him. Gritting his teeth, he hung on.

Hunching his shoulders, the soldier heaved himself upward. His clawed right hand closed on the strip of metal, his scrabbling feet narrowly missing the side step.

The tanker abruptly took another turn. It keeled wildly, like a ship about to capsize. Bolan was catapulted toward the front with such force, his hands were torn from the strip.

With nothing to hold on to, he plummeted downward.

DON PENDLETON's

MACK BOLAN.

Code of Conflict

A GOLD EAGLE BOOK FROM

WORLDWIDE.

TORONTO • NEW YORK • LONDON
AMSTERDAM • PARIS • SYDNEY • HAMBURG
STOCKHOLM • ATHENS • TOKYO • MILAN
MADRID • WARSAW • BUDAPEST • AUCKLAND

First edition October 1999

ISBN 0-373-61468-3

Special thanks and acknowledgment to
David Robbins for his contribution to this work.

CODE OF CONFLICT

Patriotism is the last refuge of a scoundrel.

—Samuel Johnson

I have no patience with those who sit around griping about how America has gone to hell. Being patriotic means that you get up off your backside and do whatever it takes to make your country the best it can possibly be.

—Mack Bolan

In memory of the men and women of the FBI
killed in the line of duty

Some people didn't mind being called crazy. Some even took it as a compliment.

Charlie Luft was one of them. For more than fifty years, his fellow Nevadans had been calling him Crazy Charlie. They poked fun at him for "chasing rainbows," as the polite ones put it. Others weren't so kind. They called him a nutcase to his face and liked to joke that his brain had been baked by the sizzling desert sun.

All because Luft was a desert rat, one of the last of a dying breed. For decades he had roamed the wilderness, prospecting and grubbing for a living as best he could. No one knew Nevada better than he did.

Luft had a good reason for not being upset by their barbs and taunts. The way he saw it, everyone else had it backward. *He* was the only sane person in a world of lunatics.

On that particular hot summer's day, Luft was reminded of the fact again when he pulled his battered old Jeep into *Baxter's Gas and Feed* on County Road 12. The engine sputtered and wheezed after he flicked the ignition. As the door creaked open on its rusty hinges, he slid out to find a sleek Corvette in the next space. A young tough in a leather jacket gawked at him, then snickered.

"Hey, old-timer. What planet are you from?"

They always did that. Whether it was due to Luft's battered hat, his greasy buckskins, his knee-high moccasins with the tiny bells attached to the fringe or the bright red sash he always wore around his waist, the old man couldn't say. Cracking a grin that exposed his missing front teeth, he responded, "I might ask the same of you, whippersnapper."

The young tough had a shiny ring in the lobe of each ear. As if that weren't silly enough, the youngster had the bottom half of his hair shaved in a crew cut while the top half was long and stringy and had been dyed with streaks of red. To Luft, the kid looked like a walking mop.

Shuffling into Baxter's, the old man held the door for a shapely young woman in shorts so tight he was sure they had to cut off her circulation. Rather longingly, he watched her sashay out to the Corvette. She was with the mop, which proved to Luft, yet again, that most people had no sense whatsoever.

"Howdy, Charlie. What brings you here?"

Ira Baxter sat on a stool behind the counter. That

was where he could always be found. It never ceased to amaze Luft that the puny stool held up Ira's considerable bulk day in and day out, year after year, without so much as cracking.

"I need some grub," Luft announced, moving to the aisle where canned goods were stacked.

"Off after lost Spanish treasure again?" Baxter quipped.

"Nope. Lost Mayan treasure." Luft held his own, and the proprietor laughed.

"You'd better be careful. The weatherman says the temperature is supposed to climb up near 110 today. It's going to be a scorcher."

Baxter was studying him. "You know, you astonish me. How many years have you been coming in here now? Twenty? Twenty-five? Yet you never look a day older than the day I first laid eyes on you. Why should that be?"

"Clean living," Luft said. Baxter laughed, but the old man meant it. He was outdoors all the time, enjoying fresh air and sunshine. Although he would eat canned goods when he was in a hurry, like now, for the most part he ate game freshly killed. He went where he wanted, when he wanted, sleeping in as late as he liked, with no one looking over his shoulder or telling him what to do. In short, he was as free as a bird, and he loved it.

Luft paid for his groceries and gas and pulled out. Turning south, he traveled until he came to a dusty track of a road that no one except a few hunters used anymore. It led westward, into the remote Desolation Mountains.

Clarabell rattled and clanked as Luft sped along, spewing clouds of dust. Beside him on the passenger's seat was his metal detector. In the back seat roosted his camping gear, backpack and mining implements. He was well prepared, as always.

Preparation was the key to his success. Some weeks he spent as many hours doing research in libraries and at historical societies as he spent out in the field. He had to, in order to track down the caches that brought in the big bucks.

Little did anyone realize it, but Luft had more than twenty thousand dollars squirreled away in a hole next to a stump in back of his shack. It was enough to meet his meager needs for the rest of his days, but the old man could no more stop prospecting than he could stop breathing.

There was always that next cache to find, that next treasure to track down. Not treasure in the traditional sense. Most people imagined him traipsing all over creation after gold and silver, but that wasn't always the case.

Over the years Luft had made money off old bottles, discarded books and even a keg of rare nails. Lost jewelry was a prime source of income. Once he'd found a watch worth hundreds. Another time, a necklace worth thousands.

This day Luft was after slightly different game. He had learned about an old World War I Army post situated at the base of the Desolation Mountains. It had been used as a training center and supply depot. After the war, the government tore it down and abandoned the site. As far as he knew, no one had been there in ages.

Luft's eyes glittered with possibilities. About a dozen years ago, at another abandoned base in southern Nevada, he had found vintage bayonets, ammo clips, insignia and even a few hand grenades. A collector had paid him hundreds for the whole shebang.

So the old man had high hopes as he came to the site his research had pinpointed. It didn't look promising, but then, they seldom did.

The post had stood on a broad V-shaped plain nestled against a barren range. No evidence of any structures existed. A row of shallow depressions marked where a perimeter fence had been, and lying on the ground at the bottom of a steep slope was a rusted coil of barbed wire. That was it.

Luft broke out his metal detector, but an hour of intense search proved unrewarding. Charlie had been concentrating on the open area, but now he moved into the narrow belt between the mountains. He struck pay dirt, first by finding several empty ammunition boxes buried under four inches of dirt.

The dry soil had preserved them well, and he knew a collector who would pay twenty bucks for each.

A little later the detector pinged, and Luft uncovered a perfect World War I Army helmet, the kind his collector friend would pay fifty dollars for, maybe more.

So far so good.

Luft strayed toward the north slope, slowly sweeping his metal detector from side to side. He covered dozens of yards without a reading and was almost to the slope when he decided that he was wasting his time and started to turn back.

The unit gave off a frantic series of beeps, the kind that told him something big was down there. When he swung the detector away from the slope, the beeps tapered, so he moved closer to the north slope, the signal growing stronger with every stride. In confirmation, the needle on the dial pegged.

It took some doing, but by walking back and forth and up and down, Luft established that the signal originated from a roughly rectangular area, maybe six feet by four. He suspected that he had discovered buried scrap tin or the like, but he fetched his shovel anyway and set to digging.

Six inches down, the shovel clanged dully against a hard object. Luft scooped more of the dirt aside, revealing a flat, smooth length of heavy-gauge metal embedded into the slope itself. More work disclosed that the metal was iron.

As the exact dimensions became clear, the old man's eyes widened. It was a door! He worked the shovel in a frenzy, eager to find out what was on the other side. Unfortunately, the setting sun sank before he could finish.

As reluctant as he was to quit for the day, common sense dictated he should. After a meal of baked beans and black coffee, he stretched out on his blankets and listened to coyotes serenade the moon. The gentle night breeze soon lulled him to sleep.

Bright and early the next day, Luft attacked the door again. By the middle of the morning, he had all the dirt cleared off. In addition to a heavy metal latch, the door was bolted at both the top and the bottom. He worked the upper bolt easily enough, but the bottom had wedged fast and resisted his every effort until he applied a crowbar.

That left the latch. Gripping it with both weathered hands, Charlie lifted. Nothing happened. He threw his entire weight into the effort. Again and again he tugged. Finally, grating noisily, the latch gave way and slid to the left.

Tingling with excitement, Luft grasped the handle and heaved. The door refused to budge. He tried repeatedly, with the same result. It was either too heavy for one man to work, or the hinges were too corroded. Either way, he was stymied.

Inspiration struck. The old man drove the Jeep over, unloaded his winch and threaded the heavy cable through the handle. Ever so carefully, he proceeded to reel in the cable until the moment of truth, when it was stretched tight and the door was quivering like a person with the chills.

A rending sound, a loud snap, and the door swung outward. Luft didn't let himself get too excited. For all he knew, the door covered a privy hole. Or maybe the Army had removed the items stored inside when the base was shut down.

Flashlight and crowbar in hand, he edged to the opening. A dank, musty scent tingled his nostrils. The beam swept over the ceiling of a large concrete chamber rife with spiderwebs.

He eased inside, on the lookout for snakes and scorpions. Something scuttled across the floor almost at his feet and he jumped back, raising the crowbar. The creature vanished in the gloom.

As Luft lifted the flashlight off the floor, his mouth dropped. The vault was filled with crates and canisters and barrels, the likes of which he had never seen. Either someone had forgotten to take the stuff when the Army left, or it had been left behind on purpose, buried where no one was ever likely to stumble across it.

Bending, he read the stenciled letters on one of the crates—Mustard Gas. He had to think about that a minute before he recalled that mustard gas had been used as a chemical-warfare agent during World War I.

Stacked canisters drew his interest. Each was labeled Chlorine Gas. That stumped him. He'd heard tell that chlorine was used in swimming pools to purify water, but he'd never heard of it being used as a weapon.

The large barrels he inspected last. Painted on them was the cryptic code TL-14. Luft had no idea what that meant. He rapped on one and could tell by the hollow thump that it was full.

Scratching his beard, he backed out. It was some haul, but how was he supposed to dispose of it? Who did he know who would be interested?

Locating long-lost caches and treasure was only part of the old man's stock in trade. Having someone to sell the stuff to was crucial, and he had a long list of contacts who would take various items off his hands. None of them, though, not even the military buff who had bought the bayonets and such, would be interested in chemical-warfare agents.

Sitting on the flat boulder, Luft racked his brain. There had to be someone, somewhere, who would pay handsomely for the stuff. It was just a matter of time before he found the right person.

CHAPTER ONE

The three dark angels of death breezed through customs at Los Angeles International Airport. Outside the terminal, they were warmly met by a swarthy man who led them to a sedan, handed over the keys and vanished. The trio loaded its suitcases in the trunk, then cruised toward L.A. The men behaved no differently than countless foreign tourists did every year. They smiled a lot and were polite to everyone they met.

No one would have guessed that they were three of the most ruthless terrorists alive. No one knew that the tallest of the three, a starkly handsome man whose wolfish features matched his predatory nature, was single-handedly responsible for the slaughter of hundreds of innocents.

No one, that was, except for Mack Bolan, aka the Executioner. Mingling with the crowd that awaited new arrivals, he had seen the men present their phony passports. Discreetly, he had shadowed them to the parking lot and tailed them when they left the airport.

Traffic was so heavy that Bolan didn't worry about being spotted. His blue eyes, piercing like those of an eagle, never lost sight of his quarry, no matter how far ahead they were or how many vehicles jammed the highway.

Bolan could ill afford to lose them. Too much was riding on his broad shoulders. As Hal Brognola, director of the Justice Department's Sensitive Operations Group, had pointed out when he asked the Executioner to take the assignment, "If we nail the Fox, we'll put a major dent in the worldwide terrorist network. He's one of their big brains."

The Fox. That was how the tall man was known. The Feds, Scotland Yard, Interpol—no one knew his real name. His official file was thinner than a toothpick.

It was rumored that the Fox's nationality was Libyan, and that he had gotten his start in the heyday of the PLO, back when that organization was more interested in piling up a body count than in racking up votes. It was also claimed that he was one of three men who had the authority to sanction terrorist hits worldwide.

Rumors, rumors and more rumors, Bolan mused. Sometimes it seemed as if half the intel the Feds gathered came from a friend of a friend of a friend.

All that mattered was that the Fox had made a

rare mistake—he had flown to the U.S. from Iran, by way of London. Since British authorities made it a point to carefully screen every flight from that volatile country, an alert MI5 agent recognized the Fox and sounded the alarm.

For while the elite security agencies of the world knew next to nothing about the terrorist, they did have an old photograph on file, snapped by a journalist who spotted a man running from the scene of a bomb explosion in Israel.

The British government alerted its American counterparts. Hal Brognola had contacted Bolan and requested his help. "I want the best on this one, Striker, and that's you."

There was just one catch. In this case, the Feds were intensely interested in learning why the Fox was in the U.S. "So we want you to shadow him until you learn what he's up to," Brognola had said. "At that point, what you do is up to you. Sanction him or bring him in, at your discretion."

Bolan would have preferred to be on an adjacent rooftop when the Fox disembarked at the airport. It would have been so simple to put a single shot from a powerful sniper rifle through the man's brain. But Brognola wanted to do this the hard way.

He reluctantly conceded that they did have a point. It defied reason for the Fox to come to America. Something big had lured him out of his sanctuary in Iran, and it was crucial the Feds find out what. For all they knew, the mastermind was about to launch a series of attacks on U.S. soil.

To Bolan's surprise, the terrorists drove straight through the city and onto Interstate 15. Proceeding northeast, they traveled mile after mile, giving no indication that they planned to stop anytime soon.

It put the soldier at a disadvantage. Trailing them through the congested streets of L.A. had been one thing. Keeping them in view on the interstate without being detected was another matter entirely.

He hung back as far as he dared, often keeping his car behind a big rig or an RV, only venturing into the open when an exit was ahead to see if the sedan took it.

He also used a cellular phone to keep in contact with Brognola.

"What the hell is the Fox up to?" the big Fed asked gruffly. Paper rustled in the background. "According to my map, the next city you'll come to is Las Vegas." He paused, then joked, "Say, you don't think he came all this way to visit a chicken ranch, do you?"

"Somehow, I doubt it," Bolan said dryly.

"It gets curiouser and curiouser," Brognola paraphrased. "I'll have a backup team waiting at each of the Las Vegas exits. That way, if by some fluke the Fox gives you the slip, our people will pick him up again right away."

That settled, Bolan hung up. Time passed slowly

once the scenic San Gabriel Mountains fell to the rear. In due course the terrorists reached Barstow but they kept on going, leaving no doubt that Brognola was right. They were bound for Vegas, or some point beyond.

Across the Mojave Desert they cruised, skirting Soda Lake and on past Baker to Mountain Pass. Once into Nevada, it was essentially a short, straight run to the sprawling metropolis that some had branded Sin City, USA.

It had been quite a while since Bolan had to pay the city a visit, but Las Vegas hadn't changed much. Magnificent casinos dominated the skyline. Neon blazed day and night. The traffic was a bit heavier than he recalled, and everywhere pedestrians hustled and bustled.

The Fox turned off at the Spring Mountain Road exit, which shortly brought the sedan to Las Vegas Boulevard. From there the trio headed downtown and pulled into the Golden Crown Casino. A valet hopped behind the wheel as a doorman took their bags. They planned to stay.

Bolan was completely mystified. It defied belief that the Libyan was there to gamble and partake of the city's notorious nightlife. He drove around the block several times until the terrorists had gone inside, then he wheeled into the lot and parked.

A black Chevy soon coasted into the space next to his. Out hopped a young federal agent whose meticulous blouse, jacket and skirt and neatly cropped hair identified her as surely as if she had a sign on her back that read I'm An FBI Agent. She walked to the passenger's side and rapped on the window.

He unlocked the door, and his car filled with the fragrance of perfume as the woman slid in and smoothed her skirt.

"Mr. Belasko? I'm Agent Brenda Mathews. We've been filled in by our superiors, and we're under orders to grant you whatever assistance you might need."

To her credit, the agent didn't voice any of the many questions her eyes mirrored. Bolan knew that she was dying to know who he was and why he rated so much clout.

"I need to find out what room the Fox and his men are in, and anything else we can learn, without them being the wiser," he said.

Mathews grinned. "Leave that to me, sir. There are certain wiles a female can use that work wonders in a situation like this."

Bolan went in with her, leaving her partner to watch the rented vehicle. He bought a newspaper at the curb, unfolding it as he stepped to the right of the front desk where he could observe the lobby without being obvious. He also overheard every word that passed between Mathews and the desk clerk.

"Excuse me, there, good lookin'," she said with a friendly wink and an exaggerated drawl. "I'm Agatha Winters, and I've been sent by the consulate to meet Mr. Akhbar and his party. Have they arrived yet?"

The Fox was traveling under the alias of Mehmet Akhbar, an importer of Turkish extraction. His henchmen also had false Turkish identification papers.

"Yes, ma'am, they have," the college-aged clerk replied, admiring her figure as if she were a showgirl on display. "They just checked in five minutes ago. Would you like for me to ring them for you?"

"No," Mathews said, smiling sweetly, "they probably want to freshen up before we get down to business." She began to go, then snapped her fingers and asked, "By the way, what room are they in?"

"Four-fourteen."

"Thank you." Mathews started to walk off, and again she paused. "They didn't happen to mention when they were plannin' to come down, did they, handsome?"

The desk clerk lapped up the compliment like a starved dog would gobble up a chunk of meat. "Not exactly, but I did hear Mr. Akhbar say that they had to leave by seven tonight. I can leave a message that you've been here so they won't go without contacting you first."

"How helpful," Mathews said, and shook her head. "That won't be necessary, though. I'll be in touch with them long before then." She smiled again, then pranced out of the casino.

Bolan smiled to himself as he pushed through the doors in her wake. She had lost the smile when he caught up. "Nicely done," he said.

"It's all in the hormones," Mathews replied. "At the tender age of ten, I found out that I could make any male eat out of my hand, and I've been doing it ever since."

There was no denying that she was exceptionally attractive. Red hair spilled over slender shoulders, framing a complexion as smooth as glass and as alluring as that of a fashion model. Yet underneath that facade was steel and grit, or Bolan didn't know how to judge human character.

"What now, sir?"

"We wait until seven."

That meant they had more than two hours to kill. Bolan contacted Brognola again to report the latest.

"I should have every federal agent in the state on hand to help out," Brognola commented, "but we both know that we have to keep a low profile or the Fox will make us." He paused. "What about the two agents you're with? Do you want me to have them pulled?"

Bolan glanced at Mathews. Her posture was as prim and erect as a schoolteacher's, her gaze locked on the casino. Although he preferred to work alone, in certain instances it was better to have backup. In this case, with so much at stake, she and her partner might come in handy. "No," he answered.

"Whatever you want. Keep me posted. I won't be going anywhere until this is resolved, one way or the other."

The soldier settled back to catch some rest while he could. Idle moments were a rare luxury, and he invariably used them to catch up on his sleep since he usually was a day behind, if not more. Folding his arms, he rested his chin on his chest and said, "Wake me up if anything happens.."

"Will do, sir."

It seemed to Bolan that he had barely closed his eyes when a firm nudge on the elbow snapped him upright. Agent Mathews pointed at the entrance, where a lanky individual in Western attire and a white cowboy hat nervously paced the length of the sidewalk. He blew puffs of cigarette smoke into the air like a steam engine gone amok.

"What's up?" Bolan asked.

"That sterling specimen of manhood is a local named Clem Weathers. His nickname is 'Dog'."

"Dog?" Bolan repeated.

Mathews nodded. "Something to do with a German shepherd that bit off one of his toes when he was a teenager." She chuckled. "Anyway, we have a sheet on him. About a year ago, he was involved in a trespassing incident on federal property. You might have heard the news stories. The Humboldt Standoff, the press dubbed it.''

Bolan shook his head. He was on the go so often, frequently out of the country for days and sometimes weeks at a stretch, that it was impossible for him to stay abreast of every little incident that caught the media's attention. He kept up with the headlines and saw an occasional newscast, but by and large he was too busy to fritter time away in front of a TV.

''Well, it had to do with a group calling itself the Sagebrush Patriots. They believe that too much land is in federal hands, that over the years our government has unconstitutionally seized property that legally belongs to the state and the people.''

Bolan knew about the sagebrush rebellion, as most called it. In states all across the West, from Montana to Texas, from Kansas to California, citizens were marshaling against what they saw as a government overstepping its bounds.

''The Sagebrush Patriots are led by a man named Harry Standish. Along with seven others, they tried to liberate the Humboldt National Forest from federal control.''

''How did they go about it?''

''By taking a bulldozer to a section of the forest that had been posted off-limits to the public by the National Forest Service because of destruction to the habitat.'' Mathews's voice acquired a peculiar tone. ''Standish is shrewd. He contacted the major media outlets in advance so there were plenty of cameras on hand. Standish and his people smashed through the barrier, rigged up a barricade of their own, raised an American flag on top of it and hunkered down to await the federal troops they were sure would be sent to stop them.''

''Were they armed?''

''No. Standish isn't one of those fanatics who want to violently overthrow our government. He seeks his ends by peaceful means.''

''So what happened?''

Mathews smirked. ''Not a whole hell of a lot. For over a month, the Sagebrush Patriots squatted out there, living in small tents and having their food brought in by friends. When it was clear that there wasn't going to be an armed confrontation, the media lost interest. Everyone went home. Standish and his people slunk off with their tails between their legs, and later they were billed for the damage they had done. That was it.''

''Weathers was one of them?''

''One of their more vocal members, yes. Dog wanted to take guns in and go down in a blaze of glory, but Standish wouldn't hear of it. Later, when Dog punched a Forest Service worker, he kicked Dog out of the Patriots.''

"For that you woke me up?" Bolan couldn't help inquiring.

Mathews was staring intently at the chain smoker. "There have been rumors on the street of late, rumors that a new group is organizing, that it will be more hard-core than the Patriots."

Rumors again. Bolan sighed. He still did not see any link to the Libyan, and bluntly stated as much.

"Sorry. I should have made it plainer." Mathews looked at him. "The word is that this group is in the market for high-tech hardware and explosives. We heard about it when they tried to bribe a construction worker skilled in demolition work into giving them lessons on how to trigger large blasts."

Bolan gave Weathers closer scrutiny. It was a tenuous link at best, but the Fox was known to line his own pockets from time to time through shady arms deals. And the Libyan was an acknowledged explosives expert.

As if she could read his mind, Mathews said, "I know it's a long shot. But seeing Dog there, and since it's almost seven, I thought—"

She fell silent as the ornate glass doors parted and out strolled the Fox and his two cronies. They had changed their expensive tailored suits for dark shirts and pants. Despite the lingering heat, each wore a trench coat. One carried a long vinyl bag.

Dog Weathers spun on his boot heels, cast down

his cigarette and stalked up to the Fox to warmly shake hands.

"I'll be damned," Bolan said.

Acting as if the Libyan were royalty, Weathers ushered the trio to a Jeep. They piled in, Weathers behind the wheel. With a squeal of tires, they pulled out, heading for the east exit. "Signal your partner to stay put," Bolan directed as he turned the engine over. A single car shadowing the Jeep might go unnoticed, but two vehicles would stand out like a proverbial sore thumb.

Weathers drove a couple of blocks to the Maryland Parkway, then turned north until he came to Bonanza Road. Taking a left, he was soon on U.S. Highway 95, bearing northwest.

Bolan hung so far back that at times he couldn't see the Jeep. It was a calculated risk that paid off. The gangly cowboy headed out into open country, sticking to Highway 95 as it wound between the Sheep Range and the Spring Mountains.

Mathews didn't utter a word. She didn't pester him with questions or call his judgment into account for leaving her partner behind. She simply did as she was told, a true professional through and through.

"Where does this highway lead?" Bolan asked.

"Clear up to near Reno if you follow it long enough. Along the way, it passes through all kinds of small towns." She ticked off some of them. "Indian Springs, Beatty, Scotty's Junction, Tonopah, plus plenty more.''

Hardly had she spoken than they passed Indian Springs. In due course, they came to a secondary road, Highway 160, which bore to the southwest. Enough light remained that Bolan could see the Jeep rapidly disappearing in the distance. He turned off Highway 95 and accelerated.

''I don't know where Dog could be taking them,'' Mathews commented. ''There's nothing out here until we come to Pahrump, some thirty miles as the crow flies.''

Traffic was sparse. Bolan had to switch on the headlights before too long. He lost track of the Jeep again, but he wasn't worried, since Mathews assured him that the next turnoff wasn't until Pahrump.

She was wrong.

They had gone perhaps half the distance when Bolan zipped past a dirt road and saw swirls of dust hovering in the air above it. On a hunch, he applied the brakes so abruptly that Mathews was thrown forward and had to fling out a hand to brace herself against the dashboard.

''Goddamn,'' she blurted.

Since no vehicles were approaching from the opposite direction, Bolan cut the wheel sharply, making a tight U-turn. He whipped onto the dirt road. In the glare of his low beams, the dust shimmered and sparkled like living fog. "Do you know where this road goes?"

"Sure don't," Mathews admitted. "Probably up into the mountains."

Just the sort of place someone might pick for a secret meeting, Bolan reflected. He held the speedometer at thirty until taillights flared ahead. Killing his own lights, he stuck to the middle of the road to avoid a mishap. A metallic rasp drew his attention to the Mathews.

The agent had taken a SIG-Sauer P-225 pistol from a shoulder holster and was feeding a 9 mm round into the chamber. She grinned, saying, "A girl likes to be prepared when she's around strange men."

The road climbed, winding deeper into the range. Forest replaced the grassland and mesquite. Now and then Bolan glimpsed the Jeep's taillights, but for the most part they traveled in murky darkness.

A switchback brought them to a broad shelf that afforded a sweeping vista of the land below. Above them, beaming faintly through the trees, was a pinpoint of light.

"A campfire, you think?" Mathews speculated.

Another quarter of a mile farther, a rutted track branched from the road into thick pines. Bolan shut off the engine and coasted beyond it to where a grassy hummock permitted him to pull over and brake. As he opened the door, he debated whether to go solo or have his temporary partner tag along.

Mathews didn't request to go, but she bestowed a hopeful look on him, the SIG-Sauer cradled in her lap.

"All right," Bolan said reluctantly. "But you do as I say every minute."

"Yes, sir."

Jogging along the shoulder to the junction, Bolan cocked his head to listen. Just then the throaty purr of the Jeep died. Faintly, a door slammed, then another. He gestured for them to go on and took a few steps, only to freeze when low voices carried to his ears.

Advancing down the rutted track toward them were two husky bruisers armed with high-powered hunting rifles.

CHAPTER TWO

As soon as the Executioner spied the riflemen, he grasped Mathews by the wrist and darted into the undergrowth, crouching behind a thicket big enough to screen a tank. He put a finger to his lips, but Mathews had already frozen.

"—hope to hell Garth knows what he's doing," one of the men was saying. "I don't trust those damn foreigners as far as I can throw a bull buffalo."

"If you want to play with fire, you have to make deals with the devil," commented his companion.

The first man snorted. "What the hell is that supposed to mean? I swear, Avery, you come up with dumber sayings than a fortune cookie."

"All I meant, Bo, is that we have to get the stuff any way we can. I don't like that Arab any better than you, but he's got what we need and he'll show us how to use it." The man spit. "Trust Garth. He's usually right about things."

Bolan cat-footed along the thicket to an incline

that brought them to a flat-topped ridge. There, in the center, sat a cabin built decades earlier that showed signs of neglect. The roof sagged at one end, there were cracks between many of the logs and both windows were broken.

Sinking onto his left knee, Bolan scanned the weed-choked clearing that surrounded the cabin. Light spilling from a window bathed a rifleman posted on a small porch. As Bolan looked on, another sentry sauntered around the rear corner and joined the man on the porch.

The Jeep was parked north of the cabin, as were a Ford pickup and a Chevy Blazer.

Bearing to the right, hugging the tree line, Bolan led the FBI agent around to the rear. They flattened against the back wall and cautiously crept to the northeast corner. Muffled conversation wafted through a broken window halfway to the front.

Crouching, Bolan moved underneath the sill, where he could hear every word distinctly.

"—apologize for this place being the dump it is, Mr. Fezzan, but a man like you can appreciate our need for secrecy."

"I appreciate it all too well, Mr. Garth," replied another man in a heavy Mediterranean accent. "In my line of endeavor, one can never be too careful."

Bolan surmised that the second man was the Fox. Could it be that "Fezzan" was the Libyan's real name? Common sense ruled against it. The Fox was too clever to ever reveal his true identity. More than likely, "Fezzan" was another alias.

"Now that the pleasantries are out of the way," the man called Garth said, "how about if you show us samples of the merchandise you have to offer."

"Certainly."

A zipper ripped open, most likely a zipper on the vinyl bag one of the terrorists had been carrying when they left the casino.

Bolan heard the clink of metal on metal, heard the scrape of a chair and a low excited oath.

"I'd never have believed it if I wasn't holding this in my own hands," Garth said. "Might I inquire how you smuggled this into the country?"

"That is a trade secret," the Libyan replied. "But I will tell you that a friend of mine lives in Los Angeles. He arranged for our car rental, and he insured that the weapons I had previously shipped to him were placed in the car's trunk." The Fox stopped. "Now, what about the payment you have promised?"

"Right here in this briefcase," Garth said. "A third now, a third when the first shipment arrives, a third for the second. That is the arrangement we struck, remember?"

The case was opened. A smug chortle issued from the mastermind. "So much pure gold! It is a joy to behold. You have no idea how difficult it is for someone like to me to obtain." Something tinkled. "How is it that you can get your hands on so much?"

Garth laughed. "America is the land of opportunity, of capitalism at its finest. That means we can buy as much as we want of anything we want, provided we have the money."

"You Americans," the Fox said. "So rich in so many ways. Imperialism is its own reward, is it not?"

"You're mixing apples and oranges," Garth said.

"I mean, for centuries America has exploited the resources of her Third World neighbors. Now she wallows in sloth and decadence, just as Rome did when Rome started her long, inevitable decline."

"I would watch that kind of talk if I were you," Garth said with venom. "America might not be perfect, but she's the best nation to ever exist, and don't you forget it."

"Strange talk from someone who wants to buy weapons so he can foment rebellion."

"You misunderstand, Fezzan. It's not my country I despise, just the federal government that runs it."

"A patriotic anarchist. Now, there is a contradiction in terms."

Bolan had hoped to hear more, to possibly discover how Garth had contacted the Libyan, and how many more people were involved with the Westerner. But fickle fate threw a joker into the deck in the form of one of the sentries, who picked that moment to walk around the front corner, a Winchester slanted across a shoulder. The man took one look, bellowed like a bull and tried to unlimber his hardware. The Executioner was faster, his right hand darting under his lightweight blue jacket and drawing a sleek Beretta 93-R. It spoke a fraction of a second before the Winchester. The rifleman's slug plowed into the ground, while Bolan's cored between a pair of high ribs to pierce the sentry's heart.

Dead on his feet, the sentry tottered against the wall, then slowly slid to the ground, a scarlet stain smearing the logs.

The guard who had been on the front porch barreled around the corner, his rifle up and ready, his finger on the trigger. Before either he or Bolan could fire, Mathew's SIG-Sauer thundered twice, jolting the man backward with each impact.

Frantic shouts broke out from inside the cabin, as well as by the vehicles, farther down the slope, and in the gloomy woods.

Bolan sprinted forward. It had all gone to hell, and his sole recourse was to make sure that the Libyan didn't get away. But as he rushed into the open, gunners raced toward him from the forest and from around the parked vehicles, as well as from the cabin.

"There! By the front corner!" someone bellowed.

The soldier snapped a shot at the four or five men

who had emerged from the cabin as the gunners near the trees and the pickup opened up. The only thing that saved him was that they were armed with single-shot rifles. If they'd had SMGs, he would have been cut to ribbons.

Pivoting, Bolan ducked against the wall, firing as he backpedaled. Mathews joined in, her SIG-Sauer cracking in regular cadence.

A withering firestorm of lead drove them rearward. Once behind the cabin, they turned and ran, retracing their steps, seeking to gain the woodland on the south side of the clearing before they were cut off.

A tall figure reared from out of the pines in front of them. Bolan and Mathews dived at the same time, both rolling as they hit the ground, both spared the buckshot that whizzed overhead when the gunman cut loose with a 12-gauge shotgun.

From a prone position, Bolan stroked the Beretta's trigger once. He had gone for the forehead, and a snap of the man's head confirmed the kill. Pushing to his feet, he sprinted for all he was worth, Mathews doing her utmost to keep up. They had a dozen yards to go when the night behind them rocked to the sound of rifle fire.

"Keep going!" the warrior shouted. He spun as a searing sensation racked his left shoulder. It did not stop him from streaking his left arm behind him and palming the big Desert Eagle that rode in a belt holster snug against the small of his back.

A gun in each hand, Bolan covered Mathews as he retreated himself, firing at shadowy forms that converged from all directions. Some scattered; some broke; some crumpled to the ground.

Mathews gained the forest. Bolan had a few feet to go when three more men spilled from the cabin. This time it was the Libyan and his friends. Shoulder to shoulder, in skilled military precision, the terrorists rolled toward the soldier like a human tidal wave, unleashing 9 mm slugs from three mini-Uzis. It was a crippling barrage that would have turned Bolan into a sieve had he lingered a fraction of a second longer. But, turning, he plunged into the vegetation, snagging Mathews's arm on the fly and pulling her along with him.

Garth's outraged commands rose from the clearing. "Find them! Kill them! Move! Move!"

The crackle and crash of brush and twigs were evidence that the triggermen had obeyed. Bolan weaved among the trunks, vaulting low logs and boulders in his way. Limbs tore at his face, slashed at his body. He ignored the discomfort.

It rankled him, fleeing. Had he been alone, Bolan might have carried the firefight to Garth's men, no matter what the odds. But he had the woman to think of.

Brenda Mathews was a highly trained agent. She

knew the risks of her job and accepted them. *He* was the reason she was there, though. That made him responsible for her welfare, and Bolan was unwilling to have her life on his conscience should she be sacrificed on the bloody altar of rabid fanaticism.

"This way!" the soldier whispered, veering to the right, heading across a patch of open, rocky terrain to a stand of saplings barely wide enough apart for them to squeeze through.

Hunkering a few steps in, Bolan hurriedly ejected the spent clips from the Beretta and Desert Eagle and inserted fresh ones. Mathews followed his example, changing magazines in her SIG-Sauer with expert precision.

None too soon. Half a dozen gunners burst from the foliage on the other side of the rocky terrain and spread out in a ragged skirmish line. They advanced warily, rifles and shotguns pressed to their shoulders.

Bolan took a bead on the man in the center. He wanted them a bit closer so he could drop half of them before they knew what hit them. Beside him, Mathews shifted her weight from one knee to the next, and a twig under her leg snapped.

"There they are!" a stout rifleman shouted. Immediately all of them were breaking for cover, firing on the fly, working the levers and the pumps of their weapons just as fast as they could.

The Desert Eagle responded in kind. The man Bolan had targeted was flung off his feet as if by an invisible sledgehammer. Bolan swung toward another target, but a blistering swarm of lead drove him flat. He crawled backward, yanking on Mathews's arm so she would do the same. Above them wood slivers and leaves flew everywhere.

Bolan changed tactics. A running firefight would get them nowhere, except maybe in a pine box six feet under. He had to reach his car. His duffel was in the trunk, crammed with the lethal tools of his trade, enough to turn the tide and put an end to Garth's private war on the government before it started.

But as the soldier lunged up, more forms materialized between the stand and the road. He had no idea where they were all coming from.

With escape to the north, east and west foiled, Bolan's sole option was to head to the south. Shots followed in their wake but most were wild, fired by nervous gunners at vague shadows. Still, wild shots were just as deadly as aimed rounds if by some fluke the bullets hit home.

Bolan adapted to the flow of the landscape, relying on whatever was available to screen them as they fled. Where trees grew thickly, he sped from trunk to trunk, always keeping one at his back whenever possible so it might take a slug meant for him. Where the ground was open, he ran doubled over so low that high blades of grass brushed his chin.

All went well for a while. The soldier and the Fed gradually outdistanced their pursuers. A narrow belt of firs was next in their path, and as they hurtled past the last stand, they drew up short at the sight of a steep, towering slope.

"Damn!" Mathews swore.

Bolan looked to the right and the left. The slope stretched as far as he could see. Worse, it was practically barren of plant growth and other places to hide.

"What do we do?" the Fed anxiously asked.

The sound of approaching footfalls in the firs spurred Bolan into doing the only thing he could—charge up the slope, legs churning, his whole body bent forward to better keep his balance.

Mathews scrambled up after him, but the chase was taking its toll. She panted heavily and slipped, so many times that Bolan slowed to assist her.

Mathews pulled from his grasp. "Go on without me. I don't know how much farther I can manage, and I won't be responsible for your death."

"We're together," Bolan responded, gripping her arm again with steely force. They climbed twenty feet, forty, sixty. A break in the slope appeared above them. Below, the firs spit out six or seven inky silhouettes.

"Which way did they go?" a triggerman shouted.

"Up there!"

Winchesters, Marlins and Remingtons blended in a thunderous chorus. Slugs tore into the soil on both sides of Bolan and Mathews. She grunted, stumbled and would have fallen if not for him. Looping an arm around her slim waist, he propelled her higher, his own legs nearly giving out as he drove them both up and over the lip of what turned out to be a rock-strewed shelf no wider than his shoulders.

Rounds jackhammering the slope, Bolan threw both of them onto the shelf, wincing when a rock gouged his ribs. He lay there, inhaling deeply, catching his breath.

"Where the hell did they go?" a gunner wondered aloud as the firing tapered off.

For the moment, they were safe. The angle was such that they were completely hidden, and the rim shielded them from any and all shots. Bolan rolled onto his side, taking pains not to expose his position, then sat up. His left shoulder hurt where a shallow furrow marked a near miss, but otherwise he was intact.

The same couldn't be said of Mathews, as Bolan found out when he put a hand on her side to help her up and his palm grew slick and warm with seeping blood. "You were hit."

"It's nothing," Mathews blustered, gritting her teeth as she slowly rose beside him.

"I'll be the judge." Bolan slid his fingers under her jacket, slapping her hand aside when she tried to stop him. "Be still. This is no time to go macho on me."

Despite their predicament, despite her wound, Mathews chuckled. "Why, Mr. Belasko. You're so grim most of the time, no one would ever suspect that you have a keen sense of humor when you care to show it."

"Who was joking?" Bolan bantered. To his relief, the slug had caught her an inch below the ribs, gouging flesh but sparing her vital organs. The bleeding was steady but not profuse. "I'll have to staunch this," he said, and started to remove his jacket.

"No, use mine," Mathews said. "I'm the idiot who got herself shot. So it's only fair that we ruin my jacket, not yours." Her features contorting, she gingerly shrugged out of the garment, quipping, "Besides, it's not as if I can afford designer clothes on my salary."

Bolan drew a stiletto from an ankle sheath strapped to his right leg. Spreading her jacket across his legs, he began to cut a long strip.

"My, my," Mathews said, nodding at the blade. "You are a bundle of wonderful surprises. What do you carry in your underwear? A bazooka?"

Bolan doubted that it was a loaded question, but he chose not to reply anyway. He finished slicing the material. As he turned to the woman, she looked up, her features pale, her jaw quivering. A delayed reaction to their ordeal was setting in.

"I've never had to use my gun before," she said rather timidly. Then, hoarsely, "They almost nailed us, didn't they?"

"We're alive, aren't we?"

Suddenly, she reached for him and lowered her face to his chest. She didn't cry or groan or launch into hysterics. She merely held him, and he held her, feeling her quake under him as if she had the chills.

It wasn't a sign of weakness. Professional soldiers sometimes succumbed to the same shakes. Bolan had seen it many times before. She would be all right. All she needed was time to cope emotionally.

Time she might not have. Dirt rattled on the slope below, forcing Bolan to let her go and peer over the edge. Two dusky shapes were heading toward the shelf, covered by others at the bottom. "Company is about to come calling," he whispered, replacing the stiletto.

Mathews had dropped her SIG-Sauer when she scrambled over the lip. Now she reclaimed it, the shakes fading, driven from her by the impending threat, by the call to action. "I'm okay," she said.

Bolan holstered the Beretta. Assuming a two-handed grip on the Desert Eagle, he rested on his chest and inched to the brink. He counted on blending into the background, but one of the gunners could see like a cat.

"There he is! At the edge!"

A rifle roared, followed by another, and the rest added covering fire that drove the soldier back. Some of the shots thudded into the slope above the shelf, cascading a fine spray of dirt and dust.

Blinking to clear his vision, Bolan tensed, then pitched to the left, the Desert Eagle fully extended. His first shot lifted the nearest rifleman off his feet and threw him to the ground. His second slammed into the other one, twirling the would-be killer and knocking him onto his back.

The men at the bottom let anger cloud their judgment. They fired and fired, churning the rim, wasting ammunition. At last the bedlam faded, and in its place came the plaintive groan of the second man Bolan had pegged.

"They won't try that again," Mathews predicted.

Bolan agreed. They would try something else, though, and he had to be prepared. There might be a way to the top he didn't know about. Or the triggermen might wait until sunrise so they could see what they were shooting at. The prospects weren't appealing.

"Where's a candy bar when you need one?" Mathews said. "Here we are, fighting for our lives, and my stomach is growling to beat the band."

The Executioner propped himself on an elbow to replace the two spent cartridges.

Mathews waxed loquacious, another trademark of a novice embroiled in combat. "Who would have believed it? Me, a simple Iowa farm girl, trading lead with a bunch of nuts in the wilds of Nevada?" She laughed. "Do I know how to pick careers, or what? Do you know what my mother would say if she could see me right now? She wouldn't ask me if I were hurt. She wouldn't offer to go for help. No, she'd stand there and gloat that she had told me so, that she had warned me something awful like this was bound to happen. Time and time again, she tried to talk me out of working in law enforcement. It's no fit place for a woman, she claimed."

"Your mother was wrong," Bolan said. He'd lost track of the number of outstanding female operatives he had met, and Mathews had potential for being another. She was green, but she was capable.

The woman blinked. "I'm doing okay, then?"

"You're doing just fine."

"But I'm scared, scared half to death."

"You're human, aren't you?" Bolan countered. He would have gone on, would have shared some elementary combat psychology, but a commotion at the base of the slope intruded. Three newcomers were busy doing something close to the trees. He clearly heard one speak Arabic. The Libyan had arrived.

It took a while for Bolan to realize what they were doing, and when he did, his blood ran cold.

The terrorists were setting up a mortar.

CHAPTER THREE

The Executioner and Mathews didn't stand a prayer. At that range, the Fox could blow them off the side of the mountain. A single fragmentation round would do the job.

"We have to move," Bolan told his companion, heading westward on his hands and knees. Standing was out of the question. Marksmen would pick them off like sitting ducks. He moved rapidly, banging his knees and shins on rocks every few yards. It couldn't be helped. The shelf was littered with so many, there was no avoiding them.

To the soldier's consternation, the shelf soon narrowed until it was barely more than a ribbon of packed earth hardly sturdy enough to support a snail, let alone the weight of a human being. Twisting, he said urgently, "Back! We have to find another way."

Mathews assumed the lead. Her hurt side hindered her movements, slowing them. By the time they came to the spot they had vacated, the terrorists had the bipod erected and the Fox was fiddling with the azimuth control.

"Hurry," Bolan urged.

The shelf wound around a slight bulge in the cliff wall. Mathews pushed herself as hard as she could, given her condition. Bolan, close to her heels, nearly collided with her when she unaccountably stopped. "What's wrong?" he inquired.

The woman pressed her body against the slope, replying, "See for yourself."

In order not to be spotted by the gunners, Bolan had to slide by with his body flush against hers. A few yards beyond, the shelf abruptly ended at a massive rockfall. Boulders of various sizes and shapes were strewed from top to bottom. Taking a gamble, he rose high enough to see where the slope resumed, which he estimated was forty yards away.

Trying to cross would be a nightmare. The boulders were lodged at all angles, their sides as slippery as marble. Wide gaps existed, where a person might plummet dozens of feet.

"Do we go on?" Mathews asked.

"What choice do we have?"

Bolan crawled out onto a flat boulder. From there, he worked his way up onto the top of another. It was barely six inches wide; if he slipped, he would fall onto a jagged stony spine. Edging forward by degrees, he had nearly attained safety when the night was rent by the rolling crash of a mortar round detonating.

For a few brief moments, the side of the slope behind them was lit up. In the glare, Bolan counted five riflemen and the three terrorists, all fixed on the point where they mistakenly believed Bolan and the Fed still were. A cheer went up, but the Libyan stifled it and fed another round into the mortar. A split second after the concussive whomp, the shelf again exploded in a shower of earthen clods and stones.

Mathews had clambered into the boulder field. She inadvertently recoiled as the second blast shattered the night. Then, biting her lower lip, she scrambled to catch up with Bolan.

The soldier forged on, selecting a route that would be easy on the woman. A third fragmentation round lit up the mountain, but the fleeting glow wasn't bright enough to catch them in its glare.

Bolan halted at the edge of a drop-off, a chasm only six feet wide but whose bottom was lost in Stygian depths. It seemed to run the full length of the boulder field. As he lay prone contemplating how to get Mathews safely across, she crawled up beside him, peeked into the abyss and gripped the edge so tightly that her knuckles turned white.

"When I was a girl, I always envied the birds their wings. Since we can't fly, how we are to get across? I certainly can't jump that far."

"You could if you had a running start," Bolan said, pointing at a long flat boulder below their vantage point.

Mathews looked, then grew paler. "I should tell you that I was never much into track and field. Soccer was my game."

"It's either this or stay here and get caught in the open when the flare goes up. They'll spot us then."

"What flare?" Mathews asked, glancing over her shoulder.

"Mortars fire all sorts of rounds," Bolan explained. "Frags for destroying an enemy, phosphorous smoke for signaling and flares for illumination at night. Once our friends back there tire of blowing the mountain up, they'll use a flare so they can admire their handiwork and see if we're still alive."

"Maybe they don't have one."

It was a lame hope and they both knew it. Bolan slid onto the next lower boulder and dropped a few feet onto the flat one. Turning, he caught Mathews when she alighted, steadying her. "I'll go first," he volunteered.

"This is no time to be fussy. I'll let you."

Smiling for her benefit, Bolan backed to the end, then faced the drop-off. He had ten feet in which to gain enough speed and momentum to clear the cleft. It might not be enough for most people, but for someone who was in perfect physical shape, whose muscles were tested daily in lethal combat, it was more than enough. He fairly flew to the brink, coiled and sprang.

Cool wind whipped the soldier's face as he sailed up and out. For an instant that seemed an eternity, he hung in empty space, the cavity yawning below like the maw of a gigantic beast eager to devour a new victim.

Another heartbeat, and a boulder swept up below him. It wasn't quite as flat as the first. It tilted near the upper edge. His right foot slid from under him. Flailing his arms, Bolan sought to stay on his feet. Mathews cried out softly. The chasm was set to claim him when he coiled at the waist and flung himself onto his stomach.

Bolan had done it, with only a few scrapes and scuffs to remind him of how close it had been. Swiveling, he beckoned.

Mathews moved to the edge and looked down, then at him. She made no pretense at hiding her fear. Sliding back until she was as far from the drop-off as she could get, she tucked her legs, pressed her arm to her wound and focused on the span to the exclusion of all else.

In a surge of motion, Mathews sped forward. So intent was she on making the jump that she didn't hear the crump of the mortar for a fourth time, nor did she realize that the darkness had given birth to a minisun. The bright light engulfed her at the very split second she leaped.

Startled, Mathews was thrown off stride at the critical moment. She pushed off on the wrong foot, recognized she had and frantically attempted to compensate by windmilling her legs. It had the opposite effect. Her body arced short of her goal, missing it by inches that in this instance meant the difference between life and death.

Bolan had anticipated she would have difficulty. Perched at the rim, he thrust out both arms and caught hold of her left wrist. It wasn't enough to haul her to safety but he did stop her from plunging into the chasm, at formidable cost to himself. Smashed flat, he clung on for dear life, every muscle shrieking in protest, his arms straining at their sockets.

He was aware that the flare was at its zenith, that the side of the mountain was lit as brilliantly as if the real sun were overhead. So he froze, afraid that any movement, however slight, would attract the gunners.

"I don't see anyone!" a man bellowed.

"We must have blown them to kingdom come!" another shouted.

The Fox wasn't so sure. Bolan saw the Libyan scan the slope, saw that wolfish profile turn in the direction of the boulder field. He had the illusion that the terrorist's burning gaze locked on to him.

If so, he was doomed. He couldn't return fire while holding Mathews, and he wasn't about to let go.

But the Fox gazed westward, then made a comment that elicited laughter and smiles. Some of the riflemen clapped him and his associates on the back.

"Nice job, pard!" declared a man in a broad-brimmed black hat. "For an Arab, you and your boys ain't half bad."

Even at that distance, Bolan noted the displeasure the remark provoked. Then the flare blinked out, and he was lucky if he could see his own fingers.

"Belasko?" Mathews said nervously. "Are you all right? What are you waiting for?"

"Hold on." Bracing his shoulders, Bolan drew his legs up under him. The strain was tremendous. His shoulders throbbed. Digging in, he hunched backward, hiking her upward a fraction at a time. He would have been able to raise her faster were it not for the angle at which the boulder was set. It threatened to spill both of them if he wasn't extremely careful.

A crown of red hair rose above the rim, then the agent's face, then her shoulders. Impulsively, she tried to help by gripping the rim with her other arm but the unexpected movement caused Bolan to teeter toward the edge. He was a hand's width from going over the side when he stopped himself.

"Be still!"

Bolan firmed his hold, slid his left foot backward

and managed to haul her high enough for her to slide onto her belly. She sagged, limp with fatigue. Her side was bleeding worse than before, and he regretted being denied the time to bandage her earlier. Without telling her what he was going to do, he shed his jacket, pulled the stiletto and soon had two long strips that would suffice.

"Sit up," the soldier instructed.

Sluggishly, Mathews complied. "You shouldn't have," she said when she saw what he had done. But no protest passed her lips when he hiked her arms, tugged her blouse from under her skirt and applied the first strip.

"Is this what it is like to be in a war, do you think?" the woman asked.

"Exactly like it," Bolan confirmed.

"I don't see how people stand it. The noise. The bloodshed. The savagery. If we get out of this mess alive, I think I'll put in for a cushy, safe desk job."

"You would be bored to tears inside of six months," Bolan stated. He tied a knot to hold the strip in place, then covered it with the second strip. It was crude, but it had to do until he could whisk her to a hospital.

"Thanks," she said meekly when he was done. "What's our next step?"

"We get off this mountain."

Suiting action to words, Bolan slid onto the next lower slab. The going was easier on this side, where the boulders were spaced more closely together. Mathews needed a hand only once.

They were almost to the bottom when an explosion boomed to the northwest. On its heels, the wind brought faint laughter.

"What do you suppose that was all about?" Mathews asked.

Bolan had an idea, but he didn't say anything. She would be upset enough once they verified his hunch. Taking her by the elbow, he warily entered the firs. The Nevada night was deathly still, the wildlife driven into hiding by the gunfire and blasts.

By the Executioner's reckoning, they were more than halfway to the shack when automobile engines revved in unison. Mathews clutched his arm and grinned.

"They're leaving! We're safe now!"

Headlights winked in the distance as the vehicles that had been parked at the site traveled down the rutted track to the dirt road, then headed toward State Highway 160.

Bolan didn't let down his guard. He wouldn't put it past the Libyan to insist that men be left behind, just in case. But after coming to the ridge and watching the shack for more than ten minutes, he grew convinced that Mathews and he had the mountain to themselves.

Garth had seen fit to cart off the wounded and

the dead. Anyone who might happen by later would never suspect that a raging firefight had taken place.

The soldier approached the front door, which hung open a crack. Aged boards on the small porch creaked underfoot as Bolan crept to the jamb and nudged the door with the Desert Eagle.

Gone were the lanterns and whatever else had been there. A lone rickety chair and a warped table were all that remained. He paced the single room, seeking clues in vain.

"What are you looking for?" Mathews asked. She had a hand over her wound, which was bleeding again. Her hair was disheveled, her face was streaked with grime and blood and her clothes were a mess.

"Sometimes we get lucky," Bolan said. But this wasn't one of those times. Not only had the terrorists given him the slip, which was bound to ruin Brognola's day, but he had also blown his chance to learn who the Fox had met with and what the man was up to. All he had to go on was a name—Garth.

"Come on," Bolan urged, ushering the woman across the clearing and down the ridge. To the southwest, a thick column of smoke rose above the trees, the tendrils a dusky gray against the backdrop of black sky.

"What's that?" Mathews mused.

Bolan knew. He had hoped that he was wrong,

but when they stepped from the pines near the hummock where he had parked the sedan, before them smoldered a charred wreck, the acrid stench of burned rubber and plastic heavy enough to make him cough.

"Good Lord!" Mathews cried. "There went your cellular phone. We can't call for backup. And now it will take us half a day to reach the highway."

"We might as well start now," Bolan suggested. It was advisable to cover as much ground as they could before daylight. Once the sun climbed, so would the temperature. In her weakened state, Mathews would be hard-pressed to maintain a steady pace.

For the longest while, the only sound was the tread of their shoes. Bolan swung lithely along, as tireless as a Marine. Mathews, however, didn't fare as well. By the end of the first mile, she plodded with her chin bowed, haggard, weakened by the loss of blood.

Dense growth hemmed them in on either side. Twice owls voiced the question always asked by their kind. A dozen times or more, the lonesome yip of coyotes echoed off the slopes. Less frequently, cattle lowed far below.

Midnight came and went. By one in the morning, Brenda Mathews was a spectral husk of her former self. She could barely lift one foot in front of the other. When Bolan touched her arm, she jumped as if struck. "What's the matter?" she blurted. "What is it now?"

"We're resting here until first light," Bolan said, indicating a grassy area beside the road.

"Nonsense," Mathews said, straightening. "I can keep going for hours yet. Don't fret yourself on my account."

"We're resting," Bolan insisted. But when he tried to guide her over, she stubbornly resisted. Yanking free, she stumbled, her heel caught on a stone, and she keeled backward.

The soldier caught her before she fell. Her pride cost the woman the last of what little strength she'd had left, and Bolan swept her into his arms with no further argument. Gently depositing her on the grass, he sat, drew the Beretta and placed it in his lap.

Mathews moistened her lips, then mustered a wan grin. "Sorry. I guess I'm not thinking straight."

"After all that's happened to you tonight, I'm not surprised," Bolan said to bolster her spirits.

"You went through the same hell I did, and you're hardly fazed," Mathews said. She hesitated. "I know it's not my place to pry, but you do this sort of thing a lot, don't you, Mr. Belasko?"

"Yes," Bolan admitted.

The Fed closed her eyes but went on rambling, her voice falling to an exhausted whisper. "I don't know how you do it. I mean, I've been trained to handle situations like this, but all the training in the world can't prepare a person for what it's really like to have someone try to take your life. Why put yourself through this?''

What could Bolan say? Should he tell her that he had dedicated his life to preserving freedom at all costs? Would she think it old-fashioned of him that he clung to ideals many considered outdated? Ideals like patriotism, a belief in ultimate justice and a profound devotion to upholding the values that had made America great?

Would Mathews laugh at him if she knew that he had forsaken everything most men valued? A wife, a family, kids—they were all denied him. He would never know what it was like to change diapers or to burp a baby on his shoulder. He would never feel the joy of watching his boy play Little League, or his girl skate in her first competition.

Some would say the cost was too high, that he was sacrificing everything that made life worthwhile for the sake of a dream. A dream where, one day, all those who were wicked at heart, all those who lived off the sufferings of others, all the petty dictators and drug kingpins and crooked politicians, were a thing of the past.

Some would say that it was a fight Bolan could never win. That for every crime czar and fanatic and cold-blooded hit man he eliminated, five more rose to take their place.

Some would insist that if he had any sense, he would give it up as a lost cause and get on with a normal life.

They missed the whole point.

It was because of decent men and women like Brenda Mathews that Bolan did what he did. He made it possible for them to enjoy their lives unfettered by the chains of tyranny. He helped to make the streets their children played on safer. He strove to stem the flow of drugs that turned their kids into violence-crazed addicts.

Were it not for men like Bolan, the decent people of the world wouldn't have a decent world in which to live.

The soldier glanced down to try to explain. He was spared the effort. Mathews was sound asleep, angelic in repose, the worry lines temporarily gone.

Bolan stayed up, keeping watch. Toward dawn he dozed, but only until the trees trilled with an avian chorus. Birds always greeted the new day with bursts of song, as if in homage to the fact they were alive.

The eastern sky had paled, but it would be a while before the sun crowned the mountains. Rising, Bolan stretched. On the plain below, a black speck appeared, spewing dust. It grew in size until he identified it as a pickup. Remembering that there had been a truck parked near the shack, he knelt to rouse the Fed.

Mathews stirred, smacking her lips. He had to shake her shoulder before her eyelids fluttered open. Confusion puckered her brow. Then she exclaimed, "Oh! It's you. How long was I out?" Sitting up, she gasped. "You let me sleep all night. That wasn't fair."

"You needed the rest more than I did," Bolan said frankly, a point she could hardly dispute. Hoisting her up, he added, "A truck is on its way up here. It might be Garth and some of his friends."

"I hope it is," Mathews said, fingering the butt of the SIG-Sauer. "I owe them in a big way."

"Do you know who Garth is?"

The Fed shook her head. "Wish I did. He's a new player." She ran a hand through her tangled hair and grimaced. "If he's involved in the sagebrush rebellion or even the antifederalist insurgency movement in general, Harry Standish might be able to help us track him down."

Bolan's gears whirled. The same Standish who tried to "liberate" federal land would help a federal agent? "Why would he consort with the enemy?" he quizzed.

Mathews blushed. She averted her face, devoting herself to her smudged, torn clothes. "Oh, he's not as bad as all that. He opposes some of our government's policies, but he doesn't hate someone just because they work for Uncle Sam."

The soldier didn't press the issue. If Standish

could help, so much the better. Locating Garth was the key to finding the Fox.

Since it would be a while before the pickup climbed the mountain, Bolan hiked lower, keeping an eye on Mathews. The rest had done her good. She strode briskly at his side. When she caught him studying her, she smiled.

"Don't worry, Mr. Belasko. I'm not about to keel over on you. Us farm girls are made of sterner stuff than that."

"You can call me Mike."

"Will do. But that's not your real name, is it?"

Bolan had to remind himself that this wholesome country girl was also a shrewd federal agent. She didn't miss much. "No, it's not." It went against his grain to lie. Besides which, even with the vast resources at her fingertips, she could never uncover his true identity. Brognola had seen to that.

Mathews didn't pry. Half an hour later, they neared a switchback obstructed by pines. The throaty growl of the pickup enticed Bolan to move into the shadows at the edge of the vegetation.

Into view clanked a vehicle that looked to be as old as the mountains themselves. Rust caked the body, its windshield was cracked and a front fender hung partly off. Behind the wheel sat a man whose salt-and-pepper beard was stained with streaks of tobacco juice. A small, dusty black hat topped a bulbous head.

Bolan stepped into the open.

"Howdy, folks," the man crowed good-naturedly as his rattletrap rumbled to a stop. "The name is Melvin. I live down on the flats yonder." Twinkling blue eyes regarded them with amusement. "The missus and me heard an awful ruckus up here last night, and she sent me up to see what it was. You wouldn't happen to know, would you?"

"No," Bolan said.

Melvin showed his entire set of tobacco-stained teeth. "Okeydoke. I never sass a man who looks as if he could break me in two without hardly tryin'." Melvin glanced at Mathews, then up the road. "Say, you folks ain't stranded, are you? Do you need a lift?"

"We sure do," she responded. "I'll pay for the gas if you'll get us to a phone."

"No need to be insultin', missy. Bein' charitable is the Christian thing to do. I'll take you to my place and you can call from there." Melvin looked them up and down, then snickered. "It's too bad nothin' happened up here last night, 'cause judgin' by you two, it was a humdinger worth hearin' about."

Melvin's cackle vied with the engine as he turned the pickup around and headed down.

CHAPTER FOUR

Charlie Luft hated big cities. He shunned them like
he would a politician. On one hand he could count
the number of times he had been to a city in the
past forty years. So it was with a sense of unease
that he wheeled the Jeep off an exit ramp into Reno.

Right away Luft saw pedestrians thronging a
street outside a casino. His scowl deepened. The
heavy traffic made it deepen even more.

Reno had grown so much since last he was there
that Charlie hardly recognized it. Fortunately, the
directions he had been given were precise. West
Second Street took him to South Wells. Crossing
East Plum to Lakeside Drive, he continued south
until he was in a ritzy residential neighborhood, the
kind where every home was a mansion, where every
yard was the size of a football field and enclosed
by a wrought-iron fence.

The particular house Luft sought loomed on a
low hill. A winding driveway led up from a massive

gate. He braked, then poked his head out. No one was around.

Maybe it was for the best, he reflected. The place reminded him of a prison. But so did many homes nowadays, what with their perimeter fences and barred windows and guard dogs as big as bulls.

Luft had about decided to forget the whole thing and go find another buyer when a gruff voice hailed him from above.

"What do you want, old-timer?"

Attached high on top of a white post was a speaker and a security camera, its red eye fixed on Luft like the unblinking orb of a cyclops. "The name is Luft," he said peevishly. "Bob Clemens sent me. I have an appointment to see your boss."

"One moment."

Patience wasn't one of Luft's strong suits. Drumming his fingers on the steering wheel, he glared at the red eye, half wishing he had his rifle so he could shoot it out. A minute dragged by, then two. He noticed other cameras mounted at strategic points on the property: in trees, on walls, even on a gazebo.

"Never trust a man who doesn't trust others," Luft muttered. It was an axiom his grandpa had passed down to him, and experience had taught him to take it to heart. Again he thought about backing up and driving off, but the disembodied voice addressed him as he gripped the gear lever.

"Yes, Mr. Luft, you are expected. Please follow the drive to the double doors in the west wing. A staff member will greet you there."

Staff member? What kind of man was he dealing with here? Obviously, the man had more money than King Midas. Probably another silly collector, like Clemens, only with more bucks to spend.

Something buzzed, and the ponderous gates swung slowly inward. As Luft drove on, he noticed that the camera on the post tracked him. No sooner was he out of range than another surveillance monitor, suspended from a tree, locked on to him.

The place gave the old man the creeps.

A trim man in a black suit waited at a wide parking area adjacent to a pair of gilded doors, a wide-brimmed black hat pulled low over his brow. A polished pair of black cowboy boots smacked the asphalt as he clumped over to the Jeep. "Howdy, partner. You must be Mr. Luft. My boss just got in from a business trip down south, and he's plumb tuckered out. He doesn't have much time to spare."

Luft had never taken to being patronized. "If that's the case, I'll be on my way," he said in a huff.

"Hold on, hoss," the man said, opening the door. "I didn't mean to rile you. Truth is, Bob Clemens said a few things that has the boss a mite curious. Please, follow me."

Against his better judgment, the old man slid out

and dogged the upstart down a spacious, plush hall-way, past rooms that would have put the fanciest hotels in the world to shame. They wound up in a trophy room. Animal heads adorned the walls, everything from antelope to elephants.

Luft found himself staring up at a hideous monster with curved tusks half as long as his arm and a snout that would outdo a hog's.

"That there is a warthog," the man in black remarked in his thick-as-molasses drawl. "It came at the boss out of nowhere, yet he dropped it with one shot to the heart."

"Your boss must be some hunter."

The man in the black hat smiled oddly. "He has his moments, Mr. Luft. Now, if you'll excuse me, I have to rustle up some grub for the boss's dog."

Luft idled away the moments examining the stuffed trophies. The elephant was immense, a mighty tusker slain in its prime. He couldn't resist the temptation to rise on his toes and stretch upward to touch the smooth ivory. Unaware that someone had entered, he nearly jumped out of his boots when a deep baritone rumbled across the room.

"I took him using a Boswell .500 Nitro Express double rifle, in heavy brush country. Contrary to the lies of the liberal media, elephants are still plentiful in countries where they are managed well."

Turning, Luft gawked. He had figured on meeting another mousy bespectacled bookworm like Bob

Clemens, but the man before him was a brawny, robust giant, six foot five or better, with a build a linebacker would envy. Riveting blue eyes seemed to see right through him. "Mr. Garth?" he said, for lack of anything more original.

His host held out a callused hand. "Trevor Garth, at your service, Mr. Luft."

It was like shaking the paw of a grizzly. Luft sensed that Garth went out of his way to avoid applying too much pressure, yet the old man's fingers still stung when he lowered his arm. Getting straight to the point, he said, "Bob Clemens tells me that you might be in the market for some military stuff."

Garth's crew-cut head bobbed. "Come with me."

A command, not a request. Luft was going to object and point out that his time was too valuable to waste in chitchat, but something about Trevor Garth compelled him to do as the man wanted. The carpet in the corridor was so plush that their feet whispered across it.

At the third door on the right, Garth stood aside so Charlie could precede him. The trophy room was small compared to this chamber, which was filled with weaponry and military accoutrements from ancient times to the present.

A sterling suit of armor worn by a knight of yore occupied a central position. Flanking it were strange getups that Luft assumed to be armor from all different countries and all different ages. On the walls were antique muskets, carbines and rifles. Flintlock pistols hung next to modern six-shooters and automatic firearms.

"Quite a collection you've got here," Luft commented.

"Thank you." Garth walked to the suit of armor and caressed it as most men would a woman. "This was worn by an ancestor of mine during the Hundred Years' War between England and France." He pointed at a musket in a prominent position. "Another forebear of mine used that with distinction during the Revolutionary War."

"So Bob Clemens was right. You are a military nut."

Garth's head swung around like that of a tiger drawn to prey. His expression didn't alter, but the old man had the impression that under the inscrutable surface bubbled a volcano. "You've missed my point, Mr. Luft. But then, I doubt you've ever read the Magna Carta, or even our Constitution, from beginning to end."

Luft didn't see what that had to do with anything. "Listen, Mr. Garth. I don't want to take up any more of your time than I have to." He paused. "The thing is, I have a bunch of stuff to sell, and Clemens thought you might be—"

"Ah, yes. Mr. Clemens," Garth interrupted. "I met him just once, over a year ago, at a military expo in Las Vegas. I'm surprised he remembered me.''

The old man reckoned that the prospect of making a few hundred dollars on the deal was growing dimmer by the moment. Clemens had steered him wrong.

Garth motioned at the walls. ''As you can see, Mr. Luft, only exceptional objects qualify for my collection. Exactly what do you have for sale?''

''Nothing that would suit you,'' Luft said, and was puzzled when the wealthy recluse laughed. ''Just a bunch of poison gas and such from World War I that—'' Suddenly, the old man fell silent on his own accord. His host had stiffened, and a downright strange expression had come over him. ''Is something the matter, Mr. Garth?''

''How much do you have?''

''Oh, I don't know. Enough to wipe out all the folks in Reno, I reckon,'' Luft joked. To his amazement, Trevor Garth beamed as if that were the greatest news he had ever heard. No doubt about it, the old man told himself. Garth was a weird one. ''But I've got to be honest with you. The stuff might be dangerous. You should get your hands on some gas masks before you fiddle with it.''

Garth thoughtfully stroked his chin. Walking to a control panel near the door, he pressed a button. ''Mr. Starkey, on the double.''

Luft's fortunes had reversed. "You're interested, then?" he asked excitedly.

"More than you can possibly imagine," Garth said cryptically. In short order the man in black was back, and Garth introduced him. "This is Ren Starkey, one of my most trusted associates. Kindly go with him and he will arrange for us to leave within the hour." Garth paused. "I trust you have the stuff at a safe location?"

"It's where I found it, way off in the mountains. I can take you right to the spot."

"Excellent." Garth clapped Luft on the back, and the old man almost lost his balance. "My cook will prepare a meal for you while you wait." Then Garth did an extremely peculiar thing. Gazing at the ceiling, he declared merrily, "Yes, Virginia, there most definitely is a Santa Claus."

Luft let Starkey lead him out. Why was it, he wondered, that the rich ones were always the craziest?

"You've made Mr. Garth very happy, partner," the man in black remarked.

"Glad I made his day. Say, where are you from, anyway? With that twang of yours, my guess would be Oklahoma or Arizona."

"You're not much off the mark," Starkey said. "San Antonio is where I grew up." He sighed. "Texas. The best damn state there is. Those boys at the Alamo knew what was at stake, didn't they?"

The Alamo? Where did that fit in anywhere? Luft reflected. "They knew how to die, that was for sure," he said.

A stairway reared on the left. Luft happened to look up and spotted a swarthy man on the first landing, a character with mean, wolfish features. An Arab, or some such, by the looks of him.

Now, what in tarnation was an Arab doing in Nevada?

FEW TOURISTS EVER SAW the seamier side of Las Vegas. Most spent all their time on the Strip, hopping from casino to casino, enjoying the shows and seeing how much money they could lose before their vacations were over.

The underbelly of Vegas was no different from others Mack Bolan had seen. Exotic Istanbul, gay Paris, the Big Apple—all had seedy sections, parts of town shunned by polite society, where pushers and pimps and con men thrived. The buildings were run-down, graffiti was rampant and the city's street crews were grossly remiss in their duties.

It was just the sort of place that Clem "Dog" Weathers would call home.

According to his rap sheet, Weathers lived on the second floor of a dilapidated hotel. Parked half a block away, Bolan kept an eye on the building. The sun had set an hour ago.

It had been a busy day.

Melvin Sirak had insisted on driving Mathews and Bolan into the city. Bolan had tried to slip the crusty oldster a twenty-dollar bill, but Sirak had handed it back, saying, "When you take money for a good deed, you don't get credit up above."

Bolan's first order of business had been to insure that Mathews admitted herself to the hospital. She had given him a hard time, claiming she was just fine even though she was still as white as a sheet.

Next Bolan contacted Brognola. As he anticipated, the big Fed was disturbed to hear that the Fox had given him the slip. The big Fed had offered to have the local FBI office handle the case from there on, but Bolan declined. He was the one who had blown it; he was the one who would track down the Libyan.

Mathews's partner, George Myers, had provided what little information there was on Weathers, and Bolan was staked out, waiting for the man to show himself in the hope that Weathers would lead him to the Libyan or Garth. He didn't have long to wait.

Weathers ambled from the hotel, yawned, took his white hat off to scratch his hair, then crossed the street and turned away from Bolan.

The soldier slid out of the vehicle and fell into step behind several women. Pacing himself so that he was always half a block back, he trailed Weathers to a billiard parlor sandwiched between a barbershop and a coin laundry. Weathers paused to check his watch, then looked both ways before going in.

It gave Bolan the idea that the go-between was meeting someone, possibly Garth or the terrorists, who were probably lying low until they could sneak out of the country.

The Feds had McCarran Airport staked out, and Brognola had put agents on alert at every major terminal within five hundred miles. Train and bus depots were also being watched. The Justice man was determined to prevent the Fox from getting away.

Pulling up the collar of the new jacket he had bought that afternoon, Bolan casually walked into the billiard hall. He was taking a gamble, but he had to be sure that Weathers hadn't slipped out the back.

Nearly all of the eight pool tables were in use. A row of booths rested against the right wall. Clem Weathers sat at one, alone, lighting a cigarette.

Bolan moved to the far end and sat facing the entrance. He slouched to disguise his height and build on the off chance Weathers had caught a glimpse of him on the mountain. The Nevadan paid no attention to him, though.

A perky brunette wearing a short dress and an apron approached Bolan's table. "Hello, mister. Care for a beer? We've got every brand under the sun, and then some."

Bolan wasn't thirsty but he ordered one anyway. As the woman left, a pair of men in Western garb entered, glanced around the parlor until they spotted him and glared in open hostility. It made no sense. Neither were familiar to the Executioner.

The pair sauntered over to Clem Weathers, and one leaned down to say something in his ear. Weathers's head snapped up, and he focused on Bolan. Rising, he walked toward the soldier, flanked by the new arrivals.

The brunette got there first. "Here's your brew, mister," she said, setting down a mug beaded with drops of moisture. "Will there be anything else?"

Weathers stopped behind her. "Get lost, Elsie," he growled. "This man and me have something to discuss."

The woman turned. "What's this all about, Dog? I don't want trouble in my place."

"All I aim to do is shoot the breeze," Weathers said, his eyes locked on Bolan.

"That had better be all," Elsie responded. "So help me, if you cause a ruckus, you'll pay for the damages if I need to have you hauled into court." She didn't ask what it was about, or tell the three men to leave Bolan alone. Wiping a hand on her apron, she made herself scarce.

Weathers didn't mince words. "Who the hell are you, mister? And why were you followin' me?"

Bolan raised the mug partway. "I don't know

what you're talking about," he said amiably. "I've never set eyes on you before."

Weathers leaned on the end of the table. "Is that so? Then why did you dog me from my hotel?" He thrust a thumb at his companions. "Don't try to deny it. My pards were headin' this way and saw the whole thing. You must be a cop."

"I'm not a law officer," Bolan said.

"Maybe I don't believe you," Weathers replied. "Maybe I think you're lyin' through your teeth."

The taller of his companions, whose leather vest bulged under one arm, sidled to the left. "I say we beat the truth out of him, Dog. My brother and me will hold him for you to pound on if you want."

Bolan could tell that for all his bluster, Weathers was unsure of himself. To fuel that uncertainty, he said, "If I was an undercover cop shadowing you, would I come in here and sit where you could see me?"

Weathers pursed his lips. "I suppose no one in his right mind would," he conceded. "But how do you explain the fact that the Haskett brothers saw you follow me for five whole blocks?"

"They came here, too. Were they following you?"

The Haskett in the vest sneered. "Can't you see what he's trying to do, Dog? He's twisting words around to get off the hook. Don't let him skunk you."

"He's got a point, though," Weathers said, slowly rising. "All right, mister. I'll take you at your word. But if I catch you trailing me again, you'll regret the day your mama gave birth to you."

He and the Haskett brothers went to his booth. Drinks were brought, and for the better part of an hour they quenched their thirst and talked in low voices.

Bolan had to stay. To leave sooner than they did would heighten their suspicion. He drained the mug, then nursed another, killing time. Weathers used a pay phone twice. When he came back after the second call, he was all smiles. They paid their bill and departed without so much as glancing at the soldier.

Quickly, Bolan rose. They had gone to the left, so he went to the right as far as the first corner. Once past it, he peered out. He figured the scruffy toughs hadn't gone farther than half a block, but they were nowhere to be seen.

Bolan gave chase. He had to find where Weathers had gone, even if it meant risking exposure. Jogging past the billiard hall and the coin laundry, he reached the mouth of a gloomy alley. Nothing moved that he could see.

Running to the intersection, Bolan scanned the street in all directions. It was as if the sidewalk had cracked open and swallowed the three men. They had to be in one of the buildings, but which one? He backtracked. There was an accountant's office, an empty structure with a sign in the window that read Space For Rent, then the alley and the coin laundry.

Bolan stopped in front of the alley. He was going to investigate it when a police car cruised down the street. Since most cops took a dim view of people who frequented alleys and were prone to stop and ask annoying questions, he walked to the laundry, loitering out front until the patrol car went around the corner.

Wasting no more time, Bolan hastened to the alley. A garbage bin blocked one side. Sliding his right hand under his jacket, he glided into the shadows, his back to the wall. He found five doors and tested each. Every one was locked. He was nearing the far end when something scraped above him. Instantly, he crouched and whirled, the Beretta filling his hand.

A tabby cat perched on a fire escape stared at him with feline disinterest.

"You've just used up one of your lives," Bolan said dryly. Shoving the pistol into the speed rig, he stepped into the bright sunshine and turned left to circle the block.

It was rare for anyone to give Bolan the slip, yet twice in twenty-four hours his quarry had eluded him. It was aggravating. Everyone, though, had bad days now and then. The only alternative could be that he was losing his edge, which was highly unlikely. He trained hard to keep himself in top shape, mentally and physically.

Walking around the block, Bolan checked the street one more time before heading toward his car. He would give Brognola a call, then stop by the hospital to see Agent Mathews. The doctor had said that it would be best if she stayed for four or five days, but she had vowed to check herself out by morning.

Bolan came to his vehicle and reached into his pocket to palm the keys. As he did, a sharp object pricked the back of his neck, and breath that reeked of garlic and beer fanned his cheek.

"Don't so much as twitch, buddy boy, or you're dead."

CHAPTER FIVE

In the Justice Building in the nation's capital, in an office that by Washington standards was Spartan, Hal Brognola sat at his desk and tapped his pen on a sheaf of reports.

The hunt wasn't going well. So far the small army of agents sent to airports, train stations and bus depots hadn't caught sight of the Fox.

It was Brognola's hunch that the Libyan had gone underground in Nevada. Somehow they had to flush him from cover. It would end a spree of vicious slaughter that spanned decades, and show those who thought they could butcher innocents with impunity that they were wrong.

Everything depended on Striker. Bolan had never let him down yet, so the big Fed was optimistic.

Another cause for concern was the possibility that the Libyan had farmed out his service to a home-grown group with the same goals as those responsible for the Oklahoma City bombing. It added a whole new dimension to the domestic terrorist situation.

Not that Brognola hadn't considered the likelihood before. It was, in a sense, inevitable. A rash of organizations opposed to the policies of the federal government had taken root in recent years. Many were law-abiding and protested with ballots rather than bullets. But a few were prone to violence, and more like them sprouted up all the time.

The big Fed had to admit that he had little sympathy for those who would violently overthrow the government instead of trying to reform it from within. As had been demonstrated in Oklahoma, when someone took up arms against what he saw as federal oppression, innocents were invariably caught in the cross fire.

He opened a file and scanned a list of groups who had caused trouble in the past and were bound to do so again: white supremacists, fringe militia, violent survivalists, some posse comitatus adherents.

They were the tip of the iceberg. It was estimated that more than twelve million Americans were "mad as hell and not willing to take it anymore," to paraphrase a movie whose title he couldn't recall.

Their reasons varied. Some sincerely believed UN tanks were one day going to roll across the heartland to impose a new world order. Some were ordinary people pushed to their limit: loggers outraged at losing their livelihood because of a few owls, ranchers upset by land-and-water-use policies, men and women who blamed the loss of their jobs on NAFTA and GATT, extremist environmentalists and many more.

It didn't help matters that certain bureaucrats were fanning the flames of discontent. The fiasco at Ruby Ridge, where an unarmed mother holding an infant in her arms had been shot dead, and the debacle in Waco, where so many children had needlessly perished, were grist for the hate-monger mill.

Where would it all lead? Brognola shuddered to think. He loved America with a passion. For his country's sake, he had dedicated the greater part of his adult life to keeping her safe from her enemies.

He couldn't bear to think of the consequences should a full-scale rebellion ever erupt. Washington's pundits thought it unlikely, but politicians were notorious for misjudging how far average citizens would let themselves be pushed before those same citizens struck back.

Where did Striker stand? Brognola wondered. As patriotic as Bolan was, as dedicated to the ideals that had made America the envy of the free world, it had to be tearing him apart. Fighting foreign fanatics was one thing. Fighting otherwise loyal Americans who believed their government had become the next evil empire was quite another.

And that just might happen. If the Libyan had joined forces with homegrown terrorists, Bolan might have to train his sights on men who had fought in the same wars he had, who had made the same sacrifices, suffered the same pain.

What would something like that do to a person?

THE EXECUTIONER DIDN'T resist as he was hauled backward into another alley and thrust behind a garbage bin identical to the one he had seen earlier.

Partly ringing him were Clem Weathers and the Haskett brothers. One sibling held a bowie, the other a Randall Arkansas Toothpick. By the way they held their blades, they were pros at the lethal art of knife fighting.

Weathers chortled. "Didn't reckon on seein' us again, did you, fella?"

Bolan didn't answer. He was gauging distances, calculating odds, coiling his muscles.

"Well, it's like this," Weathers went on. "My pards and me didn't believe you for one minute back there, but we weren't about to raise a stink and have the cops called." He folded his scrawny arms across his equally scrawny chest. "No, sir. We want to question you at our leisure, with no one buttin' in."

The Haskett with the bowie wagged the big knife. "It don't hardly make no never mind to us whether this goes down hard or easy. It's all up to you."

"Tell us what we want to know, and we'll let

you off no worse for wear,'' chimed in the other brother.

"For starters," Weathers said, "who are you? And what outfit do you work for? Are you local heat? Or a Fed?"

Bolan shifted so he could see the end of the alley. Unlike the first, this one was blocked off fifty feet in. "Where is the Fox?" he asked.

Weathers did a double take. "What?"

"Where is the Libyan you took to the Spring Mountains? The man who calls himself Fezzan."

The gangly Nevadan guffawed, then smacked the Haskett holding the bowie on the shoulder. "Doesn't this beat all, Ike? This man is about to have his gizzard carved out and shoved down his throat, yet he acts as if he's holdin' all the high cards! He's plumb loco."

"Is he, Dog?" Ike said. "How come he knows so much? How does he know about that Arab being on the mountain unless he was there?"

Weathers lost his cocky air. "You've got a point there." He thrust a finger at Bolan. "Okay, mister. Spill the beans. How *do* you know so much? Were you one of those people who jumped us last night? 'Cause if you were, you'll pay for the all the good old boys your people killed. You'll pay hard."

Bolan shifted once more so that he had an arm's length between himself and the garbage bin. "Do you know where the Libyan is or not?"

"Of course I do," Weathers said. "But I'm not about to tell you. Mr. Garth would have my head if I betrayed his trust." His fingers dipped into a rear pocket and snaked out flourishing a switchblade. It popped open with a crisp click. "Ever seen what one of these babies can do? It's no wonder the government made them illegal."

"Yeah," Ike said. "That's the government for you. Anything worth having, they don't want us to have."

The second brother was annoyed. "Quit you're jawing, dammit. Let's get this over with before a drunken bum strays into the alley and sees something he shouldn't."

"What do we care?" Weathers said. "We'll off him the same as this one." He advanced, the switchblade low against his waist. "I've never cut out a tongue before, but there's a first time for everything."

The Haskett brothers, wearing a matched set of sinister smirks, closed in, too.

The three of them were supremely confident. And why shouldn't they be? They were hardcases who had earned their reputations as tough men the hard way, on the mean streets of Las Vegas and elsewhere. Each had no doubt beaten more than his share of toughs. Each had probably taken a life or two somewhere along the line. They converged in somber silence, their weapons glinting dully in the dim light that penetrated the alley.

Bolan let them get almost within knife range. Then he exploded, doing the last thing they expected, carrying the fight to them instead of waiting for them to bring the battle to him. As the old saw went, the best offense was always a good defense. It was a maxim Bolan had taken to heart, and one he now employed to the fullest.

A feint, and the soldier's right foot flicked out to catch Weathers across the wrist. The lanky cowboy cried out in pain as the switchblade went flying.

The Haskett brothers sprang, seeking to overwhelm Bolan by sheer brute force. But they failed to take into account the soldier's speed.

He sidestepped a stab, slipped a slash, then was past the siblings in a bound. Spinning, he delivered a backhand that smashed into Ike's nose as the man turned. Cartilage crunched; scarlet sprayed. It stopped Ike in his tracks. But not the other one, who vented an oath and pounced, swinging much too wildly.

Bolan parried with his forearm, jarring the brother's arm aside. Slipping in close, he slammed an elbow into the man's chin, drove his fist into a soft midriff and followed through with an uppercut that had all of his power and weight behind it.

The second Haskett seemed to go airborne before

crashing into the dumpster and melting like so much warm wax to the ground.

"Son of a bitch!" Ike roared. In his fury over his brother, he threw his skill to the four winds and came on like a tornado, swinging his knife arm again and again in wide cuts that would open the soldier like an overripe melon if they connected.

Bolan backpedaled, narrowly evading each attempt. Abruptly, he backed into the opposite wall. Bracing his right hand against it, he tucked his knees.

Ike thought he saw his golden opportunity. "Now I've got you, you bastard!" he raged, never realizing that the precious seconds he took to gloat might be all that Bolan needed to set himself. "Die!" Ike snarled, lancing his bowie out and in.

Bolan had positioned himself so that the left side of his chest was exposed to his adversary. It was a ruse, a potentially deadly trick that had as much a chance of backfiring as succeeding. Ike took the bait, stabbing at his ribs. The big blade whistled.

At the absolute last moment, Bolan pivoted, twisting and snapping his left arm up so the bowie passed under it. The edge tore his jacket but not his body. Before Ike could cock the knife to try once more, Bolan clamped his arm on his adversary's wrist, grabbed Ike's belt with his free hand and drove his head into Ike's forehead with enough force to shatter wood.

Haskett's knees buckled, but he didn't go down. Frantically, he sought to tear his knife arm loose.

Bolan became a human whirlwind. Driving Ike against the wall, he arched his leg upward even as he snapped Ike's arm downward. Knee met elbow with an explosive crack. Ike threw back his head to scream, but a fist to the jaw silenced him.

A whisper of movement behind Bolan brought him around in a flash. Weathers had retrieved the switchblade and charged, seeking to stab him in the back while he was preoccupied with Ike.

A deft shift, and the switchblade missed Bolan by a whisker. He ducked under his attacker's arm, seized Weathers's wrist in both hands and levered the man up and over in a flawless shoulder throw. He thudded into the wall, fell like a stone on top of Ike Haskett, then struggled weakly to regain his footing.

Bolan took two quick steps and planted his foot on the underside of Weathers's jawbone. Teeth crunched, pink spittle flew and Weathers deflated like a punctured balloon.

Barely winded, Bolan scanned the alley. No one had noticed the fight. He dragged the three unconscious forms into the shadows, then hurried to his car.

BROGNOLA ANSWERED his telephone on the first ring, and listened in silence as Bolan filled him in.

"I'll have local agents there in under ten minutes," the big Fed said. "It's a step in the right direction, Striker."

"Interrogating Weathers and his friends will probably take the better part of the night," he added. "You might as well take it easy. As soon as I learn anything significant, I'll contact you."

Bolan hated to stand down. He could no more sit idly by for twelve hours than he could hold his breath that long. "I'm going to check Weathers's apartment."

"Fair enough. Keep your cell phone handy, just in case we learn anything at this end."

FOUR FBI AGENTS from the Las Vegas office arrived in the time limit Brogola had set to take Weathers and the Haskett brothers into custody. Weathers revived and wouldn't stop complaining about his broken arm. A short time later, the Feds departed.

With that done, Bolan pulled his collar up and entered the hovel Weathers called home. A grizzled desk clerk riveted to a black-and-white television didn't even look up when Bolan rapped on the counter.

"What'll it be?" the man said, sipping from a flask. "If it's a room, we don't have any left on the ground floor."

"One of your tenants was arrested today," Bolan said.

The clerk paused with the flask tipped to his mouth. His eyes widened. Some of the liquor spilled over his chin. "A cop, huh? I can smell you guys a mile off."

"I'd like to see Clem Weathers's room."

"Don't you need a warrant or something?" the clerk responded.

Bolan merely stared. He let the man's imagination do the rest.

Fidgeting, the clerk mustered a wan grin. "But why put you to that much bother, right? I mean, it's not as if you won't get in anyway eventually." Tittering, he took a key from a slot and handed it over. "Never let it be said that Art Jacoby doesn't bend over backward to help the boys in blue."

"I'll bring it right back," Bolan said. He took the stairs two at a stride. The place was a riot of noise: shouts, oaths, pounding and the wailing of an infant. Rank odors seemed to waft from the walls themselves.

At the first landing he paused, listening to a catfight in a room down the hall. Two women were going at it tooth and nail. A lamp stand, or something like it, fell with a resounding crash. One of the women screamed. No one else seemed to notice. Or maybe the other tenants were so used to it, they didn't care.

Weathers's room was 212. The lock rattled as Bolan worked the key. A decrepit bed, a chipped dresser and a nightstand that wobbled on three legs sufficed as furniture. Going to a closet, Bolan opened it.

Half a dozen shirts and two pairs of pants were the sum total of the man's wardrobe. That, and a spare pair of cowboy boots. None of the pockets yielded anything of interest.

Only one drawer contained personal effects. Underclothes were stuffed on one side, odds and ends on the others. Included was a comb with teeth missing, pencils and pens, a small writing tablet with only a few blank pages left and a bottle of acid-indigestion medicine. That, and a flyer for a gun range in Reno called The Sportsman's Shootery.

Nothing else. Not one pertinent clue to the man called Garth or the new group Garth had organized.

Disappointed, Bolan arranged everything as Weathers had left it and locked the door behind him. He deposited the key on the front desk and kept walking, deep in thought over what his next step should be.

"Say, Officer, sir?" the desk clerk said.

Bolan glanced at him.

"What about Dog's messages?"

The soldier saw the clerk turn to a small stack of notepaper beside the phone.

"I forgot all about them when you came in. But they might be important, eh?"

"They could be," Bolan conceded.

"Here you go. " The clerk held out three sheets. "Now be sure and tell the boys down at the department how helpful I've been. Maybe this way they won't come down so hard on me the next time one of the working girls and her john causes a ruckus."

The top sheet was a message from a woman named Ginger Snap. Weathers was to call her by ten at a certain number.

The second message was a man called Harry. In quotes were the words, "Where the hell is my money, you cheapskate?"

"Bolan shuffled the second page to the bottom. On the third page was a phone number and a name: Garth.

The desk clerk was watching closely. "That last one came in about an hour ago. Feller said it was important that Dog get back to him as soon as he could."

"Has this man called here before?"

"Um, let me see." The clerk scratched his chin, the rasp of nails on stubble like the rasp of sandpaper. "Yep. Come to think of it, he has. Two or three times, I think. Maybe more." He shrugged. "To tell the truth, I don't bother to keep track of every call that comes into this dump. When I was younger, I could. But the years take their toll, you know?''

So did the contents of the flask poking from the man's shirt pocket. ''Thanks. You've been a great help.'' Bolan had the number memorized. He gave the messages back and made for the door.

''It was a pleasure doing business with you, sir,'' the man called after him. ''You're a lot more polite than most of the hard heads who show up here. They bust my chops for no real reason, and I—''

The man was still talking as the door swung shut. Bolan went to his car and punched the number up on the cellular phone. When a gruff voice answered, he modified his voice as best he could to sound like Clem Weathers and said simply, ''Weathers.''

''About damn time, dipstick,'' the man responded. ''You missed the boss. He went off with some old geezer into the desert.''

Bolan didn't comment when the man paused. The less he said, the less likely the man was to realize he wasn't Clem Weathers.

After a few seconds, the man said, ''Are you still there?''

''Sure,'' Bolan said.

''Well, haul your butt up here. The boss wants everyone—and I mean everyone—on hand for a big meet. It will be at the Shootery this time, not his place. Tomorrow at nine. Do you have a problem with that?''

"No," Bolan said. He was dying to ask the boss's address, but doing so would give the ruse away. He mentally crossed his fingers that the man at the other end would go on talking and give him a clue.

"Make sure you're on time, Dog. He's still ticked off at you over the other night. If he could prove that you were trailed after you picked up those Arabs, I wouldn't want to be in your shoes."

"Anything else?" Bolan said when the man stopped. He had to hold up his end of the conversation or arouse suspicion.

"No. Just be on time for the meet. You know he's a stickler for being punctual."

The line went dead. Bolan hadn't learned what he wanted, but the call hadn't been a total waste. He now knew that the fanatics were getting together at the shooting range in Reno. He would be on hand, too, to nip their fledgling organization in the bud.

The soldier decided to inform Brognola. But first he put in a call to the hospital and was connected to Agent Mathews's room. "It's Belasko."

"I'm glad you called," the woman said, and sounded as if she meant it. "I've badgered my doctor into releasing me first thing in the morning—"

"Is that wise?" Bolan cut her off. "You lost a lot of blood." Novices were always too eager to leap back into the fray. They were too green to realize that it did more harm than good, that it delayed their healing and might cost them dearly if they were caught in a firefight.

"Dr. Howard says I should be perfectly fine," Mathews said. "If I get light-headed, though, I'm to call him right away." She paused. "Besides, I thought I could do you a favor. I know how much you want to nab Garth and his crew, so I've set up a meeting that might prove productive."

"A meeting?"

"At ten in the morning with Harry Standish. He has more underground contacts than anyone I know."

Bolan didn't answer right away. It bothered him that she was putting herself at risk for his sake.

"What do you say?" Mathews prompted. "He wouldn't do this for anyone else except me. We should take advantage of it."

There would be plenty of time for Bolan to reach Reno by nine at night. And he couldn't deny that the more he knew about Garth in advance, the better able he would be to cope with the situation when he got there. "All right," he said.

"Outstanding," Mathews declared. "Trust me. You won't regret this."

The Executioner sincerely hoped not.

CHAPTER SIX

Charlie Luft simmered the whole ride.

It had galled him terribly when Trevor Garth insisted on having a man ride with him on the trek into the Desolation Mountains. He'd almost told the millionaire to take a hike, that he never, ever let anyone else ride in his Jeep. Then Garth had clapped him on the back and voiced music to his ears.

"If this find of yours turns out to be everything you have claimed, I will be immensely grateful, my friend."

Dollar signs had danced before Luft's eyes. He saw this as his big score, the one he had longed for since as far back as he could remember, the one that would swell his bank account to near bursting.

So the old man reluctantly let Ren Starkey tag along in the Jeep. It helped that the man in black was the quiet type. The Texan hardly uttered three words the entire trip.

They had left the interstate and were on a dusty

secondary road when Luft happened to see Starkey unbutton his jacket. The flap swung open, revealing a pair of fancy ivory-handled pistols stuck into the man's belt, butts forward, the style favored by old-time gunfighters.

Something told Luft that those pistols weren't just for show. Most Texans were gun wise; Starkey looked to be more so than most.

Something also told the old man that maybe he was making a mistake. He couldn't say exactly why. It was a vague feeling, a constant prick at the back of his mind. From the moment he walked out of Garth's lavish mansion until the Jeep clanked onto the former site of Camp Wembly, a tiny voice told him that he would have been better off finding someone else to take the stuff off his hands.

The trouble was, Luft couldn't think of anyone able to pay as much. Bob Clemens had steered him to a bonanza this time around. The old man was going to milk Trevor Garth for all the money he could get.

No one had disturbed the cache in Luft's absence. Before leaving, he had closed the heavy iron door and covered it with dirt and brush on the off chance that someone else might come by.

Trevor Garth slid from his limousine like a king sliding from a royal carriage. Smoothing his knee-length leather coat, he surveyed the mountains and took a deep breath. "I do so love virgin wilderness.

It makes me think of our illustrious forebears, and the hardships they endured while carving out an empire.''

A second car had pulled up behind the limo. Between the two vehicles, Garth had brought seven men, plus the Texan. He commanded two of them to remove the brush and dirt.

Luft fidgeted. He couldn't wait to show them the stuff so he could be paid and be on his way. Which reminded him. ''We haven't settled on a price yet. How much are you willing to fork over for this stuff, mister?''

Garth smiled suavely. ''Payment depends on a number of factors, Mr. Luft. But rest assured that if your find turns out to be the godsend I suspect, you will be rewarded beyond your wildest dreams.''

Luft doubted that was possible. When it came to dreaming about wealth, he had it down to a fine science.

''How ever did you locate this spot?'' Garth asked.

Briefly, Luft detailed the hours spent doing research, then how he had stumbled on the hideaway. ''If I had turned and gone in another direction, I never would have found it.''

'' 'There is a divinity that shapes our ends, rough-hew them as we will.' ''

''What?''

Garth sighed. ''That was Shakespeare, Mr. Luft.

William S. Perhaps you've heard of the illustrious gentleman?''

"Oh, sure. Who hasn't? I just ain't heard anyone speak him since that time a pard of mine drug me off to see one of his plays.'' Luft lowered his voice. "Between you and me, that *MacBeth* about put me to sleep. The witches were funny. But all that go-dawful language!''

Luft was perplexed when his benefactor clapped him on the shoulder and chortled. The man had a habit of doing that. Shrugging, he watched as the last of the brush was removed. "I'll do the honors,'' he said.

The hinges creaked like a chorus of banshees, but the door didn't resist this time. Luft had a battery-powered lantern, which he held aloft as he cautiously went in. Even though the chemicals were all in canisters or kegs, he felt uncomfortable being in so confined a space with such deadly elements. What if something happened? What if a seal broke? Or if there were a leak he didn't know about?

Ren Starkey was next to enter. Hands poised near his ivory-handled pistols, he scanned the interior, then announced, "It's safe, sir.''

Garth made his entrance. A cobweb snagged his sleeve, and he brushed it off with disdain. As his gaze lifted to the cache, his eyes widened. His lips curled upward. "Can it be?'' he said, more to himself than to Luft. "Can it honestly and truly be?''

The next moment the rich recluse was dashing around like a five-year-old at Christmas. He'd go from the mustard gas to the chlorine to the TL-14 and back again, patting each, chortling crazily.

It flabbergasted Luft. He'd never seen a grown man carry on so. And all over a bunch of chemicals that weren't much good for anything other than conversation pieces. He let the man rave on a spell before he cleared his throat and said, "I take it this is something you're interested in?"

Garth was fondling the TL-14. Slowly straightening, he bestowed a peculiar expression on Luft. "You have no idea of the favor you have done me. Of the service you have rendered to your country. To your fellow man."

"Huh?"

Smiling benignly, Garth draped a brawny arm over the old man's shoulders. "Have you ever heard the old adage, 'Ask and ye shall receive'? Well, this find of yours couldn't have come along at a better time if it had been planned this way. Sometimes the working of destiny truly does proceed in mysterious fashion."

Garth had lost him again, but Luft held his tongue. He could afford to be patient. Haggling time had arrived, and he collected his wits for the clash.

"Chemical Warfare Weapons," Garth read a warning stenciled on a crate. "Delivered into my lap as if they were cartons of milk. How marvelous! How droll!''

"How about settin' a price?" Luft saw his opening. "What do you reckon all of this stuff is worth?"

"What do you think?"

The query caught the old man off guard. The truth was, he hadn't given it all that much thought. What in the hell was the stuff going for on the open market? If there even was a market? "Oh, I don't know," he hedged. He reminded himself that he was dealing with a man who was filthy rich, and that Garth probably knew of a way to make a hefty profit. So why not seize the bull by the horns? "Look at how much is here. I'd say one hundred thousand dollars should set us right."

"Is that all?" Garth asked.

Luft studied the man to see whether he was joking or not, and couldn't tell. "How much would you say?"

"Oh, considerably more than that paltry sum. In fact, to me, this is a treasure trove. Virtually priceless."

"It is?" A warm, gooey feeling came over Luft, just like that time he won fifty dollars in the lottery, only grander. He envisioned himself in a bathtub filled with brand-spanking-new greenbacks, splashing the money over him as if it were water. Lordy, it was enough to make him giddy!

Garth clasped his hands behind his back. "Mr. Starkey, would you have Jinson and Bailer come in here, please."

A pair of men in dark suits did as they were bid and stood at attention like toy soldiers.

Luft turned toward the wall so they wouldn't notice his smirk. Their antics were beginning to get to him. The next thing he knew, one of those muscle boys would get down on his hands and knees and lick off Garth's boots. It was too ridiculous for words. Belatedly, he realized that Garth was speaking.

"—and bring him over here."

Suddenly, steel clamps fastened on to Luft's forearms. A flunky had grabbed him on either side, and before he could protest, they snapped him around and hauled him over in front of the barrels. "Hey! What in hell do you gorillas think you're doing?"

Garth materialized in front of him. "It is fitting, my dear Mr. Luft, that you receive just payment for the invaluable service you have done me."

"Damn straight!" Luft fumed, striving in vain to wrench loose. "So tell these morons to let me go before I see fit to file charges!"

Garth's smile froze in place. Indeed, his entire body became like a block of ice, except for his eyes, which blazed with infernal inner fires that caused Charlie Luft to involuntarily cringe. "I'm afraid I can't do that," Garth said as politely as ever.

Luft's throat was incredibly dry. He had to swallow twice before he croaked, "What? Why?"

Garth looked down his nose at the prospector. "I'll try to keep this simple so you can comprehend." He folded his hands at his waist. "Do you remember my telling you that you would be rewarded beyond your wildest dreams? Well, think, my friend. What is the one payment I can render that is more valuable than any other?"

Again Luft was lost in the man's tangle of words. "I don't rightly know," he bleated, wishing he had listened to the tiny voice that had warned him to bail out of the deal while he still could.

"Oh, come now. It can't be that hard, even for you." Garth grasped Luft by the chin and held him so that their eyes locked. "Give a thought to your paltry life. Day in and day out, you struggle to make ends meet. You eke out a pathetic existence, never knowing where your next meal will come from, worrying about your welfare—"

"I don't fret much," Luft broke in, and was rewarded by having Garth cover his mouth.

"Don't interrupt," the collector said civilly. "As I was trying to point out, your paltry life is spent in anxiety from the minute you wake up until the minute you fall asleep at night. Therefore, what better payment can I render, what more fitting gift can I give you, than release from all your cares and woes?"

A glimmer of insight sent a chill rippling down Luft's spine. "You're plumb loco! You can't be sayin' what I think you're sayin'! I'm perfectly happy with my life. I don't have any complaints."

"So you claim, but what about in the small hours of the night when you are alone with the reflection of your meager soul?" Garth nodded at the Texan. "Mr. Starkey, have a crowbar brought. I want one of these barrels opened."

Luft's breath caught in his throat. "What do you want to go and do something like that for?" he said. "That stuff might be dangerous."

"That is exactly what I intend to determine," Garth responded.

Another bruiser in a dark suit brought the crowbar, which Starkey applied to the rim. Working around the edge inch by inch, he gradually pried the lid loose.

Luft wanted to bolt, but he was helpless in the grip of his captors. He quivered as two more men came forward and gingerly lifted the lid clear. A noxious stench hit his nose, reminiscent of burned eggs and worse odors. A thick greenish substance, a vile mucus, filled the barrel to within several inches of the top.

"Hold our friend down," Garth commanded.

Men seized Luft's ankles. An oath escaped him as he was lifted bodily and placed on his back. Pinned flat, a heavy flunky on every limb, all he could do was gape in stark horror as the rich recluse leaned over him.

"Actually, Mr. Luft, I'm in your debt in more ways than one. Thanks to you, I can kill two birds with one stone."

"How's that?"

"I not only have obtained the chemicals, I have a subject on whom to test them."

Raw, unbridled terror racked Luft, heart and soul. He opened his mouth to scream for help, but strangely, his vocal cords wouldn't obey. Aghast, he watched as Garth took the crowbar from Starkey, dipped it into the open barrel and swirled the mucus.

"Isn't it beautiful?" Garth asked. "See how it shimmers and glistens where it catches the light?" He raised the crowbar out and grinned as mucus rolled off it back into the container. "Oh, this is too wonderful for words!"

Luft could guess what was going to happen next. Fanning his courage, he said, "You'd better think twice, mister. Friends know where I am, who I've talked to. Harm me and you'll have the law down on your head."

Garth glanced down, pursing his lips. "Oh please, Mr. Luft. Don't insult my intelligence. A man like you would never disclose the location of a find like this. But you do bring up a critical point I shall address shortly." Dipping the crowbar into the barrel, he carefully drew it out again, holding it nearly level so the mucus on top would not slid off.

"Oh, God!" The old man thrashed and strained. He tried to kick, to heave upward. It was hopeless. He was a babe in their clutches.

"Now, now," Garth chided. "Try not to make this any harder on yourself than it has to be." The big man stood over Luft, regarding him intently. "How shall I test it? Certainly not by ingestion. Practically any toxin can work that way." His brow knit. "Skin contact, then? But where?"

The old man gazed in mute appeal at the men who held him, at the Texan. None betrayed a hint of sympathy. He gulped, tears moistening his eyes. It couldn't end like this! he told himself. It just couldn't!

"I know!" Garth cried, and lowered the crowbar toward Luft's right hand. "I hope this doesn't cause you much pain," he said, and tilted the bar just enough for a few drops to fall onto the old man's palm.

"No!" Luft howled, going berserk. For all the good it did him. The quartet held him effortlessly. He stopped struggling when a slight burning sensation crept down his hand to his wrist.

"Anything?" Garth asked, bending low.

"Go to hell!" Luft spit. He would have added a whole string of curses but the burning grew a lot worse, so bad that he had to grit his teeth to keep from crying out. In another few seconds, it spread down his arm to the elbow, growing hotter and hotter as it went. Perspiration broke out all over him.

Someone had produced a knife, and Garth sliced Luft's sleeve open. "Look at this!" he said. "His skin is bright red."

"It looks as if he's been out in the sun for a week, boss," commented one of the men holding the old man down.

"And look at how fast it's spreading," another said.

Panic clawed at Luft. The terrible sensation had climbed to his shoulder. It was like the time flaming kerosene had spilled on him, only much, much worse. Oh, Lord! It hurt! He tossed his head from side to side, teeth clenched, every vein in his neck and temples bulging. What in the world was happening?

"Absolutely fascinating," Garth said clinically, much as might a scientist doing research on real guinea pigs. "But is the TL-14 still lethal?"

Luft could no longer contain himself. Screeching at the top of his lungs, he flopped up and down in a frenzy as the searing heat spiked into his chest. A lung was engulfed, and suddenly he could barely breathe. "No!" he cried. "Please! For the love of God, no!"

Garth had been consulting his wristwatch. "Eight seconds so far," he stated.

The creeping, boiling inferno reached Charlie Luft's sternum. A thousand tiny needles pierced his heart at the same instant. His spine arched, and he gulped in air. A shriek was torn from his throat, then he collapsed, as limp as a wet rag, blood trickling from the corners of his mouth, his nostrils, even his ears.

"Eleven seconds from initial exposure until death sets in," Garth said happily. "Not bad. Not bad at all." He nudged the body with a toe. "Our friend Mr. Luft wasn't exaggerating. With the quantity we have, we could wipe out an entire city."

"What do you want done with the body, sir?" Starkey drawled.

Garth was already contemplating another important matter. "Oh, have some of the men drag it off and bury it." Taking the Texan by the elbow, he moved to a corner and said quietly, "As for you, get on the horn to our people in Vegas, Reno and Elko. I have a job for them."

Starkey waited patiently, the ivory grips on his pistols gleaming in the lantern light.

"Mr. Luft brought up a point I have foolishly overlooked," Garth said. "There are certain people who know enough about me and our organization to pose a threat should the law come snooping around. Not many, mind you. Just a few, but that is a few too many. We must take steps to insure their lips are sealed."

"I savvy, boss."

"Have one of our people pay Bob Clemens a visit. Odds are that he's the only other person who knows that Mr. Luft came to see me." Garth paused. "Then there is Tim Considine in Elko. He knows about the ammo we've been stockpiling. And let's not forget Harry Standish, in Las Vegas. He's sharp enough to put two and two together."

"Is that all?"

"For now, Mr. Starkey. After we get back, I'll have to make a list of everyone who could pose a threat and decide which ones should go on living."

Starkey started to go. "Is the big meetin' tomorrow still on?"

"I should say so," Garth responded. "Now that we have what we've been praying for, we must move up the timetable. It's time to reclaim America for Americans. Before we're through, the streets will run red with blood."

TIM CONSIDINE SOLD GUNS for a living. In any given month, he might sell ten or twelve, hardly enough to live on. Ammunition and accessories comprised the core of his livelihood. Until recently, he had been selling cases of ammo every few weeks to a wealthy customer in Reno.

On this particular night, Considine was in his office, a small room on the ground floor of his house. Bent over his ledger, he was trying to balance his books. His home was quiet. His wife and kids were upstairs, sound asleep.

He couldn't say what made him turn. It might have been a puff of air on the back of his neck. It might have been a hint of movement. Whichever, he swiveled in his chair, thinking one of the children or the cat had waltzed in. The last sight he beheld was the snout of a sound suppressor.

BOB CLEMENS WAS in his basement, where he kept his prized collection. An avid World War II buff, he had spent thousands of his hard-earned dollars on military paraphernalia. Lining his walls were rifles, bayonets, pistols and uniforms, and whatever else he could get his hands on.

In his lap sat a small glass case containing medals and insignia. Only the day before, he had added a rare find, lieutenant's bars belonging to a man who had fought in the Battle of the Bulge.

Bob leaned forward, admiring how the bars reflected the overhead light. Unexpectedly, a shadow fell across him. Yet that couldn't be. He lived alone. Startled, he glanced up just as a baseball bat descended.

AT THAT SAME MOMENT, northeast of Las Vegas, a man clad in black crept down a long, tree-lined driveway to a waiting car and climbed in the passenger's side.

"How'd it go?" asked the burly figure behind the wheel.

"It didn't. Standish isn't home."

"You're sure?"

"Of course I'm sure! What do you think I am, an idiot? I checked every damn room."

The man behind the wheel pondered. "All right. Simmer down. I say we wait until morning. If he doesn't show by then, we'll leave and check back every couple of hours until he returns."

"I know him. He travels a lot. Sometimes he's not here for days at a time."

"So?" The man at the wheel turned the ignition key. "Our orders are to hit him, and a good patriot never questions his orders."

"I have no problem with whacking Goody Two Shoes," said the man who held the pistol. "But I don't much like the idea of doing it in broad daylight."

"What are you worried about? The car is stolen, we'll be wearing masks and his nearest neighbor is half a mile away. We'll be in and out before the poor bastard knows what hit him."

CHAPTER SEVEN

Agent Brenda Mathews was in remarkably fine spirits for someone who had taken a bullet less than forty-eight hours earlier. She placed her handbag on the seat beside Bolan, slid in and gave him a warm smile. "I'm glad you agreed to this. I was afraid we'd never see each other again."

It was an innocent comment, made offhand, yet it set warning bells ringing in Mack Bolan's brain. He looked at her, but she had faced front and was primly adjusting her skirt.

"Let's go. It's a twenty-minute ride, at least."

The soldier pulled out, following her directions. They took Interstate 15 to Exit 64, then drove north on Highway 93.

"It's only a few more miles," Mathews said.

Bolan couldn't help but notice that her fingers were entwined with her purse strap, plying it as if it were a string of rosary beads. Her features were drawn, and not due to her condition. "There's something you're not telling me, isn't there?" he demanded bluntly.

Mathews went as rigid as steel. "You don't miss a thing, do you? Or am I that obvious?"

"It doesn't take a Sherlock Holmes to figure out that Standish and you have a history."

The woman shifted her handbag to her lap and clutched it with both hands. "It was short and sweet, as the saying goes. I was tracking down leads on a pair of antigovernment loons who were going around robbing banks all over Nevada and Utah. Since Standish knows next to everyone in the underground movement, I went to talk to him."

"Your personal life is your concern," Bolan said.

"No, it's necessary. I don't want you to think that you can't trust me." Mathews coughed. "I know what I did was wrong. I know it was against bureau policy. Thankfully, we broke up before my superiors found out."

An intersection appeared. "Take a right," the Fed said. "His house is the split-level on the hill."

Bolan could see it, outlined against the azure sky. A winding driveway bordered by dogwoods led to the front door. No other vehicles were in evidence. They climbed out in front of the house.

Mathews pumped a metal knocker in the shape of a dragon. Hollow pounding echoed dully indoors, but no one answered the door. "That's odd," she said. "He promised me that he would be here."

"Maybe he changed his mind," Bolan said. "A man in his position can't afford to be on friendly terms with the Feds. It undermines his credibility."

"Harry wouldn't care about something so trivial," Mathews said. "And he always keeps his word."

It would have been plain to anyone that the woman still carried a torch for the fiery insurgent. Bolan discreetly kept his opinion to himself and walked to the edge of the driveway, where a steep slope banked down to the road. A two-door sedan with tinted windows was going past.

"I don't know what to tell you," Mathews said. "Let's stick around awhile and see if he shows."

As if on cue, a horn honked up the road. A red sports car zipped into the driveway doing over forty miles per hour. Tires squealing, it sloughed around the turns. Mathews's smile was all the confirmation Bolan needed that the leader of the Sagebrush Patriots had arrived.

The car rocketed to a stop. Mathews started forward, then paused when both doors opened.

From the driver's side uncoiled a tall, well-built man who looked as if he had just stepped off the cover of a men's fashion magazine. Blond hair tied at the back in a ponytail framed a square-jawed face. His flashy clothes were flawless, down to the creases in his pants and his polished shoes.

From the other side stepped a petite brunette

whose skimpy halter top and tiny shorts would raise eyebrows in Rio.

To say that Harry Standish wasn't what Bolan had expected would be an understatement. The man should be working in Hollywood, not inciting his fellow citizens to rebel against their government.

"Hi, Brenda," Standish said in a voice any disc jockey would envy. "Sorry I'm a bit late. After you called yesterday, Amy here invited me out for supper."

Mathews visibly struggled to keep a tinge of resentment from marring her expression, but she couldn't do it. "We just got here ourselves. If you don't mind, we have a few questions we'd like to ask."

"No problem," Harry Standish said, twirling a key chain on his finger as he strolled to the door. "Enter my parlor. Amy will whip us up some instant and we can get down to cases."

Bolan idly watched the brown sedan pull into a driveway several hundred feet away. It promptly braked, no doubt so the driver could get out and check the mailbox. Pivoting, he went in last.

"Make yourselves comfortable," Standish said, indicating a living area. He bounded up a flight of stairs while the brunette padded down a hall.

Mathews sat in a chair. Bolan walked to a fireplace and leaned against it, his arms folded.

"We'll keep this short," Mathews said. "I know

you want to catch that flight to Reno you mentioned.''

Actually, Bolan hadn't told the whole truth. Brognola had a private plane waiting for him at the airport. Usually, Jack Grimaldi, ace pilot and one of the soldier's few friends, would ferry him around. But Grimaldi was off on assignment with Able Team, so Brognola had sent one of the backup pilots from Stony Man Farm.

In no time Harry Standish sauntered down the stairs. He had traded his shirt and jacket for a tank top that displayed his bronzed physique to good effect. ''You're Mr. Belasko?'' he asked, shaking Bolan's hand. ''Brenda was a bit vague on the phone about why you needed to see me.''

''What can you tell me about a man named Garth?''

Standish eased onto a sofa. ''So. It's come,'' he said softly. ''What have you heard about me, if you don't mind my asking?''

''I know that you're head of a group called the Sagebrush Patriots,'' Bolan admitted. ''I take it that you think the federal government has overstepped its bounds, and you want to remedy the situation.''

''Spoken like a diplomat,'' Standish said. ''Mr. Belasko, do you love our country?''

If Hal Brognola or Jack Grimaldi or any of Bolan's other few close friends had been present, they would have rated the question absurd. Few cared more for America than Bolan. He had proved his devotion time and again where it counted, on the battlefield, putting his life on the line for Lady Liberty and all she stood for.

"I'd say so."

"So do I, believe it or not. But yes, I think our government is out of control." Standish launched into a litany of complaints. "Crooked politicians fleece us every day. They've put us in debt to the tune of trillions of dollars. They tell us how we should live, what we should think—"

Bolan held up a hand. Demagogues loved to get on a soapbox, but he wasn't in the mood to stand there listening to Standish prattle on.

"Hear me out," the man said. "Did you know that in some counties in Nevada, the federal government controls over ninety percent of the public lands?"

So what? Bolan mused. Land not privately owned or under state and county supervision was held in public trust by the federal government.

"Ninety percent!" Standish repeated, as if it were horrible beyond belief. "And that's just the tip of the iceberg. Nationwide, the government controls half a million acres!"

"Out of some two trillion," Bolan mentioned, and saw that he had surprised the firebrand.

"Even so, five hundred million is about four hundred million too many," Standish said. "It's my aim to see that our government gives up its control of land that should rightly be under local control.''

Bolan glanced at Mathews, who was being no help whatsoever. ''What do you do for living, Mr. Standish?'' he asked out of curiosity.

''I'm a lawyer.''

The soldier stared out the rear picture window at a robin that had the end of a worm in its beak and was tugging furiously to yank the worm out. He should have known.

''I used to specialize in environmental issues until I stumbled on the government conspiracy to hoard our land.''

''Conspiracy?'' Bolan said. He had stood about all he was going to. ''Can we come down to earth and talk about Garth? Do you know him or not?''

''Trevor Garth? Most certainly. And if you think I'm off in the ozone somewhere, then you should meet him. The man is positively rabid where the federal government is concerned. Why, he thinks that there is a plot in the works to have everyone stripped of their constitutional rights and have a—''

The next instant, all hell broke loose.

Amy, the brunette, appeared at the end of the hall bearing a tray laden with cups and saucers. She smiled and opened her mouth, but whatever she wanted to say was drowned out by the tremendous crash of the front door buckling inward.

Two men dressed entirely in black hurtled into

the house, their faces covered by ski masks, their gloved hands holding Mossberg Model 500 pistol-grip shotguns. They issued no threats; they gave no warnings. They simply opened fire.

Bolan was in action the moment the door went down. His right hand swept under his jacket and found the Beretta, but as he dropped into a combat crouch, Harry Standish jumped up right in front of him, blocking his shot.

It was to prove a costly mistake.

The two shotguns boomed. Loaded with buckshot, at that range they had the devastating effect of small cannons.

Amy was flung against the wall, her chest mangled, the lower half of her face torn to ribbons.

Standish took a blast full in the torso. The impact did to him what it had done to his girlfriend. Like a ripped and bloody rag doll, he was thrown backward to slam into Bolan, smashing them both against the fireplace. The soldier ended up on the bottom, and out of the corner of his eye he glimpsed Mathews on her knees by the chair, fumbling for her weapon.

"We got him!" one of the masked killers bellowed. "Go! Go!"

The pair turned to flee.

As if in slow motion, Bolan saw Mathews lunge upright, saw her adopt a two-handed stance and take deliberate aim when she would have been better off snapping shots at random. He shoved against Standish, but in death the man seemed to weigh a ton.

One of the gunners bolted through the shattered doorway. The second, though, glanced back and spied Mathews. His shotgun was at his hip, pointing in her general direction. All he had to do was squeeze the trigger.

Someone once said that buckshot was the next best thing to a hand grenade, and anyone who knew anything about the destructive power of double-aught shot at close range would never dispute it. Bolan shouted a warning, his cry eclipsed by the thunder of the Mossberg.

The soldier had seen far too many people die. He had lost loved ones, friends, casual acquaintances. He had seen strangers cut down like so much straw under a scythe. Yet he would never forget what happened next.

Agent Brenda Mathews took the full force of the discharge in the head. She died in a heartbeat, her cranium bursting like an overripe melon. Her body was crushed to the carpet where it rolled against the wall, upending a lamp.

The second gunner sped from the scene.

Icy fury seized the Executioner. It was an emotion he rarely let himself feel. In combat, all emotions hampered one's ability. But he had liked Mathews, and she had died helping him.

Bolan heaved the corpse from him at last. He was

on his feet and racing to the door as a car engine roared to life. Beretta extended, he cleared the jamb to find the brown sedan chewing up the gravel, roaring in reverse down the driveway. He loosed two shots at the driver. The windshield sprouted a web of cracks, but the car didn't slow.

The soldier spun and dashed back inside. He ran to Harry Standish, hoping he remembered the correct pocket. Heedless of the blood, he yanked out the car keys.

Fortune favored him. The brown sedan had reached the first bend, and the driver had spun the wheel to swing the car around, but he had miscalculated and the vehicle slid partway into the ditch. Now, tires spinning, it clawed up onto the driveway and zoomed downward like a runaway train.

By then Bolan was in the Saab Turbo, working the five-speed shift in a flurry, grinding gears as he whipped it into reverse to back it up against the house. Its 160-horsepower engine roared as he stepped on the gas and streaked in pursuit.

The killers bounced over the ditch onto the road. They turned left, accelerating rapidly. But as fast as they were, their Ford was no match for the sports car. Bolan hit the road doing over fifty and in seconds was pushing ninety, his front bumper riding their tail end.

Spinning the steering wheel, Bolan attempted to

pull alongside. The sedan swerved to prevent him. Again he tried, with the same result.

A harrowing game of cat and mouse ensued, with the Executioner seeking to get close enough to shoot, and the desperate triggermen balking him. It was a stalemate until they came to the junction.

Bolan knew that they would try to turn left and head back to Las Vegas. So when they did, he veered into their path, sending the Saab broadside into the driver's door. Metal crunched; pieces of chrome flew. For long seconds the two vehicles were locked together, engines revving, tires grinding for traction.

The Ford gave way first. It swerved to the right, and Bolan saw the driver pumping the wheel frantically to keep the car from flying off the road into trees. The man succeeded, but by then the sedan was pointed in the opposite direction. It shot north up Highway 93.

Downshifting, his tires screaming, Bolan tore after them. Thankfully, the traffic wasn't as heavy as it would be later in the day during rush hour, when commuters left the city in droves for their country homes.

A corner of the sedan's front fender was dragging on the asphalt, showering sparks.

Bolan detected a slight stiffness in the steering linkage as he tromped on the accelerator. It had been damaged when they collided, and he could only hope it didn't worsen.

The killers caught up with a slow-moving truck. Not bothering to brake, they went around it doing over seventy. An oncoming driver leaned on his horn as they narrowly missed him.

Bolan had to be careful. As much as he wanted the pair, he wouldn't endanger bystanders if he could help it. Bringing the Saab from fourth to fifth gear, he passed the truck and discovered a straight stretch ahead. He poured on the gas.

The killers had done the same. There was movement in the front seat, but Bolan couldn't quite make out what they were doing. His speedometer soared to ninety-five, to one hundred and higher. The surrounding countryside was a blur. They passed a car, so he did too, careful to swerve wide in order not to scare the elderly female driver any more than she already was.

An RV was next. The Ford flew by without any regard for oncoming traffic. A Volkswagen van had to brake sharply, the driver leaning on his horn as he slanted toward the shoulder to avoid an impact.

The gunner cut in too close to the RV. Bumpers scraped. The angry RV driver pounded on his horn, too, and nearly went into the ditch.

Then the Ford was in the clear, and it was Bolan's turn. The RV had slowed, but if he did the same he stood the risk of losing the triggermen.

Flooring it, he zipped ahead of the RV, whose driver flipped him the finger.

The sedan had gained a few dozen yards. In short order Bolan narrowed the gap again. The Ford's trusty engine was just no match for the Saab's high-performance engine.

As Bolan caught up, he saw the rear window being cranked down. A masked head popped out, and thin lips curled in a sadistic smile. The next moment the business end of a shotgun was thrust in his direction.

Bolan decelerated. The Saab dropped from ninety to forty in a span of seconds. It was barely enough. The Mossberg boomed, spraying lead, some of which clipped the sports car's hood and roof.

The killer worked the pump action, then brazenly smiled and beckoned for Bolan to come closer.

The soldier was lucky the shooters weren't armed with high-powered rifles. The shotgun's range was limited.

Hollywood's nonsense notwithstanding, a shotgun couldn't cause a speeding auto to explode into tiny bits. It would do damage, yes, but a lot depended on the gauge and the ammo used.

The soldier suspected that the shooters had 12-gauge weapons. The last he knew, Mossberg didn't manufacture 16-gauge persuaders. The 20-gauge variety, while they offered the advantage of less recoil, suffered from a scarcity of ammo in any shot greater than Number 2 buck.

But 12-gauges had it all: heavier payloads, higher velocity, deeper penetration. They were the closest thing to a real megablaster.

The only drawback was their range. With buckshot, the average was about fifteen yards. Eighteen yards, tops.

So Bolan stayed approximately twenty yards back, debating how he could stop the Ford before it went much farther. The loss of his duffel hampered him. Without it, his firepower was limited to the Beretta and the Desert Eagle.

Shooting out one or two of their tires would slow them, but the only sure means of stopping them was to take out the driver. Which he couldn't do while that grinning baboon in the back seat held him at bay.

A bend loomed ahead. It wasn't much of one, but the angle was such that Bolan felt justified in being a shade reckless. As the sedan whipped around the corner, he shot forward. Only instead of swinging wide to the outside, he held to the inside of the curve.

Before the killers knew what he was up to, the Saab was abreast of the sedan on the passenger's side. Bolan jerked the Beretta from his lap, pointed it out the open window and fixed a hasty bead on the driver.

The gunner saw him and shouted something. The Ford slanted toward the opposite shoulder, too late. Bolan squeezed the trigger. He saw a hole blossom in the sedan's window, saw the man at the wheel jarred by the slug.

Bolan slowed, expecting the other car to do the same. Instead, the driver went even faster. The shotgunner in the back seat switched windows, rolling down the other back one to get at the Saab.

Slipping into place directly behind them, Bolan kept the Saab on their rear bumper. They zigzagged repeatedly, but they couldn't shake him.

Bolan was on the verge of ramming them when the man in the back seat suddenly faced the Saab and raised the shotgun.

Instantly, the soldier braked, punching the pedal so hard that the sports car weaved wildly coming to a stop. It was well he did, for the sedan's rear window had dissolved in a spray of lead that would have done the same to the Saab's windshield.

The gunner laughed and gave a taunting wave.

Bolan sat there a few moments, revving the engine, calculating and projecting, doing what he did best. One of his strengths was his unmatched ability as a tactician. Strategy was his forte, whether it involved complicated battle maneuvers or spur-of-the moment firefight combat.

In short, Bolan had a knack for always picking

an enemy's weakness and capitalizing, for doing whatever it took to get the job done.

In this instance it was imperative that he end the chase before lives were lost. He couldn't do it playing tag. He had to disable the Ford swiftly, effectively. Since he lacked their firepower, he had to rely on his one clear advantage—speed.

Bolan revved the engine a final time. At the apex of its roar, he rammed his foot onto the gas and sped northward—fifty in under five seconds, eighty in under seven.

The needle climbed to ninety, and still Bolan held the pedal to the floor. One hundred miles per hour didn't faze him, nor did one-ten. The Saab was a blur, a red hare to their brown tortoise.

He glanced at the dash. One-fifteen and still rising. Girding himself, he prepared to sweep into the other lane and zip by them as if they were standing still. Then he would bring the sports car broadside and hop out. They would have to stop or be riddled with bullets.

There was only one potential flaw. Bolan had to get past the sedan before its occupants realized what he was up to and the man in the back seat popped out to stop him. The sports car was sixty feet away, then forty, thirty, fifteen. He was almost there. Another two seconds and he had them. That was when the killer in the back seat lunged into view, leveling the 12-gauge.

CHAPTER EIGHT

The Executioner had a split second in which to react. One of his options was to slam on the brakes again and drop back out of range. Another option was to swerve to the left in the hope that the passenger's side would absorb the buckshot. The gunner would expect him to do either, so he did neither.

Bolan resorted to the only tactic that would get him past the sedan, if it worked. He veered toward the sedan, trying to force the gunner in black back into the Ford.

Traveling at the rate he was, Bolan was on the killer in the blink of an eye. The triggerman drew back as if scorched. Accidentally, the man's weapon went off, and the buckshot sailed over the Saab's roof.

The recoil caused the gunner to lose his grip. His Mossberg slipped. In order to catch it, he had to lunge outward, and he did so without thinking. If he had been thinking, he would have realized that the Saab was much too close and getting closer. He would have foreseen the result.

Bolan hadn't intended for the cars to brush together. It just happened. He saw the gunner lunge, saw the upper half of the man's body disappear between the vehicles, then felt a bump and a grating lurch.

Steering clear, Bolan added the final burst of speed needed to pass the sedan. In the process, he left the limp figure of the gunner flopping against the Ford, the man's ski mask a flattened ruin, the shoulders splattered with blood and gore.

One down, one to go.

The driver cast a spiteful glance at Bolan as the Saab surged ahead. Bolan noted that the man drove with one hand. The other arm had been rendered useless by the round from the Beretta.

Bolan continued to gain steadily. As soon as he was well in the lead, he braced for braking. The brown sedan filled the rearview mirror. He was watching it closely, so he was surprised when the wily driver left the road.

The sedan bounced over the shallow ditch, smashed through a fence and plowed off across a field, spewing dust and dirt like a tornado. It missed a stump, tilted going over a deep rut, and made for a belt of vegetation in the distance.

It took Bolan much too long to reduce speed to where he could execute a U-turn. By the time he reached the field, the Ford was roughly seven hundred yards away, barreling to the southeast.

As a general rule, sports cars weren't made for off-road travel. Their suspensions weren't up to the jolting and pounding, and their bodies rode too low. But that didn't stop Bolan from driving the Saab across the ditch as if striving to get airborne, then plunging into the swirling cloud of dust.

It got into his eyes, mouth and nose. Pressing the lower half of his face against his left forearm, he bore to the right to miss the worst of it.

They were in relatively open country. Bolan didn't see how the driver could get away, but if there was one lesson he had learned, it was to never, ever take anything for granted. The belt of vegetation might be thicker than it appeared. Or there might be a residence on the other side, where the gunner could switch vehicles or perhaps take a hostage.

Back on Highway 93, cars and trucks were stopping so their occupants could watch the chase. By now someone had probably contacted the local authorities. A sheriff's deputy was bound to show up. Bolan preferred to be gone by then.

The sedan gained the vegetation. The brake lights flared, and the wounded gunner jumped out. He took one look at the onrushing red sports car and stumbled into the brush. He didn't take his shotgun.

Bolan chafed at the extra time it took him to

reach the same spot. He was out of the Saab while it was still coasting to a halt, and in among cottonwoods and willows. The gurgle of sluggish water revealed that the plant growth hugged an irrigation ditch.

The killer was somewhere in there.

The soldier stooped low and listened. A brisk breeze stirred the leaves and grass. No footfalls sounded. No brush crackled. The man was either out of earshot, which was unlikely given his condition, or he was wisely lying low, waiting for Bolan to show himself.

The soldier resorted to one of the oldest tricks in the book. A stone sufficed. Palming it, he cocked his arm and threw it to the left into a thicket. The cracking and snapping provoked no response, so he tossed another to the right.

A pistol cracked somewhere close to the water, the shot aimed at the point where the stone hit. That told him the gunner was running scared and liable to blast away at shadows.

Flattening, Bolan crawled into a patch of high weeds. He applied pressure slowly to the stems so they wouldn't shake violently and give his location away. Faint splashing reached him, letting him know that the gunner was changing position.

The killer was in the ditch, probably hugging the near bank, using it to screen himself.

Accordingly, Bolan angled toward the water. The

weeds ended a few feet shy of the edge. Wary of being caught in the open, he eeled around a small knob, shifted and eased his legs over the top.

The ditch was three feet deep, twice that wide. He pressed his spine against the smooth bank, scouring the section before him for sign of a black ski mask. Low-hanging brush cloaked the sides, providing ample cover.

Bolan came to the first clump. Setting his shoes down with the utmost care so he wouldn't slip on the slick surface underfoot, he crept past it. The gunner wasn't on the other side.

A siren howled in the distance. The local law was on the way. Unless Bolan wrapped this up quickly, he would be hauled in for questioning.

It was a routine he had been through more times than he cared to count. He would be treated just like any other suspect, cuffed and questioned and kept under close watch until Brognola got word to the higher-ups that he should be released. He could do without that headache, thank you.

Bolan drew the Desert Eagle. Bending at the knees, he dipped until the water rose to his chin. Six feet wasn't much, but with a wounded trigger-man eager for the chance to cut him down, the other bank might as well be a mile.

Crabbing sideways, Bolan cautiously started across. A few dozen yards farther, something moved close to the bank. He froze, balancing his left foot on his toes, riveted to a shadow that acquired form and substance.

The shooter was concentrating on the trees, not the ditch. He had pulled his ski mask up to his forehead, exposing a pudgy face, a bald pate that glistened with sweat and a mustache modeled after Hitler's. His hurt arm was tucked to his side. In his other hand was what appeared to be a Browning Hi-Power semiauto pistol.

Bolan didn't quite have a clear shot. But with the siren growling ever louder, and the prospect of nosy busybodies arriving on the scene at any moment, it had to do. He tracked the killer with the Desert Eagle, the hammer cocked, his finger caressing the hair trigger. A few more inches would do it.

A songbird trilled north of Bolan. It wasn't a cry of alarm, yet the gunner glanced toward the bird, and spotted him.

The Browning leaped up, its muzzle spitting high-velocity death. But in the span it took the pudgy man to fire twice, the Executioner fired three times, the roars of the Desert Eagle amplified by the narrow ditch.

Kicked rearward, the man toppled against the side and was still, one arm snared in growth.

Bolan hurried forward. A rear pocket yielded a wallet, which he thrust into a pocket to inspect later. Climbing out of the ditch, he holstered both guns and headed for the field.

Flashing lights warned him that it wasn't a good idea. A sheriff's cruiser had arrived, and another was coming from the other direction. Retreating into the willows, he crossed the ditch, then turned to the south and broke into a mile-eating jog that he could sustain for hours.

He had an appointment to keep in Reno.

THERE HAD BEEN a few occasions when Hal Brognola had wished he could read people's minds to learn what made them tick. This was one of them.

An hour earlier Bolan had contacted him from McCarran Airport and filled him in on what had gone down at the Standish residence.

Brognola had caught an unusual note in Bolan's voice when his friend told of Agent Mathews's death. He had been about to ask if the two had struck up a friendship, but Bolan said he had to go, that the plane was due to leave in a few minutes.

It bothered him.

It wasn't like Bolan to let the death of a field agent get to him. Not that Bolan was made of steel. He was human, after all. But the man was professional enough to appreciate that emotions and duty were a volatile mix. In the heat of combat, self-control was crucial.

Was Bolan slipping? He quickly dismissed the notion. Bolan would always focus on the task at hand. He'd deal with the pain of Mathews's death later.

Seated at his desk, sipping at a steaming cup of coffee, Brognola thoughtfully regarded the growing file he had started on their prime suspect.

Trevor Constable Garth. Age, thirty-two. Height, according to his driver's license, six feet, five and a half inches, Weight, 224 pounds. He had no criminal record, not so much as a speeding ticket. IRS files divulged that he had vast real-estate holdings, and bank accounts that totaled in the millions. He lived in a mansion, belonged to several prestigious organizations.

What could possibly induce a man like Garth to turn into a rabid revolutionary?

The big Fed was thoroughly mystified and deeply troubled. It wasn't bad enough that more and more citizens were taking up arms against their own government. It wasn't bad enough that many were ordinary blue-collar people who had never committed a crime in their lives. Now a man like Trevor Garth, someone who had everything, someone who was rich, respected and powerful, had joined the ranks of the disaffected.

What did it all mean? Was it symptomatic of far worse to come?

The other name Bolan had given him had proved more mundane.

Lyle Bollinger was a born hardcase. He had quit

school in the eighth grade, been arrested for burglary and petty theft and gone to prison for trying to cave in the skull of a woman who hadn't wanted to part with her purse.

While behind bars, Bollinger had been recruited by the Aryans. It had given him a whole new perspective on life. He had learned to hate Jews, to hate blacks, to hate anyone and everyone in authority. Upon his release, he had joined the Neo-Brotherhood, a small group of supremacists operating in eastern Nevada.

Now Bollinger and an unidentified accomplice had murdered Harry Standish, Amy Pournelle and Agent Brenda Mathews. Why? Were they doing the bidding of the Neo-Brotherhood or someone else?

The evidence indicated the latter.

Thanks to Bolan, Brognola had uncovered a link between Bollinger and Trevor Garth. In Bollinger's wallet, Bolan had found a membership card to a gun club in Reno called the Sportsman's Shootery. The big Fed had run a quick check and discovered a startling fact. The owner of the club was none other than Trevor Constable Garth.

THANKS TO CHARLIE MOTT, the pilot from Stony Man, Mack Bolan had a new duffel in the trunk of his rental, crammed with the sort of items that a professional warrior couldn't do without.

He drove past the Sportsman's Shootery twice, at

fifteen-minute intervals. It was a long, low structure. A converted warehouse, he deduced, repaired and painted with a high fence around the perimeter to keep out minors.

There was a gate manned by a security guard, which was unusual for a gun club. Bolan was glad the membership card he had taken from the wallet of the dead gunner didn't include a photo of its rightful owner. Braking, he flashed the card at the guard, who consulted a list on a clipboard.

"Ah, yes. Mr. Bollinger. You are aware of the big meeting tonight for Double A members only?"

Bolan had wondered about two capital *A*s stamped on the corner of the card. Now he knew. The club had an elite inner circle that had to include Trevor Garth. "Yes," he answered.

The guard checked his watch. "You're early, sir. The meeting isn't until nine and it's only seven."

"I wanted to get in some practice first," Bolan lied. What he really wanted was to case the club from top to bottom and pick where he would spring his little surprise on the man responsible for the death of Brenda Mathews.

"Have fun," the guard said, waving him through.

The lot was big enough to hold sixty vehicles, and twenty or so were already there. Bolan pulled into a slot near the entrance to insure a quick getaway should things go wrong.

No one else was around. Bolan opened the trunk,

slung the heavy duffel over his shoulder and strolled inside as if he had been doing it for years.

Another security guard, a skinny man with a nervous tic, sat at a front desk. The corner of his mouth constantly twitched as he sat there reading a girlie magazine. Stifling a yawn, he glanced up. "Howdy. Card?"

Bolan showed him and was going to walk on by when the guard unexpectedly straightened.

"Mr. Bollinger? Didn't we talk once? I could have sworn you were about sixty pounds heavier and had a hell of a sight less hair. What did you do? Go on a diet and buy a rug?"

The soldier adopted a friendly smile and plucked at his hair. "No toupee here. You must have me confused with one of the other members."

"I suppose so," the man said. "With over a hundred, and at least thirty of them Double A guys like you, it's easy to get faces confused. Sorry."

The muffled booms of guns wafted from the bowels of the building. Bolan walked on down a long corridor, passing doors that bore stenciled markings. There was the front office, with two secretaries inside. One door was marked Ammo Room; another labeled Armory: By Appointment Only; a utility closet, and finally, a pair of double doors, above them emblazoned in bright red and orange, Warning! Firing Range! Safety Rules Stringently Enforced!

Bolan pushed on through. Immediately, his ears were buffeted by the concussion of multiple heavy-caliber weapons being discharged in thunderous cadence.

One thing was for sure. No expense had been spared in constructing the facility. The range was state-of-the-art, the decor a far cry from a typical ma-and-pa-type operation. Polished paneling adorned the walls, and thick carpet covered the floor. There had to be sixty firing lanes, each enclosed so the shooters enjoyed perfect privacy. In short, the Sportsman's Shootery was an ideal facility for anyone who loved guns.

Bolan moved along the line, noting shooters young and old, male and female. Due to the heavy firing, he didn't realize someone had come up behind him until a hand fell on his shoulder. Tensing, his right hand rising toward the Beretta, he rotated.

"Hi there, partner," said a kindly gray-haired man who wore a cap that identified him as a range instructor. "Did you remember to sign your John Henry before you take a lane?" He indicated a glass booth at the center of the firing line.

"I haven't decided yet whether I'll do any practicing," Bolan said. "I'm here for the meeting later."

"Oh. You're a Double A? That's good. Then I don't need to remind you that you have to be out of here by eight forty-five." There was a lull in the firing and the man lowered his voice. "Just between you and me, some of the regular members are mighty ticked off at you special guys. They don't like it that the Double As get to have the whole place to themselves now and then."

Bolan had to hand it to Trevor Garth. The man had a slick operation set up—a place where Garth could hold a meeting any time, right out in the open, as it were, with no one suspecting his motives. A place where the killers who worked for him could hone their skills, with no one being the wiser.

"Well, if you decide to shoot, remember to get some plugs or muffs from me if you don't have your own," the friendly employee said, and nudged Bolan with an elbow. "We don't want the damn Feds down on our case, do we, brother? You never know when one of them will slip on in here to try and cite us for safety violations."

"That's the government for you," Bolan said. "Always putting safety before all else."

The man laughed. "Yeah. It's getting so that a man can't spit without first looking to make sure Big Brother isn't spying on him."

Bolan nodded, thinking his helpful friend would wander off, but the man was a chatterbox.

"That reminds me. Have you heard about that newfangled law they passed in Minnesota?"

"Which one?" Bolan dutifully asked.

"Where a man can't stare at a woman for more

than seven seconds without being hauled into court on a charge of public ogling? Ain't that just about the stupidest thing ever?''

The soldier did recall reading about it. Apparently, a few women had complained that some construction workers were being too brazen in their admiration of pretty members of the fairer sex who went past their work sites.

''It's a classic example of what's wrong with this country today,'' the man declared. ''The pissant politicians are always sticking their damn noses into things that don't concern them. Do you know why that is?''

Bolan was sure the man would tell him, and he was right.

''We're to blame. You and me and the rest of us chumps. For years we've been electing lawyers to run things. Then we have the gall to complain when they make a bunch of stupid laws. But that's what lawyers do best, ain't it? They love to write new laws, no matter how dumb. It gives them more excuses to sue, and the more they sue, the richer they get. That's the whole shebang in a nutshell.''

It was a novel theory, Bolan reflected. Oddly, it also made a lot of sense.

''My idea is to pass a law that prohibits lawyers from holding any public office. Only ordinary folks like you and me could be senators and such. That would solve everything,'' the man said.

Bolan tried to imagine a senate consisting solely of used-car salesmen, veterinarians, dentists and the like, and couldn't. "It would be different," he conceded.

The employee might have rambled on forever had the double doors not parted and a tall man dressed entirely in black, including black cowboy boots and a wide-brimmed black hat, ambled into the range.

"Goodness gracious!" the chatterbox declared. "That's Mr. Starkey, Mr. Garth's right-hand man. You should see him shoot! He's poetry in motion." Excusing himself, the instructor hastened to greet the newcomer.

Bolan stayed close to the wall where he was less likely to be observed.

Several others converged on the man called Starkey. At one man's gesture, Starkey swept back his jacket to reveal a matched pair of ivory-handled Remington revolvers worn butts forward, the barrels wedged under his belt.

The gunman and his entourage moved to an empty lane. Bolan drifted along behind, halting where he could see without being seen. The instructor gave the man in black a pair of yellow foam plugs to stick into his ears.

Breathless anticipation seemed to grip the onlookers. They watched the tall man closely. Bolan was at a loss to understand why they were so excited until Starkey moved.

It was an incredible explosion of movement, a sweep of arms and body into a unified whole, a draw undeniably as fast as any the soldier had ever seen, and that said a lot. One instant Starkey's hands were empty at his sides; the next they held the nickel-plated Remingtons and the six-shooters were firing so swiftly that it was one continuous blast.

The firing died. The instructor pressed a button, and the target downrange glided forward so they could examine it.

Bolan didn't need to move any nearer to tell that all ten shots had been placed within an inch of one another, smack over the heart. It was uncanny marksmanship, some of the best he had ever witnessed.

"Wow!" a young onlooker marveled. "Trevor Garth sure is lucky to have you as his bodyguard! Is that what you'll do to anyone who tries to hurt him?"

Starkey looked up. "That's exactly what I'll do, pard," he said. It wasn't bluster; it wasn't bragging. It was cold, calculated fact.

CHAPTER NINE

The utility closet was Bolan's best bet. He slipped inside when the corridor was vacant. Mops, brooms and buckets took up one corner. In another stood a floor-to-ceiling shelf stocked with cleaning supplies. Maintenance uniforms hung on a rack. A wash basin took up a third of the floor space.

He set down the duffel and opened it. The M-16 had been broken down into the upper and lower receiver groups for storage, so he reattached them. As he worked, he noticed that the crack of weaponry was unusually loud and crisp overhead. A thin line of light where the rear wall joined the ceiling merited investigation.

Using the shelf as a makeshift ladder, Bolan climbed.

The closet was an add-on, constructed when the warehouse had been converted. It wasn't fully soundproofed, and whoever had installed the rear wall hadn't sealed it properly. A crack enabled Bolan to see and hear everything taking place in the vicinity of the glass booth.

Fate had rolled him a pair of deuces. Now all he had to do was wait for Trevor Garth to show up, hopefully with the Libyan in tow, and he could kill two birds with one stone.

Bolan threaded a sound suppressor onto the Beretta, stowed a pair of grenades in his front pockets and made himself as comfortable as he could.

It was half-past eight.

He had watched Starkey's amazing exhibition for a while, genuinely impressed by the tall man's unerring aim. Not one shot had missed the bull's-eye. Right-handed, left-handed, using both hands at once, the man in black was the embodiment of every Western gunfighter who ever lived.

After Starkey departed, Bolan had drifted around the facility. He'd visited a locker room where members stored personal effects, then a plush lounge where waitresses in skimpy outfits served espresso and sandwiches.

No one challenged him. A few members had made small talk, then gone their own way.

Bolan was a living statue. Years ago his patience had been honed to a superb degree during his sharpshooting days on a special penetration team. He could sit for hours without so much as twitching.

Senses primed, the soldier perked up when someone began shouting that it was fifteen minutes until nine, time for all members who weren't Double As to leave.

Apparently by design, the majority of Double A members didn't arrive until after the others were gone. He heard them filing down the hall, singly and in groups. There was a lot of joking, a lot of laughing. They were in good spirits.

He didn't know how many would show up. Would it be the thirty mentioned by the guard? Or were only certain Double A members invited?

Twenty-one, it turned out, far more than Bolan had bargained on, far more than one man could hope to take on, even with the element of surprise in his favor. Still, Bolan was bound and determined to bring down Trevor Garth, no matter what it took.

Shortly after nine, with the members seated or standing in clusters close to the glass booth, another commotion sounded in the hallway. Soon the doors were opened by husky men in dark suits. Several others entered. Behind them came the gunman, Starkey, who took a post to the left of the doors where the entire range was under his scrutiny.

Last to walk in was a man well over six feet tall, broad at the shoulder, lean at the hips. A flowing leather coat fit snugly to his powerful frame. He had a commanding presence about him, an air possessed by naturally gifted leaders.

No one had to tell Bolan this was the man of the hour. He knew it was Garth, just as he instinctively knew that here was an extraordinarily dangerous man. As dangerous as the Fox. Maybe more so. ~

"Gentlemen! Brothers!" the millionaire said, holding out his arms. "Thank you for showing up on such short notice. Initially, I called this meeting to set your minds at rest about the other night, since many of you weren't there." Garth shrugged out of his coat and gave it to an underling. "But now I have simply wonderful news to report."

A scruffy man chewing on the stub of an unlit cigar raised a hand. "The news can wait. What's this about federal agents jumpin' you and that Arab up in the Spring Mountains? I thought you claimed something like that would never happen."

Some of the others had been whispering. To a man, they stopped, turning worried eyes on their leader. Those closest to the speaker edged to either side.

Trevor Garth, though, didn't take offense. "Mr. Lafferty, I can always rely on you to cut to the chase, as they say. Yes, two incompetents we took to be federal agents showed up during the meeting. Our Arab friend disposed of them with one of the mortars he brought us."

Lafferty wasn't satisfied. "Feds are like rabbits. Kill one, and there's always another hoppin' around somewhere ready to take its place."

"How eloquent," Garth said sarcastically. He scanned the faces ringing him and didn't seem to like what he saw. "Brothers! What is the matter with you? Where is your faith? A minor setback like this, and all of you go to pieces?"

Another man responded, rather timidly. "Some of us just don't like dealing with foreigners, Mr. Garth. This is a homegrown outfit. We're all home-grown boys. We don't need no stinking Arabs telling us how to do things."

"Withers, I'm surprised at you," Garth said. "Do you honestly think I wouldn't know what is best for the organization *I* started? The Minutemen were my brainstorm, not yours."

So now Bolan knew what they called themselves. The irony wasn't lost on him.

Before the Revolutionary War, militia companies had been formed in Massachusetts and elsewhere. They were trained to be ready to fight at a minute's notice—ergo, minute men. The name was synonymous with patriotism.

"I took the liberty of contacting the Arab because he can provide us with any type of weapon we want, for the right price. The PLO has used his services, the IRA, the Red Brigade in Japan, the PKK and others. Why not us?"

No one responded. Garth clasped his hands behind his back and paced in front of them, his scowl like that of a grizzly about to charge. "What is the matter with you people? Each and every one of you was handpicked by me. You were chosen because you feel the same way that I do about this glorious country of ours. Because you want to see the government stopped before we have a dictatorship on our hands."

Garth had a flair for public speaking. His tone, his rich resonance, his very posture radiated vitality, mesmerizing his followers.

"Would I do anything to hurt our cause? No! Would I do anything to harm any of you? No!" He gestured grandly. "Trust me, fellow Minutemen! I always have our best interests at heart."

Did anyone besides Bolan notice that he had danced verbal rings around their worries without actually addressing them? Evidently not, since the majority acted content.

"Our Arab friend hasn't left yet," Garth rumbled on. "We have yet to finalize a deal, since he has been holding out for more money. It's proved to be a costly mistake on his part."

"How's that, sir?" someone inquired.

Garth's face lit up like a Christmas tree. "Gentlemen, I have outstanding news! A fluke has delivered into our hands the means to bring about our goal without having to pay another cent to the Arab or anyone else." He paused for effect. "The Minutemen now have the means to bring the federal government to its knees!"

Bolan had been about to climb down. He planned to leave his hiding place and jump them while they were distracted. With any luck, he'd nail Garth and Starkey and eight or nine others, then he would get out of there and let the Feds mop out. But now he stopped cold.

A note of confidence and triumph had crept into Trevor Garth's voice.

"That's right!" the giant crowed. "The means to our nation's salvation has been delivered into our laps! We now have a stockpile of chemical-warfare weapons large enough to wipe out every man, woman and child in any major city in the country!"

They lapped up the news like starved cats lapping up milk. Inspired by their leader, aglow with a shared feeling of power and conviction, they beamed and clapped one another on the back or shoulder.

"How did this happen?" one asked.

"The details are unimportant at this time," Garth said. "What matters is that we act quickly. There is a chance that the Feds are on to us. Some of our brothers in Las Vegas have disappeared without a trace. I suspect they have been taken into custody."

Murmuring broke out.

"Our brothers are brave men. They're sworn to secrecy. But we all know that the government has ways of making people talk. Truth drugs. Threats against loved ones. Even torture, if they have to."

Bolan tried to get a better look at Garth. Did the man honestly believe the federal government would resort to torture? Or was he playing to the fears of the Minutemen to sway them into doing his bidding?

"So I repeat—we must act quickly!" Garth pounded a palm with a fist. "I want all of you to report to the warehouse tomorrow at four in the afternoon. I'm having the chemical material transferred there."

Shifting his leg for better balance, Bolan felt the shelf sag under his weight. He tried to shift again, but the wood gave way with a resounding crack.

A profound silence gripped the gun club.

Bolan raised himself and risked a look. Trevor Garth was nowhere to be seen, and the members of the Minutemen were piling toward the double doors.

The soldier dropped, unlimbering the Beretta as he did, then turned. At that split second, the utility-room door burst open, framing a bruiser in a dark suit, holding an autopistol. The soldier fired first, two rounds that punched the man backward, a pair of holes drilled between his eyes.

Someone shouted. Autopistols and SMGs unleashed a hammering crescendo as slugs bored through the walls on both sides of the doorway and through the doorway itself, peppering the washbasin. They chopped broomsticks into bits and ripped into the shelves, shattering the items they held.

The hailstorm would have done the same to Bolan—if he were still on his feet. But the moment he downed the first gunner, he had flattened. Holstering the 9 mm pistol, he scrambled to the M-16. Plaster, chips and assorted pieces of plastic and wood cascaded onto him as he flicked the selector lever from semi- to full-auto.

Rolling to the left of the doorway, Bolan hugged the floor, waiting. The Minutemen were making the same mistake that most novice killers did. They were firing high, aiming their rounds from the waist up, when it should have occurred to them that anyone with half a brain would hit the floor.

Suddenly, the shooting tapered. Magazines had cycled dry and were being replaced.

It was a window of opportunity Bolan wouldn't pass up. Staying on the floor, he flipped into the doorway. To the right and the left were gunners caught flat-footed in the act of reloading.

Bolan sprayed quick, controlled bursts that stitched chests and ruptured abdomens. The front ranks were devastated. Men fell like bowling pins, some screaming as they gave up the ghost.

Snapping back before they retaliated, Bolan yanked a grenade from a pocket. He pulled the pin, tensed, then lunged, heaving the bomb to the left, toward the double doors to the firing range where most of the opposition was congregated.

"Grenade!" a man roared. Feet pounded madly,

yelling and strident cries further testifying to the panic.

Bolan rose onto his knees and retreated into a far corner, covering his head with an arm. Mentally, he ticked off the seconds. M-67 fragmentation hand grenades had a four- to five-second time-delay element in their fuse. At the five-second count, this one went off.

The soldier figured that the Minutemen had tried to retreat through the double doors. Apparently, not all of them made it. At the crump of the blast, amplified by the confines of the corridor, screams and shrieks and wails mingled in a ghastly refrain.

Lunging erect, Bolan slung the duffel over his left shoulder and barreled into the hall, throwing himself against the opposite wall.

Seven bloody forms were sprawled near the double doors, three of them still moving. The doors themselves were shattered ruins. Smoke and dust hung heavy in the air, so thick that Bolan couldn't see more than a few feet past them.

In the other direction were two bodies, as well as several gunners who had overcome their shock and were regrouping. He swiveled the M-16 and sent a sustained burst into the heart of the small group. As some fell and others turned to flee, he charged forward.

It meant certain death to linger in the hall. Outnumbered as he was, no amount of firepower would spare him from the inevitable. In order to fight another day, he had to live, to get away. To that end, he headed for the entrance.

Behind him more shouting showed that the Minutemen who had darted into the range were marshaling. The thought of having a dozen rabid fanatics at his back spurred him to go faster.

A man had stopped in front of him and was raising a Smith & Wesson pistol. Bolan drilled the gunner's cranium with a single round.

Two men in uniform appeared beyond, in the lobby. The security guards drew their service revolvers.

Bolan hesitated. The guards weren't Minutemen. They were legitimate, working for a private security firm, and were just doing their jobs. He had no right killing them if he could help it.

A door on the left offered him an alternative. It was the lounge. Lowering his shoulder, he slammed into it at the same instant that someone pulled on the knob on the other side. The door flew inward, bowling over a portly man in a red shirt who yelped as he landed on his posterior, then sat gaping in stunned disbelief.

Was the guy a Minuteman? Bolan had no way of knowing for sure. So he let the gawker live, dashing past a pair of petrified waitresses to the wide picture windows that fronted the parking lot.

Halting, Bolan tucked the M-16s stock to his side

and swung the barrel in a circular pattern, lacing the window with lead. Slinging the autorifle, he grabbed the back of a chair, pivoted and hurled it with all his might at the center of the circle.

With a tremendous din, the picture window came crashing down, shards raining onto the carpet. Bolan sidestepped a piece big enough to slice off a limb. Holding tight to the duffel, he took several long strides and vaulted the bottom of the window.

It was a four-foot drop. He landed lightly, then made for the rental. Off to his left someone bellowed, but he paid no heed. Throwing the car's door wide, he threw the duffel onto the seat, shoved the M-16 onto the dash and slid in.

The security guard at the gate was on a phone in the shack next to it. He looked up as the sedan revved. Spying Bolan, he let the receiver fall and leaped out, awkwardly clawing at his weapon.

Bolan hunched low to make himself a smaller target. He was one row from the gate when a gleaming black limousine hurtled from an aisle on his left. Madly spinning the wheel, he averted a collision by inches.

The limo never slowed, never stopped. Wheeling toward the gate, it would have run the guard down had the man not jumped back into the guard shack.

It had to be Trevor Garth, Bolan realized. He raced from the lot on the limo's heels, aware that the security guard was bringing a revolver to bear but counting on his speed and the guard's agitated state to spoil the man's aim. Two shots rang out. Neither came anywhere near him.

The limo had gained speed, and Bolan stomped on the accelerator. Come what may, he had to catch Trevor Garth. The millionaire was the brains behind the Minutemen, and without him, they would fall apart.

There was a hitch, though. As far as Bolan knew, Garth might be the only one who could tell him where the chemical-warfare weapons were stored. Since it was imperative that Bolan find them, he had to take Garth alive.

Once again Bolan found himself embroiled in a high-speed pursuit. This time, with a crucial difference. They were in the middle of Reno, not out in the country. Innocents were all around. Somehow he had to stop the limo without bringing harm to the legion of bystanders.

Any hope of that was dashed when the limo wheeled right at the next intersection. The front window on the passenger's side lowered, exposing a swarthy gunner in a black suit who leaned out and pointed an Uzi at the Chevrolet.

Bolan swerved to the left. Above the squeal of tires, he heard the chatter of a submachine gun. Rounds pinged off the hood and the roof. Three holes dotted the edge of the windshield. He floored the gas to pull abreast of the driver's side but the limo banked, forcing him toward the curb.

Bolan tried to fight it, but the sedan jumped onto the sidewalk. A woman pushing a baby carriage froze in terror. He cranked the wheel to the right, narrowly avoiding the mother and her child.

The soldier caught up with the limo. The gunner popped above its roof, squeezing off a steady stream of slugs.

It sounded as if someone were beating on the sedan with a ballpeen hammer as Bolan nudged it closer to the limo. He wanted to make the limo pull over, but he had to be careful how he went about it. And where. One wrong move and pedestrians would pay with their lives.

Without warning, the limousine cut to the right, taking a side street. Bolan was caught off guard and shot past the turn. Throwing the sedan into reverse, he backed up and turned. By then he was half a block behind.

Four blocks farther, the limo careened into a broad avenue, scattering panic-stricken motorists like so many chickens. Bolan almost rammed into a pickup. The driver of a concrete truck shook a fist and insulted his lineage. Then he was past them and had a straight shot at the limo.

There was only one problem. The triggerman holding the Uzi had a clear shot at him. Bolan juked to the left when the man fired, and he knew that his windshield couldn't absorb many more slugs without falling apart.

In a spurt of speed, Bolan pulled next to the limo's front fender. Deliberately, he rammed them. The other vehicle swerved, but its driver compensated. Again the two vehicles ground together. Bolan sought to buckle the metal around the limo's fender well. It was hopeless. The limo was built like a tank. The best he could do was scrape and dent the surface.

The rental car simply wasn't heavy enough. Bolan had to devise a new strategy.

Drawing the Desert Eagle, he shot out the passenger's window. Simultaneously, he let up on the accelerator a hair. When the two vehicles were neck and neck, his passenger's door lined up evenly with the driver's door on the limo, Bolan snapped two shots at the driver's window. It should have brought the limousine to a halt, but he hadn't counted on its windows being bulletproof. Or close to it. The glass cracked and splintered but stopped the slugs.

Another couple of shots should do the job. Before Bolan could shoot, however, the limo veered toward him. He had no time to swerve. The Chevy was propelled into a parked station wagon.

The impact threw Bolan against the steering wheel, and the breath whooshed from his lungs. Bright fireflies danced in front of his eyes. Dazed, ribs aflame with pain, he struggled to resume the chase.

The crippled sedan was sluggish. He had to use both hands to spin the wheel. Shaking his head to clear it, he saw the limo take a corner a block away.

Bolan fairly flew to the junction. He took it on two tires, causing a young couple in the crosswalk to leap out of his path. Straightening the sedan, he looked up.

The limousine was gone.

At the next intersection, Bolan braked. He checked in both directions, frustration balling his gut into a knot. Impossibly, the limo had already vanished. On impulse, he turned right and traveled several blocks. No luck.

Trevor Garth, the madman who schemed to slay untold thousands, had gotten clean away.

CHAPTER TEN

"When it rains, it pours," Hal Brognola said.

It was a tired cliché but oh so true. Bolan took a sip of the coffee the big Fed handed him and stepped to the office window. Reno was awash in garish neon. Even though it was three in the morning, the city's nightlife was still in full swing. Below, two women in short dresses paraded their ample wares for the benefit of passing motorists.

"I had him and blew it," Bolan said.

"You did your best," Brognola stated. He watched his friend closely, wondering after all if Bolan was taking this one too personally for his own good.

Brognola had taken a special flight out of Washington the minute he learned about Garth's macabre claim. It was frightening to think that the fanatic had indeed gotten his hands on a stockpile of chemical weapons. Collaring him was a top priority. The last thing the Justice man wanted was a Tokyo-subway-type disaster on his hands.

"What I can't figure out," Brognola said, "is how Garth got hold of the stuff. The Libyan deals in arms and explosives, not chemicals."

"He must have found another source."

"That's just it. Security at plants that manufacture warfare chemicals is almost as tight as security around nuclear installations. A person can't just walk in off the street and help himself."

"It's not a bluff. Garth definitely got some somewhere," Bolan told his friend.

"Oh, I don't doubt it. Anyone with that much money can pretty much get his hands on whatever he wants." Opening a briefcase he had brought along, he removed a file and laid it on the desk. "I'm still in the dark as to his motives, though. Can you shed some light?"

Bolan remembered the speech he had overheard. "He thinks our government is on the verge of becoming a dictatorship."

Brognola shook his head in bewilderment. "How can any sane person believe such nonsense? Doesn't he realize that it can never happen here, not with the checks and balances our Constitution guarantees? Why, if any President tried to seize the reins of government, he'd be impeached so fast his head would swim."

"It's not the President per se Garth is worried about," Bolan said. "It's the government as a whole.'' He paused. ''At least, that's the impression I had.''

The big Fed was still mystified. Although he had mulled it over from every angle on the flight out, he was no closer to comprehending than he had been when the whole nasty business began. Shifting gears, he asked, ''How soon will you go in?''

''At four.''

''My special team is on standby. We'll provide perimeter cover and make sure no one escapes.''

Bolan polished off the rest of the cup of coffee in two gulps, then arched an eyebrow at his friend. ''We?''

''You don't expect me to sit on my duff while this goes down, do you?''

No, Bolan didn't. But it bothered him nonetheless. Brognola was a lot like a Thoroughbred too long confined to a stable; he liked to break harness, liked to stretch his muscles, as it were, to get out in the field every now and then. But the endless days spent behind a desk took their toll. His reflexes weren't what they once were. He was, to put it bluntly, not as young as he used to be. And Bolan worried that one of these days the big Fed's penchant for breaking harness would be the death of him.

''We have the estate under surveillance,'' Brognola went on. It had been one of his first orders of business after arriving in Reno. So far there hadn't been much activity. He didn't even know if Trevor Garth was there.

"Let's just hope the chemicals are stored on the grounds," Bolan remarked. It was a long shot, though. Garth would be more likely to stockpile them somewhere safer, somewhere no one would ever think of looking.

Brognola got up and refilled his coffee cup. "I'm having more Justice agents deployed. They should be here about the middle of the morning. If we don't find Garth at his mansion, I'll have them fan out across the state and check each of his holdings. We won't rest until we track him down."

Bolan didn't bother to point out that a man as devious as Trevor Garth was bound to have any number of safe havens set up. Locating him could well be more difficult than finding the proverbial needle in a haystack.

"Do you want any agents to go in with you?" Brognola inquired.

"No," Bolan said curtly. He had learned his lesson with Mathews. From here on out, he would deal with Garth on his own.

The big Fed was standing by another window. He saw a crowd of revelers going from one casino to another. So happy, so carefree. They had no idea that a madman planned to wipe out their city. Or would Garth strike elsewhere?

That was the trouble with fanatics, Brognola

noted. They were as unpredictable as they were unstable. The psych-profile department couldn't begin to come up with remotely accurate projections.

He had to rely on his instincts on this one. Normally, that was enough to see him through. But when dealing with a loose cannon like Garth, there were no behavioral patterns to guide him, no precedents to fall back on. It was like groping in the dark. A single misstep and he would have the population of an entire metropolis on his conscience.

"I'd better get ready," Bolan commented.

"Let's keep our fingers crossed that this time things go our way," Brognola said. "I'm tired of having one setback after another."

"That makes two of us," the Executioner agreed.

MILES TO THE SOUTH, in one of the most affluent neighborhoods in the city, Trevor Garth climbed plushly carpeted stairs to the third floor of his mansion. Trailing him were two of his trusted lieutenants, Ren Starkey and Paxton Mills.

Garth was smiling. Almost anyone else would have been terrified at the prospect of going up against the limitless might of the federal government, but not Garth.

He saw it as a challenge, as the supreme test of his ability. It was the moment he had known would come one day, the moment he had spent years preparing for. The moment when he formally declared war on the United States of America.

Subdued voices brought an end to Garth's reverie. To be polite, he knocked on the bedroom door and didn't enter until he was bid to do so.

The Fox was seated in a chair across the room. One of his followers sat on the edge of a bed, cleaning an MKE pistol. The other man stood in front of a mirror, preening.

"Finally, my friend!" the Libyan declared. "I grew worried that you had forgotten about us."

"Never fear on that score," Garth said, stepping to the right and leaning against the wall. Starkey stopped in the doorway, blocking it. None of the Arabs noticed that the Texan's jacket was unbuttoned, or if they did, they didn't attach any special importance to the fact.

The Fox patted the briefcase on the nightstand. "I look forward to receiving the rest of my payment. By tomorrow night, the ship will dock in San Francisco. If the cargo of presumed computer equipment passes through customs without a problem, your armament will be on their way to you the day after."

"That's nice," Garth said.

The Libyan continued to fondle the briefcase. "I have kept my word, my friend. You will have all the machine guns, mortars and plastic explosives you could possibly want, enough to start your own private little war.''

Garth glanced at Starkey.

The Libyan's dark eyes held a crafty gleam. ''Keep in mind, though, that unless my people in San Francisco receive word from me, you will not receive a single bullet.''

''You've planned well,'' Garth conceded. ''The steps you've taken would prevent anyone from double-crossing you.''

The Fox beamed smugly. ''I have not lasted as long as I have in this business by being careless.''

''Sometimes being careful isn't enough,'' Garth said. ''Sometimes fate deals us cards from the bottom of the deck and we're stuck with a losing hand. The only thing to do then is fold, or be folded.''

''I am sorry?'' the Fox said, sitting up. Uncertainty marked his cruel features. ''I do not understand your—how would you say it?—figures of speech.''

Garth had looked forward to this. Yes, he had been the one who sought out the Libyan. Yes, he had been willing to pay a small fortune to acquire the arms that were coming in. But that was before Charlie Luft provided him with something better.

The truth was, Garth didn't like Abdul Fezzan, or whatever his real name happened to be. Necessity had given birth to their business arrangement. Circumstance required that he sever it, with extreme prejudice.

"I meant that I no longer have need of the armament," Garth said frankly. "I don't give a damn whether they're smuggled into the country or not."

Suppressed fury made the Fox's sinister visage even more evil. Leaping to his feet, he stabbed a thick finger at his host. "What game is this you play? We had a deal. I went to considerable expense on your behalf, and I demand that you honor your word."

Garth sighed. "I don't suppose you would be willing to write it off as a business loss and let it go at that?"

"Are you insane?"

The other two Libyans had risen and nervously glanced from their leader to the giant in the leather coat. Their English was limited, and they didn't quite grasp what was transpiring.

The Fox started around the bed. "I warn you, American! Do not think to cheat me! I head the most feared terrorist organization in the world! All I need do is snap my fingers, and you are a dead man." To emphasize his point, he did just that. Immediately, his two companions unlimbered mini-Uzis from under their jackets and trained them on Garth.

Starkey acted indifferent to the threat to his employer. As silent and still as a statue, he waited.

Trevor Garth stared into the muzzles of the Uzis and did a strange thing. He smiled. "I must confess, Fezzan, that I am severely disappointed. After all I'd heard about you, I expected better."

"Do not think to talk your way out of this," the Fox told him. "You will produce the rest of my payment, and you will do it this minute."

Garth ignored him. "You see, my underground contacts assured me that you were the best of the lot. That you were an idealist, devoted to your cause. That you were a man of honor." He sadly shook his head. "But I see now that they had it all wrong. You're no different than the money-hungry leeches who run our country. All you care about is lining your own pocket."

The Libyan took several short steps. It put him at the end of the bed, much closer to Garth but also much closer to Starkey. "You dare doubt my integrity? Why, you American pig! I despise your country and everything it stands for! Were it in my power, I would grind it under my heel and spit on what was left."

Garth glanced at the Texan. "Did you hear that, Mr. Starkey? Apparently I owe our friend Mr. Lafferty an apology. He was right. I should never have done business with scum like this. If you please?"

It was said so calmly, so casually, that only the Fox detected the underlying nuance. He started to shout, to warn his men, to have them open fire, but the speed of the man in black was such that he never uttered a syllable.

The twin Remingtons materialized in Starkey's hands as if out of thin air. The terrorist gunners had him covered, yet their brains hadn't quite registered the fact that he had drawn when the Remingtons cracked, once each, and the two gunners toppled with holes squarely in the center of their foreheads.

In pure reflex, the finger of one of the terrorists closed on the trigger of his Uzi. It chattered for all of two seconds, the rounds flying wild, most thudding into the ceiling. But as luck would have it, a few struck the man closest to him. The Fox.

The Libyan cried out as the Parabellum rounds chewed up a kidney and one lung. He staggered forward, onto his knees, then tried to get at the Glock in his shoulder holster. A hand nudged his aside.

"Is this what you're after?" Garth asked, wagging the pistol. Squatting, he thoughtfully regarded the crimson rivulets trickling from both corners of the Libyan's mouth. "It's too bad you couldn't be reasonable. I might have let you live."

The Fox wanted to spit in the giant's face, but he couldn't muster the energy. Of a sudden he had grown terribly weak, terribly faint.

"You see, Mr. Fezzan, I honestly don't care who you are," Garth said, no malice in his tone. "I don't care if your people want my head for what I've done. Would you like to hear why?''

The Fox did want to know, but he'd never admit as much. Hatred of all things American festered like a burning sore at the core of his being, and if he could, he would have strangled Garth with his bare hands.

''I'm about to do something that will bring the full might of the United States government down on my head. Even with all my resources, I won't be able to elude them for long. My days, I'm afraid, are numbered.''

A peculiar ringing in the Libyan's ears drowned out many of Garth's words. He didn't comprehend what was being said.

''I just don't give a damn if your people in the Middle East put a price on my head. It will be the least of my worries. I'll be—''

Paxton Mills entered, a walkie-talkie in his hand. ''Sir, sorry to interrupt. Security reports a perimeter breach.''

''The Feds? So soon? I was hoping we had another day, at least.'' Garth rose. ''How many?''

''It's just one guy.''

''One?'' Garth repeated, surprised. ''Interesting. Logically, they should have sent in a small army.'' Pondering probabilities, he absently tapped the Glock against his chin. ''This I'll have to see for myself. But first—'' Abruptly turning, he cocked the autopistol, placed the tip of the barrel against the Fox's forehead and said, "Our business arrangement is hereby terminated, you miserable crud."

At the boom of the Model 19, the Fox keeled backward, coming to rest with his head against the bed, his wide eyes fixed blankly on the overhead light.

"Let's go," Garth said, hurrying out. He descended the stairs three at a time, pausing on the first landing to snatch the walkie-talkie from Paxton Mills. "Status report, Blanchard," he commanded, hastening on.

"The intruder is making his way across the grounds, sir. He's gotten as far as the big oak."

"I'll be there in under a minute. Contact Hanson and tell him to have the Broncos ready."

"Will do, sir."

Garth gave the walkie-talkie back to his burly lieutenant. At the bottom of the stairwell, he turned left, down a narrow side hall until he came to a large impressionist painting that occupied a recessed niche. Reaching behind the frame, he depressed a hidden button.

There was a click. A section of wall to which the painting was attached popped outward, and Garth quickly opened the secret door. Concrete steps led to a dimly lit concrete corridor, which in turn brought them to a large chamber crammed with sophisticated electronic equipment.

This was Garth's command center. It had cost a pretty penny, but in his estimation no price was too high for a fail-safe security system.

A thin man with white hair sat at a bank of monitors. "You should see this guy, sir," Tom Blanchard said. "He's something else."

Garth scanned the monitors. Each was fed by a camera somewhere on the estate. Every square foot was constantly under surveillance. And as if they weren't enough, mounted high in the walls of the mansion were special infrared cameras that could register a heat source the size of a bird at one hundred yards.

"Look at this," Blanchard said, pointing at a monitor that showed the gazebo. "He's right there, at the northwest corner, yet he blends in so well that the only way you can spot him is on the infrared."

It was true. On the regular monitor, Garth saw nothing out of the ordinary, but on the infrared the intruder's heat signature made him stand out like the proverbial sore thumb. "Fascinating."

"He's on the move," Blanchard said.

The figure glided from behind the gazebo toward a cluster of trees. On the regular monitor there was the barest hint of movement, a shadow blending among shadows. Only on the infrared could they track him.

"Whoever this guy is, he knows his stuff," Mills commented.

Garth leaned on the console and chuckled. "Do you realize what this means, gentlemen?"

"Sir?" Blanchard said.

"Use your intellect. Think it through," Garth chided. "We know the Feds are on to us, thanks to the fiasco at the Shootery. By rights, they should send in a team of elite FBI agents to take us down. Yet it's just one man."

"Maybe it's an Arab," Mills suggested. "Someone working with Fezzan."

"Unlikely, since we had his room bugged and we know that he hasn't contacted anyone since he put through that call to San Franciso this afternoon." Garth shook his head. "No, our intruder works for the government. And he's not just an ordinary FBI agent. I suspect that our visitor is a black-op specialist."

"Sir?" Blanchard said.

"Black ops," Garth explained. "It's another name for clandestine government operations, for the shadow government that really runs our lives." He indicated the monitor. "See how he moves? This man is like a living ghost. He knows every trick there is. Only someone with vast experience could do what he is doing."

"He must be the same one who was at the Shootery," Starkey said.

"My thinking exactly," Garth agreed. "I wondered why there was no mention of him in any of the news accounts, why the police told the press that a club member had gone off the deep end. Now it's clear. The government clamped a lid on it. They want it kept under wraps until their man does his job."

The Texan placed his hands on the Remingtons. "Do you want me to handle him, boss?"

"No. I want him taken alive," Garth said. He was aware of the glances Blanchard and Mills swapped. They failed to grasp why, but they didn't dare voice their doubt. "Get up," he said, and when Blanchard obeyed, he slid into the chair.

The intruder was nearing the west wing of the mansion. He wore a formfitting blacksuit, and his face had been streaked with combat cosmetics. He carried an M-16, as well as a pistol in a shoulder rig and one on his right hip. Spare magazines and other items adorned military webbing and made his pockets bulge.

"The hellhound of war has come to call," Garth paraphrased, his hand hovering over a row of toggle switches.

The man in the blacksuit stopped at a ground-floor window. Instantly, Garth flicked a toggle, unlocking it. The intruder checked the edges for wires and alarms. Finding none, he gingerly pushed on the meeting rail, and the lower half slid upward.

"You've got him, sir," Mills said.

"Don't be too sure," Garth responded. "A man like this one has the instincts of a jungle cat. He won't be taken easily."

In confirmation, the intruder started to hike a leg over the sill, then hesitated. He scoured the wall above him, as if he sensed somehow that he was being watched. But the infrared unit was embedded in the wall itself, invisible except for the lens, which was tinted the same color.

Garth tingled with excitement. "Come into my parlor," he said softly to himself, grinning when the man in the blacksuit slipped into the mansion. A camera mounted in a bookcase picked him up as he crossed to the door and peeked out.

"I'm surprised the Feds didn't kill the power to the property," Mills remarked.

"It wouldn't have done them any good. Our backup generators would have kicked in," Garth said. "Besides, I doubt they would risk forewarning us."

"Look!" Blanchard said. "He can't get away now."

The intruder had moved into the hall, his back to the wall. Shutting the door, he crept toward the staircase.

"You're absolutely correct," Garth said, and reached for another toggle.

CHAPTER ELEVEN

It was supposed to be a routine operation. Go in, locate Trevor Garth, and keep the leader of the Minutemen on ice while Hal and the backup poured in and mopped up.

But from the moment the Executioner slipped over the boundary wall, he felt that something was wrong, something he couldn't quite put his finger on.

Bolan had no trouble pinpointing the security cameras and avoiding them. No guards were present, and no dogs had to be dealt with. Yet he couldn't shake a nagging sense of unease.

The soldier took his time, never taking a step until he had checked and double-checked the terrain ahead. Avoiding lit areas, he reached the mansion without mishap. Just as he was about to enter, he grew convinced that he was being watched. Pausing, he scanned the windows above.

Nothing.

The room Bolan slid into was a library. Thick

carpet smothered what little noise he made as he crossed to the door. No alarms sounded when he inched it open and surveyed a hallway. Carefully closing the door behind him, he padded toward a staircase. He didn't think it unusual that the mansion was as quiet as a tomb. At four in the morning, it was to be expected.

As he neared the corner, his sensitive ears detected a faint whirring. He froze, then glanced up. He was sure the source was somewhere above him, but he saw no explanation.

Then a small panel slid down, revealing the cold eye of a concealed camera. Instantly, Bolan sprang forward to reach the stairs, but he was a shade too slow. A metal partition shot down, blocking off the end of the corridor.

Bolan whirled. He had taken a single stride when another partition slammed into the floor, sealing him in as effectively as if he were in a box. There were no doors on either side. He was trapped.

The soldier spun, bringing the M-16 to bear on the camera. He would have shot it to pieces had a familiar voice not issued from a small speaker underneath.

"I wouldn't, if I were you," Trevor Garth said. "Not if you want to live."

Bolan's mind raced. It was a no-win situation. Gone was any hope of taking Garth unawares. The mastermind had him dead to rights. He could try to blast his way out, but the house was undoubtedly fitted with other nasty surprises. He eased up on the trigger and let the M-16 dip.

"How refreshing," the millionaire said. "An adversary with intelligence. Most Feds would have tried to bull their way out of my little trap, triggering the pressure plate you're standing on in the process."

The short hairs at Bolan's nape prickled. Was Garth bluffing? Somehow, he didn't think so. He stared at the floor.

"There are sliding panels at the end of each hall," Garth mentioned. "My associates thought I was crazy when I had them installed. They laughed, and accused me of watching too many spy movies. But I knew my precautions would pay off one day. Now, if you would be so kind, deposit all your weapons on the floor, then raise both arms. Do so, and you go on breathing a while longer. Refuse, and I will detonate the explosives under your feet by remote control. It's your choice."

It was no choice at all. Bolan had no intention of dying needlessly. As long as he lived, he could fight. He did as he had been instructed.

"Excellent," Garth said. "Now stand perfectly still. In a minute the panel in front of you will slide open. When it does, make no sudden moves."

There were two of them. One was a beefy gunner Bolan had never laid eyes on. The other was the tall Texan, the gunman known as Starkey. The beefy specimen came around behind him and prodded him with his own M-16, while Starkey stayed in front and backpedaled down the hall, those gleaming ivory-handled Remingtons fixed on the soldier's midriff.

They passed behind a painting and descended concrete steps. Bolan had to admit that he had miscalculated. So had Brognola. They were both guilty of neglect, of not taking Garth as seriously as they should have. They had taken it for granted that the leader of the Minutemen was an eccentric, devious, dangerous crank; they had failed to see exactly how devious. The man had every contingency covered.

The control room had to have cost half a million dollars to construct, probably more. Bolan saw the infrared monitors and understood how he had been trapped so easily.

Garth leaned against the console, more amused than anything else. A man with white hair stood to one side, covering Bolan with an AMT Automag.

"Greetings," Garth said pleasantly. "I imagine you know who I am. And I also imagine that you're not prepared to reveal your identity. So how about if I call you Horatio? Would that do?" Laughing, he smacked his thigh.

Was there supposed to be some special significance to the name? Bolan wondered. It had been years since he read any Shakespeare. As best he recalled, Horatio was the straight arrow friend of Hamlet, Prince of Denmark, foil to the melancholy Dane. How did that apply to him?

Garth faced the console and stabbed a button. "Are the vehicles loaded and ready to go, Mr. Hanson?"

"Yes, sir."

"Stand by. We'll be there in a bit." Garth stepped in front of Bolan. "Whether you go on living depends on your answers to three questions." He paused. "Do you consider yourself patriotic, Horatio?"

Bolan did not see what that had to do with anything, but he answered honestly. "Yes."

"Do you trust our government, Horatio? Do you believe that the powers that be have our best interests at heart?"

"Basically, yes," Bolan said. What else was he to say? He knew that too many politicians were more concerned with their own financial welfare than the welfare of their constituents, but, as the old saying went, every bushel had a few bad apples.

Garth acted pleased by the answers. "Now for the million-dollar question," he said, studying the soldier closely. "Do you have the slightest idea why I'm doing what I am?"

Was it a trick question? Bolan mused. If he didn't answer properly, would the millionaire have him cut down where he stood? "Not really, no," he confessed.

"Outstanding," Garth said, clapping his hands. "Mr. Mills, please bind our visitor's wrists. We are taking him with us."

The man holding the Automag frowned. "Is that wise, sir? I mean, he's liable to turn on us the first chance he has."

Garth chortled. "Of course he will. That's why he's here, isn't it? To take us down?" He wagged a finger at Blanchard. "Your job is to see to it that he doesn't."

Covered by three guns, Bolan had no recourse but to stand there while Mills produced a rope and bound his wrists. None too gently, either.

The tall Texan nodded at the monitors. "I reckon his pards are a mite impatient, Mr. Garth," he said. "They must be wondering where he got to."

An unmarked van was cruising slowly past the front gate. Only Bolan knew that Hal Brognola and a handful of select federal agents were inside. Other Feds ringed the property, waiting for word to move in.

"Ah, yes. The backup," Garth said. "They pose no threat, not with the steps I've taken." His finger found a black button, and a section of the rear wall hissed open. "Bring our guest. On the double."

Bolan was hustled into a narrow tunnel dimly lit by overhead fluorescents. It was dank and musty, but the lack of dust showed that it was used regularly. He attempted to figure out the direction they were going, a hopeless cause without the stars or landmarks to guide him. By counting the steps he took, he did deduce the tunnel linked the house to somewhere beyond the brick wall that enclosed the estate.

A short ramp brought them to a closed door. The rumble of engines reached Bolan's ears. They emerged into a wide garage where a pair of Broncos idled. A man of average height and build awaited them. But there was nothing average about the Madsen M-53 submachine gun he held.

"All set to go, Mr. Garth."

The leader of the Minutemen climbed into the first vehicle. Mills sat behind the wheel. Bolan was shoved into the rear seat, and Ren Starkey slid in after. To discourage him from getting any ideas, the business end of one of the Remingtons was gouged into his rib cage.

The other two men got into the second four-wheel drive. Moments later both doors rattled upward on rollers. Mills assumed the lead, turning right.

A glance disclosed that the tunnel had brought them to a small house on a street north of the mansion. As they braked at a stop sign, Bolan spied the unmarked van several hundred feet away, moving past the front gate again.

Garth held up a hand. "Wait a moment," he commanded, taking a tiny transmitter from his coat pocket. "After all the trouble the Feds have gone to on our account, it's only fitting that we give them something to remember us by." He flipped a switch.

A second-floor mansion window exploded in a shower of flames and glass. Bolan saw the van stop. It wasn't hard to imagine what was going through Brognola's mind, and what he would do next.

"Isn't there another way, boss?" the driver asked. "You've lived in that place your whole life. Hell, your father built it."

"We all have our crosses to bear, Mr. Mills," Garth said. "Without sacrifice, we can never hope to triumph." He was watching the van. "See. The next act in our drama is about to unfold. Pay attention and you will learn something."

The van had backed to the paved area in front of the gate, then swung around. Tires spinning, it shot toward the wrought-iron barrier, smashing into it with the force of a Sherman tank. Elsewhere, figures appeared at various points on top of the brick wall. The Feds were closing in from all points of the compass.

"Look at them," Garth said. "Like rats swarming to cheese. We are about to repay these storm troopers for the lives of our brothers who died at the Shootery."

Bolan saw Brognola's van rocket up the drive. Agents sped across the lawn on foot. He glanced at Garth, who was tensed to press another button on the transmitter. It didn't take a genius to guess what would happen when he did.

Despite the Remington pressed against his side, Bolan braced both feet on the floor. He couldn't sit there and do nothing with so many lives at stake. That one of them was Hal Brognola only made it worse.

The van screeched to a stop. Its side door was flung open and out spilled Feds in body armor, armed with M-16s and shotguns. They were part of the special Justice contingent, the strike team assembled by Brognola to handle mop-up operations for Phoenix Force, Able Team and Bolan.

Brognola appeared, carrying a shotgun and a radio. He was talking into it as he followed the others to the front door. It was kicked in and the team started to file through, at the ready.

"There was no need for them to do that," Garth complained. "I purposely left the door unlocked."

Other Feds had reached the mansion and were going in through windows and side doors.

The Minuteman at the wheel laughed. "Look at them! Like lambs to the slaughter, eh?"

"More like pigs to the slaughter," Garth corrected him, and went to activate the device.

Fully expecting to be shot dead, Bolan hurled

himself forward. His shoulder rammed into the back of the front seat, knocking Garth against the dashboard. It was the best he could do, and it was nowhere near enough.

A heavy blow caught Bolan at the base of the skull. It was delivered expertly, with just enough force to stun him but not enough to render him unconscious. He sagged against the front seat, his head twisted so that he saw what happened when Garth pressed the button.

The whole mansion went up. Not in one gigantic explosion, but in a series of blasts as staggered charges were detonated. First the east wing spewed fire and debris, then the west wing and finally the central section, every window gushing flames.

"Get us out of here, Mr. Mills," Garth said. "I have too many fond memories of Ravencrest to sit here and watch its death throes."

Bolan was riveted in horror to the consuming flames and rent walls. The structure was collapsing in on itself, whole portions buckling like a condemned tenement before a wrecking ball. The Feds hadn't stood a chance! All he could think of was Brognola, imagining his friend lying broken and crumpled under tons of debris.

A cold rage consumed him. Bolan didn't have many close friends. The nature of his work limited his contact with others. Those friends he did have, he cherished, as a connoisseur would cherish fine wine.

Hal Brognola had been one of the oldest, one of the best. He had stood by Bolan through thick and thin, had always been there when Bolan needed him. They were comrades in arms, brothers in spirit. He felt the loss as he had felt few others.

Starkey gripped the soldier's collar and shoved him back. "Behave yourself, pard," he cautioned. His eyes narrowed a moment, and he cocked his head. "I've seen you somewhere before, haven't I?"

Bolan had wondered if any of them had gotten a good look at him at the gun club. Should Garth learn that he was responsible for the carnage, the millionaire might change his mind about permitting him to live. He chose not to answer.

The Minuteman leader turned. "Friends of yours, I gather?" he said, jerking a thumb at the conflagration that engulfed the mansion. "That was a noble but futile gesture on your part."

Inwardly, Bolan boiled with rare rage. If it was the last thing he ever did, he would see that Trevor Garth paid for the lives of Hal Brognola and those others.

"Blindfold him, Mr. Starkey," Garth directed. "We don't want our impetuous friend to learn the location of my private airstrip."

It was done neatly, efficiently. Bolan sat back,

cataloging every sound he heard in case he had to try to retrace the route later on. As best as he could determine, they left the outskirts of the city and drove for another fifteen to twenty minutes. Gravel crunched under the tires. They stopped at a gate apparently, because a window whined down and someone said, "Oh. It's you, Mr. Garth. Go right in."

A cool breeze fanned Bolan's face as he was hoisted from the limo and half carried, half dragged across tarmac. He figured that they were going to board a plane. So he was mildly surprised when rotors growled to life and Mills told him to duck his head.

The smell of fuel and oil was strong as he was roughly thrown into the helicopter's bay. Hands pulled him to a bench seat, and a harness was strapped across his chest. He sensed someone on his left and another person on his right. Trevor Garth, it turned out.

"Make yourself comfortable, Horatio. It will be a relatively short flight." Garth patted a bulkhead. "This Augusta is one of a fleet of three. I've had it retrofitted with a few, shall we say, unconventional extras."

A rivet or something like it was digging into Bolan's shoulder blade. He shifted, and his captor misconstrued the act.

"I would heed Mr. Starkey's warning, if I were

you. You are completely at my mercy, Horatio. If you're counting on your friends tracking you down, you can forget the idea. The helicopters are owned by one of over a dozen dummy corporations I've set up over the years. No one knows I have them.''

Once again Bolan was reminded of the man's foresight. ''You've been planning this operation for a long time, then,'' he remarked.

Garth chuckled. ''Good Lord, no. The dummy corporations are tax shelters, Horatio. But they have proved useful now that I've gone to war with our own government.''

''Why, Garth? Why would someone who has all you do throw it away on an empty crusade?''

''Is that what you think? Well, I'll set you straight soon enough.''

Little else was said until the chopper landed. Bolan gauged the flight took approximately half an hour. But the chopper banked frequently, leading him to believe that they flew an erratic pattern to confuse him. The actual distance between the airstrip and where they came down was undoubtedly much less.

By then the sun was up, the chill of dawn having given way to the heat of morning. Bolan sniffed the dry air and concluded they were in the desert or close to it. He was ushered into a building and along a corridor. Suddenly, the blindfold was snatched off.

They were in a corrugated metal building, a warehouse filled with military jeeps and trucks, assorted military hardware and stacked crates and boxes. It reminded Bolan of an Army depot, only this one was in the hands of a fanatic and his merry band of self-righteous men.

Many of the Minutemen who had been at the Sportsman's Shootery were present, as well as new faces. Twenty-two, all told. Most stopped what they were doing as their leader strode through the doorway.

"Carry on, men," Garth said, clasping his hands behind his broad back like an oversize Napoleon. "Every minute is vital now that the opening gambit has been played."

Bolan wriggled his hands to keep the circulation flowing. Mills had disappeared, but Ren Starkey stood a few feet away, those lightning hands of his held close to the polished ivory butts of the Remingtons.

Most of the work being done involved crates, canisters and barrels being unloaded from a flatbed truck covered by green canvas. The care being taken indicated that whatever was in the containers had to be extremely hazardous.

Garth motioned for Bolan to fall into step beside him. He nodded at some crates. "Those contain Mausers. That second stack, Garands. The third one, SKSs." Garth sighed. "All serviceable, but not what I would have preferred. You have no idea how difficult it is to obtain automatic weapons in any quantity.''

''That's why you contacted the Libyan,'' Bolan said.

Garth glanced at him. ''Precisely. He was going to provide me with all the modern firepower I wanted, along with enough plastic explosives to flatten half of Washington, D.C. Now I don't need either.''

''Because you have chemical warfare weapons,'' the soldier mentioned, and knew it was a mistake the second he did. His captor spun and poked him in the chest.

''So it was you at the gun club! I suspected as much.'' Garth pondered a moment. ''I'd wager you were also involved up in the Spring Mountains. True?''

There was no use denying it. Bolan nodded. By rights it would outrage the madman, but he didn't care. Yet, to his amazement, Garth smiled.

''I'm flattered. You must be the cream of the crop, one of the very best assassins the government has on its payroll.''

''I'm not a hired killer,'' Bolan said flatly.

''Oh? What else would you call it? You do clandestine ops for them, don't you? You terminate enemies with extreme prejudice, as I believe they so quaintly phrase it. In my book, that makes you a paid assassin.''

''I don't kill for money,'' the soldier elaborated.

''No? Why, then? Out of a sense of patriotic duty? To right the wrongs of the world? Whatever your motives, we are a lot more alike than you are probably willing to admit.''

''We're nothing alike.''

''How so? Because you support the government and I seek to destroy the status quo? I fear you sorely misjudge me, Horatio. Let your education begin.'' Garth addressed someone behind Bolan. ''Seize him.''

Two brawny men each took an arm. The soldier was hauled to where several large barrels sat. Painted on the side of each was the code, TL-14. One had been opened. Inside was a thick greenish mucus that gave off a terrible stench.

Garth stood beside it, smirking. ''Perhaps our guest would like to try a unique type of new shampoo?'' he suggested. ''Gentlemen, if you please.''

Without warning, the two men shoved Bolan's face toward the green mucus.

CHAPTER TWELVE

Hal Brognola would be the first to admit that he wasn't perfect. He was guilty of errors of judgment, just like everyone else. True, they were few and far between, or he wouldn't be the Director of the Justice Department's Sensitive Operations Group and have the ear of the President of the United States.

He didn't deem it a mistake to send Bolan into the mansion alone. The Executioner was the best there was at what he did. No one stood a better chance of nabbing Trevor Garth without a single shot being fired. And above all else, Brognola wanted Garth taken alive in order to learn where the chemicals were being stored.

The decision to have a backup strike team on-site seemed sound at the time. They were to function as the cavalry, so to speak. They were insurance that neither Garth nor any of the Minutemen on the premises would escape.

Brognola had deployed his agents in accordance with standard rules of engagement. The armored van was an added precaution. Its mobility and extra firepower were his trump card.

He had all the bases covered. Or so he thought until a second-floor window blew out.

He assumed that his friend had run into trouble. To aid Bolan, and to foil the Minutemen in case they tried to bust out en masse, he ordered his people to close in.

Seated in the front passenger's seat of the van, Brognola nudged the driver. The van hit the iron gate doing over fifty. As it roared up the driveway, Brognola cradled his Uzi.

The old tingle was still there, the old excitement he always felt when going into a firefight. It was a heady feeling. He knew that he was taking an unauthorized risk, that the President would have his scalp if word ever leaked.

Could he help it, though, if he tired of always being desk bound? Was he to blame if he craved to get out in the field now and again?

Brognola shook his head to derail his train of thought. Now wasn't the time for idle musing. He heard Deming's voice crackle on the radio. The agent was halfway to the east wing, and there was no sign of activity. Moments later Baylor reported in, saying that the west wing was just as quiet.

How could that be? Brognola asked himself. The explosion should have those inside in an uproar.

Gunners should be rushing to repel attackers. Where were the Minutemen?

Even more important, where was Bolan? Why hadn't he reported in also?

The van slewed to a stop. Agent Niles threw open the side door and leaped out, covering the others as they broke for the entrance. Brognola was last, Agent Wilkins in front of him.

No gunfire greeted them. No alarms were sounding. No shouts issued from within the mansion.

Brognola's apprehension mounted. Something was dreadfully, drastically wrong, but he couldn't turn back now. His people were committed. They had to see it through.

He barked into the radio, demanding to know if Deming or Baylor had encountered any opposition. Deming responded in the negative. Baylor reported that he was inside and hadn't seen a living soul.

Wilkins kicked in the front door. Flowing like the well-oiled fighting machine they were, the strike team darted inside.

Brognola brought up the rear. He was just about to instruct them to hold their positions while he assessed their options when the whump of an explosion sounded to the east. Heartbeats later another explosion sounded to the west. The entire mansion rocked, the floor under his feet shifting as if from an earthquake.

Was it simple common sense or intuition that

screamed at Brognola to get out that instant? Was it instinct that whirled him around even as he bellowed, "Get out of here! Everyone! Now! Move it! Move it!"

It was too little, too late.

The next explosion was the blast to end all blasts.

Brognola was looking over his shoulder when the main charge detonated. He saw a massive fireball spurt down the hallway toward them, saw it destroy walls and tapestries and paintings, saw it engulf Niles, Florence and Wilkins, searing them to the bone in the time it took him to blink.

The fireball swirled madly, billowing outward, red-and-orange fingers clawing for his life.

He was six feet from the entrance when an invisible hand lifted him off his feet and flung him like a rag doll through the opening. He tumbled end over end, caught in the searing hot breath of a fiery man-made dragon.

Vaguely, Brognola was conscious of striking grass, of rolling over and over. Dimly, he heard screams, the voices of his people being consumed alive. He struggled to his hands and knees, conscious of blood trickling from his left ear, of pain that lanced his right shoulder.

The mansion was falling in on itself. The interior had been destroyed, and the outer walls, lacking support, crumbled of their own weight. An avalanche of wood, metal and brick collapsed to the ground, the crash nearly deafening.

A gust of hot wind struck the big Fed. It bore the acrid, unmistakable reek of burnt flesh. He pushed upright, his knees unsteady. The shotgun was gone, but by some miracle he hadn't lost the radio.

"Deming?" he hollered into it, procedure forgotten in the extremity of the moment. "Baylor? Arliss? Hines? Someone, anyone, answer me!"

No one did.

The big Fed backed away from the rising flames, the heat growing so intense that it caked him with perspiration. He staggered to the van, fumbling at the controls.

So much for thinking that dealing with the Minutemen would be routine. So much for treating them as if they were a second-rate threat. Overconfidence had cost the lives of decent, hardworking operatives. It had also cost him the closest friend he had.

Hal Brognola made himself a promise. From then on, Trevor Garth would have his undivided attention. He was going to bring the entire might of the United States government to bear on bringing the Minutemmen to bay. Bolan and Wilkins and the rest wouldn't have died in vain.

So help him God!

THE NAUSEATING STINK of the green mucus was enough to make Bolan gag, but it was insight born of the cautious treatment the Minutemen had given the barrels that forewarned him they were highly lethal. He flung himself backward, resisting with every iota of strength he had. Inch by gradual inch, he was pushed nearer, his head shoved lower, until he was so close that he could see tiny bubbles on the surface and heard one of them pop.

"That's enough, brothers," Trevor Garth said, chortling. "I was only joking."

Bolan was snapped erect. He would have turned on the men who had grabbed him, but they prudently didn't let go.

Garth tapped the barrel. "I don't suppose you have any idea what this stuff is, Horatio?"

The warrior had never heard of TL-14. Nearby were canisters of chlorine gas and crates marked Mustard Gas. Both had seen use by the Army many decades ago. It led him to suspect that, somehow, the Minutemen had gotten their hands on old military warfare weapons. If so, how potent could the chemicals be?

As if Garth were able to read Bolan's mind, he called out, "Mr. Mills, find Jinx and bring him here, if you please."

"Jinx? Ah, boss. Not him."

"Now, Mr. Mills."

Minutemen who overheard gathered around. The Texan changed position in order to have a clear shot at Bolan should he act up. No one spoke. It was not long before the man called Mills returned, carrying a young cat.

"I wish there were some other way, Mr. Garth. Jinx is just a little lost stray."

"Would you rather I demonstrate on one of us?" retorted their caustic leader. "Besides, you know how I feel about cats. My mother had one she adored. The damn thing was forever underfoot, and it got hair all over everything." Garth snatched the animal by the scruff of its neck.

Mills wasn't the only one who didn't want to see the cat sacrificed. "There's no need to do this," Bolan said.

"Yes, there most definitely is," Garth replied. "I want you to fully appreciate the scope of what I intend. The government must be convinced I am not bluffing." He scanned their vicinity. "Mr. Baker, would you bring me that hammer lying on the workbench."

A Minuteman complied. Garth hefted the hammer before slowly dipping the head into the toxic substance. When he lifted it, tiny gobs of mucus clung to the metal.

Setting the cat at Bolan's feet, Garth held the hammer over the hapless creature's head and gently shook it so that several of the gobs slid off and landed on the animal.

"Poor thing," Mills said.

The cat had flinched when the drops struck it. Now the unsuspecting feline wiped itself with a paw and licked the paw clean. It stood, shook itself, took a few tentative steps, then broke into violent convulsions. Falling onto its side, it mewed pitiably, the cries growing in volume and desperation as the convulsions rapidly worsened.

"Poor thing," Mills repeated.

In under ten seconds, it was over. The cat stiffened and was still, its mouth parted wide, blood seeping over its lower lip, as well as from its nose and ears.

Garth touched it with a toe. "You can't tell because of the hair," he said with no trace of sympathy for the feline's plight, "but the toxin turns skin beet-red."

Bolan stared at the barrel. Five others were arranged in a row behind it. The sheer quantity staggered him. If a few drops killed in seconds, then the Minutemen had enough to wipe out any major city in the country. Just as Garth had boasted.

"I trust I've impressed you?"

The soldier and the madman locked eyes. "Few people have ever made the impression on me that you have," Bolan declared sincerely.

"Good," Garth said. Sniffing, he said to Mills, "Dispose of this thing. Bury it outside and cover the grave with rocks so coyotes can't get at it. For all we know, the poison might spread through the ecological food chain if an infected carcass is devoured.''

The magnitude of the threat brought a shiver to Bolan. Hundreds of thousands, perhaps millions of innocent lives were at risk. The Minutemen posed one of the greatest threats to America's security of any enemy he had ever been up against. And to what purpose? He had to know. ''Why?'' he asked simply.

''Why, indeed?'' Garth said. He walked to a crate and sat. All he had to do was crook a finger, and the two hardcases holding Bolan steered him over and forced him down.

Garth's expression became somber. ''It's important that you understand, Horatio. Terribly important. I don't want history to judge me a raving lunatic.''

''How else would posterity judge someone who slaughters the populations of whole cities?'' Bolan countered. ''You'll be right up there with Attila the Hun, Adolf Hitler and Jack the Ripper.''

''How unkind of you. Actually, I should be held in the same esteem as George Washington, Abraham Lincoln and Ronald Reagan.''

Was the man insane? ''You can't be serious.''

Sighing, Garth rested his forearms on his knees. ''I'm a man of vision, Horatio, and a man of conviction. When I see a wrong, I do everything in my power to right it. So when I saw that our government was out of control, I decided to take steps to correct the situation.''

"Define 'out of control'.''

"For starters, Waco and Ruby Ridge.''

Bolan had half expected as much. Many American citizens had been deeply disturbed by those two tragic incidents. So much so, Congress had called for special hearings. He mentioned as much.

"Congress?'' Garth snorted. "What the hell good did those glory hounds do? All they were interested in was putting a positive spin on everything for the folks back home.'' He swore a lusty string. "Did you watch those hearings?''

"No,'' Bolan admitted. He had been in the field, half the time overseas. Spending days in front of a TV set was a luxury denied him.

"I did!'' Garth thundered, rising. "And do you know what? Not once was the FBI called to account for using CS gas at Waco. A gas forbidden for military use against enemy troops in war. Yet they used it on Americans! On helpless women and children!''

"They took drastic steps because they were worried about those children—'' Bolan began, but he was cut off.

"That's no excuse! Their stupidity ended up incinerating the very children they claimed to be concerned about!'' Garth had flushed and was growing more animated by the moment. He smashed a fist into his other hand. "It was butchery, plain and simple!"

It was common knowledge that many militia groups felt the same way. Experts believed that Waco had done more to fan the flames of right-wing resentment than any single act in U.S. history.

"Then there is Ruby Ridge," Garth went on. Abruptly whirling on Bolan, he stabbed a finger in the soldier's face. "Tell me something, Horatio. And be honest. Have you ever done any work for Uncle Sam as a sniper?"

Bolan wasn't about to reveal that he had held a sharpshooting rating in the service, or that he had made dozens of kills behind enemy lines. Sniping was his specialty.

"Won't answer me?" Garth said testily. "By your silence you incriminate yourself. And that's all the better. Because even you can appreciate the injustice at Ruby Ridge."

Everyone knew the details. A paid government informant had talked a man named Randy Weaver into sawing off the barrels on two shotguns. The Feds had moved in, and a ten-day siege resulted. Weaver's young son and wife were both killed. Later the federal government agreed to pay Randy Weaver over three million dollars for the wrongful deaths of his loved ones.

Garth leaned down. "Even you can see the injustice done there. An unarmed woman holding her baby had half her face blown off by an FBI sniper. And that sniper has never been punished!''

''I recall reading that he was trying to hit a friend of Weaver's,'' Bolan stated.

Garth growled deep in his chest. ''And you believe that? How many times have you accidentally shot an innocent bystander when you were aiming at someone else?''

''Never,'' Bolan confessed.

''And were you aware that the FBI snipers were given shoot-to-kill orders before they went in? Orders half of them refused to carry out? Orders that the Justice Department later ruled were unconstitutional?''

Bolan saw an opening and took it. ''That should prove to you that the government isn't all bad. They admitted their mistake. They paid millions in damages.''

''They had to. They were under pressure from the people and from patriotic members of the press.'' Garth shook his head. ''No, Horatio. Our government is out of control. The liberals in power want to take away all our rights. They want to strip us of our guns so we can't defend ourselves. They banned 185 firearms, not just a few measly assault rifles. Their goal is to take away all our guns. If you don't believe me, check the literature put out by liberal gun-control organizations.'' The giant straightened. ''Well, I can't allow that to happen. I won't stand idly by while our Second Amendment right is stripped away.''

"So you'll kill thousands of innocent people?'' Bolan challenged.

"The government has slaughtered innocents. Why shouldn't I, if it helps to awaken the American people to the dangers of Big Brother?'' Garth said icily.

"That would make you no better than the government you despise.''

Garth arched a brow. "Nice try, Horatio. But if George Washington and Thomas Jefferson and the rest of our forefathers took that view, we'd still be under British rule.'' He visibly relaxed, the scarlet fading from his cheeks. "No. There comes a time when patriotic men and women must take a stand. I'm taking mine.''

Bolan glanced at the barrels of TL-14. "By using chemical weapons on unsuspecting civilians? How will that advance your cause?''

"By drawing attention to what our government is up to. By exposing their hypocrisy. Before I'm done, every loyal American will praise me as a hero.'' Garth strode to the open barrel. "You see, you're taking it for granted that I'm going to use this stuff. But I won't if the government meets my demands.''

"Demands?''

"Remember the Unabomber, the serial bomber

who forced major newspapers into printing his manifesto by threatening to blow up an airliner? Well, I'm taking a page from his book. I won't unleash my chemical weapons if the government will agree to three simple terms.''

A glimmer of hope rose in Bolan. Maybe mass slaughter could be averted, after all. ''What are they?'' he asked.

Garth turned, his expression smug. ''First, every major newspaper in the country will publish what I'll call the Minuteman Manifesto. In it, I will explain why the Minutemen were formed, and list our grievances against the government.''

So far, so good. Bolan believed that the authorities would cooperate if the Minutemen would hand over the chemicals in return. ''What else?''

''Congress will repeal the assault-weapons ban. Further, they will pass a law requiring that an automatic weapon be given to every law-abiding adult in the country.''

Bolan's flicker of hope died. ''You want to hand out assault rifles and machine guns to everyone?''

''Just like they do in Switzerland.''

The Swiss didn't have a standing army. Rather, every male citizen was a member of their militia and was required to keep a fully automatic rifle in his home and to participate in regular training. ''Their situation is different than ours,'' Bolan pointed out.

Garth paid no attention. "Our last condition is the most crucial. We want liberalism outlawed. We want it made illegal for anyone to advocate liberal views. Anyone who does so will be declared insane and committed to an asylum."

Bolan simply stared. How could he have deluded himself into thinking there was any chance at all of coming to terms? "You know as well as I do that the government will never agree to your conditions."

"That's up to them. But then the consequences will be on their shoulders." Garth smiled. "Or, rather, on yours, Horatio."

"What are you talking about?"

"Why do you think I've kept you alive? Why didn't I put a slug in your brain back at the mansion? It's what you deserve."

Minutemen were gathering around again, their hostility almost palpable. Several fingered weapons they would dearly love to use on him.

"I need a messenger," Garth elaborated. "An errand boy, if you will. Someone who can convince the government that I mean what I say. Someone who will persuade them that the Minutemen are a force to be reckoned with. Someone they will believe."

"Me."

Garth laughed. "You, Horatio. It's all up to you.

If you can't make them see the light, then the deaths that will result will be on your conscience.''

Bolan would have given anything to have his hands free, and an M-16.

"The government has twenty-four hours in which to agree," Garth said. "They will announce as much on every radio station in Nevada. If not, the Minutemen will wipe out a city of our choosing the day after tomorrow."

At a gesture from their leader, the same two burly Minutemen jerked Bolan to his feet. Mills approached to apply the blindfold.

The last thing Bolan saw was the open barrel and the bubbling green mucus.

CHAPTER THIRTEEN

It was the same routine, only in reverse.

Bolan was whisked from the Minuteman hideaway by helicopter and flown to the airstrip. There, he was transferred to a four-wheel-drive vehicle, presumably one of the same Broncos as before.

Three Minutemen accompanied him. One was the Texan. Bolan knew it was Starkey because twice the deadly gunman spoke to him, once when they were in flight and Garth's right-hand man prodded him with a pistol.

"I reckon you must live a charmed life. It's too bad Mr. Garth doesn't want you dead. I'd love to do the honors. Those jaspers you mowed down at the gun club were my pards."

The second time the Texan spoke was after the Bronco stopped. Bolan was roughly ushered into a building and thrown to his knees on a concrete floor.

"This is the end of the line, pilgrim. Don't budge

until we're gone or I'm liable to put a bullet in your arm or leg.''

It was no idle threat. Bolan stayed put until the snarl of the truck's powerful engine dwindled in the distance. Then, lying on his back, he tucked his knees and rubbed them over his eyes again and again until the bottom edge of the blindfold slid high enough for him to see.

He was in a garage. In fact, it was the very same garage that the Broncos had been stored in initially, the one at the end of the secret underground tunnel from Ravencrest. A workbench stood against one wall. Pushing to his feet, he went over to it.

A hacksaw seemed his best bet. It hung from a hook, but by stretching and nudging it with his chin, he brought it clattering down. From there it was a simple matter to turn and grab hold of the handle, then align the blade so that it dug into the coils of rope binding his wrists.

By patiently sawing, always careful not to dig the serrated edge into his flesh, Bolan cut himself loose. Casting the blindfold to the floor, he exited the building.

Smoldering ruins were all that remained of the mansion. The estate had been cordoned off. Police cars and FBI vehicles were everywhere, and a small army of agents and officers combed through the wreckage.

Bolan hiked to the gate. He had no identification

on him, but it shouldn't be hard to convince one of the Feds that he was on the side of the angels and be put in touch with one of Brognola's assistants at the Justice Department.

He was in luck. A small crowd of curious residents was on hand, and FBI agents had been posted at the gate to keep onlookers out. One of the men standing guard was someone Bolan recognized.

The agent was being pestered by a heavyset woman in a paisley dress and curlers who was holding a French poodle attired in a short red jacket in her fleshy arms.

"No, ma'am, I can't tell you any more than I already have. An official press release will be issued shortly. I'd advise you to go home and watch the local news when it comes on, and you'll learn all there is worth knowing."

The woman wasn't satisfied. "That might be hours yet. And you can't tell me that explosion was an accident. We don't use gas on this street, so it had to be deliberate." She paused. "I always knew there was something fishy about that snotty Trevor Garth. Cars coming and going at all hours. And those silly men in fatigues running around his property from time to time. What was that all about?"

Bolan saved Agent Patterson from having to answer by squeezing past the woman and tapping the Fed on the arm.

Patterson glanced around and did a double take.

He was about to say something when he caught himself and raised the yellow ribbon. "Go right in, sir. Mr. Brognola will be delighted to see you."

Hal was alive? Relief spurred Bolan to hurry up the driveway. He heard his friend before he saw him, standing beside the same van that had crashed the gate.

The big Fed's clothes were a mess, his skin blackened by grime and soot. "Keep looking," he was telling a knot of agents. "We're not going to rest until we've sifted every square inch. We owe them that much, at least."

"Hal."

Brognola turned and froze in astonishment. This was the one time he had been sure that his old friend had bought the farm, and he had spent half the morning trying to come to grips with the awful loss. To have his friend show up out of thin air, as it were, shook him. "I thought you were dead," he said, his voice oddly hoarse.

"Same here," Bolan responded.

Neither said anything more about his feelings. They didn't need to. Their mutual gratitude at finding each other alive was mirrored in their eyes.

Brognola coughed, then steered the soldier to one side. "Mind telling me where you've been? And what became of Garth?"

Succinctly, Bolan did. Brognola was gnawing on

his lower lip by the time the Executioner was done, a sure sign that the big Fed was extremely worried.

"This is my worst nightmare made real. There is no way we can meet their lunatic demands, even if we wanted to. Issue SMGs to every adult? Why, that would cost a fortune. And as for outlawing liberalism?" Brognola snorted. "As much as I might want to, there is no way in hell Congress would ever do it. Surely Garth knows that?"

"I can't say for sure what Garth believes," Bolan said. "One minute he acts as sane as you or me. The next, he's off in the ozone somewhere."

Brognola rubbed the stubble on his chin, his keenly logical mind already prioritizing the steps that had to be taken. "Okay. Here's what we'll do. I'll set up a command center in Reno. The President will have to be notified. And every available agent between the Mississippi and the Pacific will have to be called in to help in the manhunt."

"Don't forget the brown Bronco," Bolan said.

Brognola hurried to the van and got on the horn, providing a description to the Reno police and the country sheriff. An APB was promptly put out.

"Now I need to get my hands on some aircraft," the big Fed remarked. "We'll initiate the most massive air search in the history of Nevada. Mark my words. We'll find that airstrip and the warehouse sooner or later."

"It had better be sooner," Bolan noted. "Or by

the day after tomorrow, the Minutemen are going to add a whole new meaning to the phrase 'hell on earth.'"

"I DON'T GET IT, BOSS," Paxton Mills said. "You told that stinking Fed we would give the government twenty-four hours to meet our terms."

"So I did," Garth said. "But are any of you gullible enough to honestly think the federal government will give in to our demands?"

The Minutemen were gathered around their leader, hanging on his every word. Each and every one fervently believed in their cause, just as each and every one had unshakable faith in the man who had formed and bankrolled their organization.

Garth had seen to that. He had handpicked them to a man, selecting only those who were as passionate about bringing the government to its knees as he was. Another requirement was that they have no qualms about how they achieved their goal. They had to be willing to kill for the cause, or they weren't fit to join.

"If you knew all along that the Feds won't do as we want, why did you bother to send that guy back?" asked one of them.

Garth squared his broad shoulders. "The ultimatum is a ruse, brothers. The government thinks that it has twenty-four hours to respond, and another twenty-four before we unleash our chemical weapons.''

"But we strike sooner!" a Minuteman guessed, beaming at his brilliance.

"That we do," Garth declared. "We are going to fill three tanks with with a mixture of TL-14 and water, then split up and head for three different targets. Tomorrow morning we strike, not the day after. The Feds will be caught with their pants down."

Excited murmuring broke out.

"What about the mustard gas and the chlorine canisters?" Blanchard wanted to know. "Aren't we going to use them?"

"Neither are as toxic as the TL-14. Since we must act quickly, we will rely on our deadliest chemical agent." Their founder stepped down from the crate he was on. "We can always use the others later on, if need be."

Garth gave orders, and the Minutemen scurried to obey. Confident of success, reveling in the glory of his righteous crusade, Garth strolled to the wide double doors that flanked the flat stretch of desert where the chopper would land on its return.

At last! His many months of meticulous planning were about to pay off. It would take all night for the trucks to reach their destinations, but by sunset tomorrow he would strike a ringing blow for liberty.

It would be the death knell of the old order, Garth was positive. Once the American people were awakened to the atrocities their government was guilty of, once they saw that someone was willing to stand up to all the crooked politicians and their puppets in law enforcement, patriots would flock to the Minuteman banner.

It would be the Boston Tea Party and Bunker Hill all over again.

He did not delude himself. The struggle would be bloody. Many would have to die in the crusade to come. But when the dust settled, the power mongers who had ground the American people under their political boot heels for decades would be overthrown.

Federal abuses of authority would be brought to an end.

No further legal assaults on the Second Amendment would be tolerated.

Liberal judges would no longer pervert the criminal-justice system by being allowed to let hardened criminals off with slaps on the wrist.

Best of all, there would be no more Wacos, no more Ruby Ridges.

The United States of America would be remade in the glorious image the founding fathers had intended. And Garth would be in the vanguard of those reshaping the country. His would be the standard around which the freedom fighters of America rallied.

He surveyed the azure heavens and the majestic

mountain range to the north. As if it were an omen, an eagle appeared, gracefully soaring high in the sky on outstretched wings.

Trevor Garth inhaled deeply. God, but it felt great to be alive!

"NOTHING YET? Nothing at all?" Hal Brognola suppressed the frustration that was taking a toll on his nerves and gazed out the window at the Reno skyline. "All right. Keep at it. Check old maps. My guess would be an abandoned airstrip the Minutemen took over for their own use." He hung up the phone.

Bolan was on a sofa across from Brognola's desk. A plate with a half-eaten doughnut and a barely touched cup of coffee rested on an end table beside him.

The telephone jangled again, and the big Fed swept it to his ear. "Brognola here. Agent Calvert? No, no. That would be a waste of time." He paused. "We know they have a helicopter, so they must buy fuel somewhere locally. Contact every aviation-fuel company in the state, if you have to." He paused again. "I don't care. No one gets any time off until we nail the Minutemen. If we don't stop Garth, Jiminez will have to postpone his wedding."

Bolan was about to swallow some coffee. He glanced up as the phone slammed down for what had to be the twentieth time in as many minutes.

"It's not my place to say, but wasn't that a bit harsh?"

"No," Brognola said more gruffly than he intended. But he couldn't help feeling flustered. More than two dozen federal agents, as well as county and city law enforcement across Nevada, were at his disposal. Dozens of additional federal people were due in over the next several hours. Yet it was proving to not be enough. So far they hadn't uncovered a single clue as to where the Minutemen were holed up.

The Reno branch office of the FBI on East Plum served as Brognola's command center. A captain with the Storey County Sheriff's Department and a lieutenant with the Reno Police Department were his liaisons with the locals.

They had gotten the command post up and running by noon. Now it was past two in the afternoon, and Brognola was no closer to bringing the Minutemen to bay than he had been two hours ago. It was aggravating beyond measure.

"Maybe you should get some fresh air," Bolan suggested. "Take a walk around the block. Patterson and the others can hold down the fort for five minutes."

"Thanks, I'm staying put." It would be just his luck to have a major development break while he was off stretching his legs.

"It's your blood pressure." Bolan set down the

cup. He had seen his friend frazzled before, but seldom quite like this. Not that Bolan could blame him. The pressure was enormous. The welfare of countless people rested on their shoulders.

"Maybe I'll treat myself to a day off when this is over," Brognola said, although they both knew full well that he wouldn't. He was the original workaholic.

There was a knock on the door, and Agent Patterson entered bearing several sheets of paper. "This was just faxed to us by Washington, sir," he said. "You gave orders to have it brought in right away."

"Thank you."

As Patterson wheeled on a heel and left, Brognola scanned the first page. The report was entitled simply TL-14. "It's what we've been waiting for," he said, and paraphrased pertinent portions for Bolan's benefit.

"TL is tetrachloroethane lycyclidine, whatever the hell that is. It was secretly developed during World War I, mainly to counter the Germans, who had developed a supertoxin of their own."

Chemical warfare had been all the rage during the first global conflict, Bolan knew. The hapless troops in the trenches had been exposed to all sorts of chemical poisons, many later outlawed as inhumane.

"The war ended, though, before TL-14 could be

widely employed. Small stockpiles were kept at scattered military bases. Later they were ordered destroyed.''

"Obviously, not all of them were," Bolan commented.

"It says here that there is no record of any TL-14 stockpiles being kept in Nevada, but it also says that most of the records from that period were routinely disposed of years ago.''

"Wonderful," Bolan said. There went any hope of learning how the Minutemen had gotten their hands on the stuff unless some of the fanatics were taken alive.

Brognola turned to the second page. His anxiety mounted as he scanned the intel. "Sweet Jesus," he breathed.

"It's that bad?"

"Listen, then you tell me." Brognola paused, then read verbatim. '"Tetrachloroethane lycyclidine is the most lethal chemical-warfare agent ever devised. A single drop is enough to induce violent death in an otherwise healthy adult in approximately ten seconds. The ideal vector is as an airborne mist or spray, with a recommended mixture of one part tetrachloroethane lycyclidine to ten parts water.

'"Tests indicated that unlike most artificially fabricated toxic chemicals, which tend to lose potency with age to varying degrees, TL-14 actually increased in potency.

"'In 1939, when the last known stockpile was being destroyed, it was learned that TL-14 also thickened with age, and in the process activated a chemical imbalance that rendered the primary catalytic agent explosive.'"

Bolan sat forward. "Are they saying what I think they're saying?"

Brognola swallowed hard. "'Nine servicemen were killed when a barrel of TL-14 being loaded onto a truck exploded. Subsequent research established that once the chemical imbalance took effect, nullifying the reaction was impossible.'"

"In other words," Bolan translated, "the stuff becomes a chemical time bomb."

"There's more. It was discovered that the chain reaction was triggered when the aged tetrachloroethane lycyclidine was exposed to air.'"

"And the Minutemen have already opened a barrel," Bolan said.

"'Diluting the TL-14 with up to one hundred parts water per one part tetrachloroethane lycyclidine had no effect,'" Brognola read. "'It is advised that any barrels retrieved be subject to immediate incineration at a designated disposal facility.'"

Brognola put down the report and sat back, stunned. The implications were staggering. "Garth is playing with fire and doesn't realize it. Imagine what will happen if one of those barrels explodes in an urban center.''

Bolan was thinking of just that. The loss of life would be as great as if the Minutemen were to spray the TL-14. ''Maybe we'll get lucky,'' he said without conviction. ''Maybe that barrel they've opened will blow up right there in the warehouse and wipe out the whole bunch.''

''I suppose you still believe in the tooth fairy, too?''

Another knock interrupted them. It was Patterson again. ''Good news, sir. Calvert and Jiminez think they've hit paydirt already. A local fuel company tells them that one of their best customers for helicopter fuel is a firm called Thrag Aerial Survey And Mapping.''

Still staggered by the revelations concerning the TL-14, Brognola didn't see why Patterson was so excited. ''So? There must be a dozen survey firms in this area.''

''There are, sir. But this one is unique.'' The agent grinned from ear to ear. ''It's the only firm whose name contains an anagram for 'Garth.'''

Brognola wanted to kick himself for not seeing it himself. ''I want an address, and I want it yesterday.''

Once more the young agent whisked from the office. Bolan rose and stretched. Soon he would be in the field again, and he could hardly wait. The clock was ticking in more ways than one. A thought struck him. "It wouldn't be hard for the Minutemen to rig a chopper with the kind of aerial-spray equipment used by crop dusters."

Brognola snapped his fingers. "I'll need fighters ready to scramble at a moment's notice." He grabbed the phone and started punching in a number. "Nellis Air Force Base will have some. Indian Springs, too."

"Don't forget Stillwater Naval Air Station," Bolan said. It was a lot closer to Reno than either of the Air Force bases.

"Got it."

While the big Fed arranged to have the military put on alert, Bolan went for a stroll. There was little he could do until the Minutemen were located. He felt about as necessary as a fifth wheel on a car.

To occupy himself, he tried placing himself in Trevor Garth's shoes. How would the madman carry out his insane scheme? Aerial spraying was feasible, but it had drawbacks. The weight factor limited how much a copter or plane could carry. An Augusta helicopter would only be able to make five or six passes before it had to go back for a refill. That was hardly efficient, even with three choppers to deliver the chemicals. And whatever else might be said about Trevor Garth, the man was a model of efficiency.

But if not by aerial spraying, then how? Bolan

asked himself. Contaminating a city's water supply was one possibility. What were others?

"Excuse me, Mr. Belasko?"

Bolan had been so preoccupied that he had not heard anyone approach. A slim brunette regarded him somewhat shyly. "Yes?"

"I'm Agent Walters, sir. The rumor mill has it that you were with Agent Brenda Mathews, of our Las Vegas office, when she died. Is that true?"

With everything that had happened since the debacle at the mansion, Bolan was startled to find that he had completely forgotten about Mathews. He wondered who could have told Walters.

"I'm sorry to bother you, but I knew Brenda," Walters said. "We went through the academy together, and were sent out here about the same time. Once a month we did lunch." She hesitated.

"What's on your mind?"

"I just wanted to know," Walters said. "Was it quick? I mean, did she suffer much? I'd hate to think that she did."

"It was quick," Bolan confirmed softly, reliving that horrible moment in his mind's eye. He saw the gunner fire, saw Mathews take the full blast of the shotgun.

The brunette nodded. "That's a relief." She started to walk away, then looked back. "We will get the ones responsible, won't we, sir? It wouldn't be right if they were to get away."

"We'll get them. If it's the last thing I ever do."

CHAPTER FOURTEEN

Rotors whirring in a muted whine, the United States Air Force HH-60 Night Hawk streaked in low over the desert, the pilot hugging the desert floor with seasoned skill.

The Night Hawk was state-of-the-art, boasting a sophisticated avionics array. It included a FLIR sensor, terrain-following radar and terrain-avoidance radar, plus automatic ground mapping.

Powered by twin T700-GE-700 turboshafts, it was big enough and fast enough to ferry an eleven-man infantry platoon into a fire zone.

In this instance, the sole passenger was the Executioner. Dressed in a blacksuit, armed to the gills, the soldier sat staring out the open bay door as the desert flashed past. By the position of the North Star, he could tell that they hadn't deviated from their northerly bearing. His headset crackled.

"Two minutes to drop zone, sir," the pilot said.

"Acknowledged," Bolan answered. He pulled the cocking handle on his M-16 all the way to the rear and released it. Trevor Garth and company were in for an unwelcome surprise.

The big break in the manhunt had come over an hour ago, thanks to the dogged persistence of Agents Calvert and Jiminez. They had been given permission by the owner of the aviation fuel company to examine the company's records.

The three Augusta 109s owned by Thrag Aerial Survey had been busy in recent months, as their fuel consumption testified. While compiling a list of the dates and gallons purchased, Jiminez had stumbled across payments rendered for maintenance. Questioning revealed that all routine maintenance had been performed by two qualified mechanics at the fuel company as part of a package deal.

Probing deeper into the records, Jiminez had uncovered a crucial tidbit. One of the choppers had broken down at a remote site in desert country north of Reno. The owner of Thrag Aerial Survey had paid three times the going rate to have one of the mechanics flown out there.

The mechanic was all too willing to help the FBI. But the breakdown had occurred more than seven months earlier, and he hadn't paid much attention to where he was taken. The best he could do was narrow the probable location down to a forty-square-mile area.

The Air Force had picked up the ball. Two Douglas EA-3B Skywarrior electronic-reconnaissance jets were called in. They crisscrossed the target zone in a computer-projected grid pattern.

As it was, the Skywarriors might have missed the camouflaged corrugated metal building hidden at the base of an isolated butte if not for their sensitive infrared sensors. They detected the heat emission given off by a large generator.

Word had been passed to Hal Brognola. Within half an hour, Bolan was being whisked to an isolated corner of Reno Cannon International Airport, where the Night Hawk waited.

Now the soldier was going in for the kill. It was pushing ten o'clock and the desert was bathed in the pale glow of a half moon. The Night Hawk's shadow glided over the stark landscape like an inky specter.

According to the U.S. Geological Survey map Bolan had studied, the small butte was located in the middle of a vast expanse of desert. Far to the north was a mountain range. But no one could approach the site by day without being spotted from a long way off.

At night? That was anyone's guess. Given the extensive security measures Trevor Garth had taken at the mansion, Bolan figured that the same would hold true at the Minuteman warehouse. So he was loaded for bear.

The M-16 was fitted with a 40 mm M-203 grenade launcher. It was also fitted with a modified

Metrologic neon laser sight specifically designed for night use.

Bolan wore Kevlar body armor under his black-suit. He carried a Ka-bar fighting knife in an ankle sheath and a stiletto at the small of his back.

An extra item this time around was a small night-vision device shaped like ordinary binoculars. The NVEC 800 came with a head strap and a neck lanyard. That meant he could strap on the device and have his hands free for what really counted.

His was a special unit. Boosted by a high-performance upgrade, it amplified the ambient light thirty-five thousand times. In layman's terms, that meant it would turn the darkest of nights into virtual day.

"One minute, sir," the pilot reported.

The soldier unfastened his safety harness and edged to the end of the seat. Gripping a handle, he peered ahead, seeking the gully. Suddenly, it was there, seeming to lunge up out of the ground as if to devour them.

Bolan had to hand it to the pilot. The Night Hawk banked and stopped on the proverbial dime, hovering a scant four feet above the ground. Stripping off the headset, Bolan stepped to the bay door and jumped. His knees cushioned the drop.

Bent low, buffeted by the rotor wash and stinging particles of sand and dust, he gave the pilot a thumbs-up and sprinted for the gully eight feet away.

Resembling an enormous metallic dragonfly, the Night Hawk rose and veered off. In half a minute, it had receded to a dot in the sky.

From the safety of the gully, Bolan watched until the chopper was gone. Moving to the other side, he beheld the squat silhouette of the butte four hundred yards off. No lights showed at the bottom, nor did any alien sounds reach him on the brisk breeze.

Squatting, Bolan opened his backpack and took out the NVEC 800. Insuring it was snug, he switched on the device. Immediately, his eyes were aglow in garish green light.

Moments before, the gully had been as murky as a crypt. Now Bolan could see every boulder, every crack in the earthen walls. In a crouch, he wound along the meandering gully toward the butte, pausing every so often to climb to the top and scour the vicinity.

In the green glare of the night-vision device, the desert took on an eerie aspect. Cactus and scrub trees were imbued with a luster that lent them the illusion of being living, breathing creatures.

The NVEC had an illumination range of five hundred feet. Bolan had to get close to the butte before he distinguished the outline of the building. Not only had it been painted in a camouflage pattern, but camouflage netting that perfectly matched the surrounding desert had been draped over the roof and down the sides.

For fifteen minutes, Bolan studied the warehouse. Only when he was convinced there were no guards did he scale the lip of the gully and cat-foot from cover to cover until he was within a stone's throw of the double doors. A glimmer of light showed in the crack between them and along the bottom, not noticeable at all without the NVEC.

No trace of an infrared laser alarm system was evident, nor were there any unusual heat signatures anywhere outside the building.

Could it be that Garth had felt so secure he hadn't bothered with an elaborate security system? That was the question Bolan mulled over as he stalked nearer. It seemed too good to be true. But try as he might, he pinpointed no cameras, sensors or trip wires.

Bolan didn't like the setup. It was too pat, too easy. Having been caught napping once, he was wary of making the same mistake twice.

He crouched at the double doors and pressed an ear to the crack. A generator hummed. Voices and movement were conspicuous by their absence.

Mystified, Bolan glided to the corner. The Minutemen had either flown the coop, or they were lying low, waiting to spring an ambush. If that was the case, he couldn't afford to wait them out. He had to go on the offensive.

The side door he'd entered on his first visit was unlocked. Silently twisting the knob, he pressed his back to the corrugated wall, then eased the door inward. No trip wires were attached; no gunfire greeted the move.

The overhead fluorescents were on. He switched off the NVEC unit and rapidly unfastened the head strap.

Shrugging out of the backpack, Bolan stuffed the binoculars inside and placed the backpack behind a boulder less than six paces from the doorway. Hunkering, he let his eyes adjust before he committed himself.

As stealthily as a prowling panther, the soldier slipped into the building and down the narrow hall. The first door opened into an empty office. The next was to a break room complete with a TV and a freezer.

Next was the warehouse proper. Bolan sank onto his heels, comparing what he saw to what he had seen previously. The flatbed trucks were still there but the jeeps were gone. Stacks of crates and boxes were right where he remembered them. So, to his surprise, were the canisters of chlorine gas and the mustard gas.

Most amazing of all, the five barrels of TL-14 were lined up where they had been when the cat was killed.

Trevor Garth would never go off and leave his

precious chemical weapons unguarded. Bolan knew something was seriously wrong here.

He scoured the warehouse from end to end. He scrutinized the girders that laced the ceiling. He lay flat to peer under the trucks and rose on tiptoe to see the far corners. Nothing at all.

Flicking on the laser sight, Bolan pointed the M-16 at a rivet on the wall, verifying the pencil-thin red dot centered correctly. Then, flying through the doorway, he dived for cover beside some crates. From there he sprinted to the piled canisters.

Silence, not the staccato beat of autofire, reigned.

Could it be that he was mistaken? Had Garth changed his mind and fled?

Minutes elapsed. At length Bolan rose, shifting every which way as he moved toward the barrels. The slightest motion would have drawn a burst of searing lead, but the place appeared to be genuinely deserted. He walked past the first barrel, aiming to make a sweep before he would concede he was alone.

It was empty.

Bolan drew up short. Tiny gobs of mucus clinging to the sides were all that was left. He stepped to the next one and discovered it was the same. And the next. And the next.

Now Garth's absence made sense.

The TL-14 was gone. The Minutemen had transferred it to other containers, maybe to tanks that were fitted on the three Augusta choppers Garth owned. Then they had either flown to a different hideaway to lie low until they learned whether the government would accept their demands, or they were already on their way to however many cities Garth had targeted.

What they didn't know was that the moment they had exposed the TL-14 to air, they triggered the chain reaction that would eventually cause the chemical warfare agent to explode, even if it had been resealed.

Brognola had to be told. Bolan reached for the radio clipped to his belt, then tensed. From behind him came the faintest suggestion of a creak, just such a sound as a door being stealthily opened might make.

He'd scoured every square foot of the warehouse, and that had included looking under the flatbed trucks and above the flatbed trucks, but he had been distracted by the empty barrels before he had checked inside the cabs of the four vehicles.

The soldier dived to the right as an SMG opened up. Rounds spanged into the barrel he had been standing in front of, punching holes in the metal as if it were made of paper.

Bolan rolled, coming to rest in the shelter of stacked crates. Scrambling to his knees, he counted six gunners. There had been two to a cab. Somehow, they had been forewarned of his presence.

Whether there had been motion sensors he missed, or some other device was to blame, was irrelevant.

They were spreading out to box him in. All except for one fanatic, an ox of a man in Army-Surplus fatigues who had triggered the initial burst. Cradling an Ingram M-10, he brashly lumbered toward the crates, making no effort at concealment.

Only someone who had never tasted real combat before would be so stupid. Only a rank amateur would act as if he were invincible, exposing himself for no reason.

Not that Bolan was complaining. He wasn't one to look a gift horse in the mouth. Popping up, he saw the laser sight's red dot blossom squarely in the center of the Minuteman's chest. He stroked the M-16.

It was a short, controlled burst, so precise that all five slugs drilled the gunner's sternum in a tight pattern. Jolted backward, the man looked down at himself in blatant astonishment. He tried to say something, but all that came out were spurts of scarlet that drooled onto his chin.

Bolan didn't see the man fall. He hurled himself to the left, behind some boxes, as rifles and another SMG opened up. A buzzing swarm of lead sought his life, rounds peppering the boxes and sizzling the air above him.

That the Minutemen didn't have many automatic weapons was a plus in his favor. Ordinary rifles were deadly in their own right, but they lacked the rate of fire of his M-16.

Surging erect, Bolan sprayed lead in an arc, driving three triggermen to ground and causing a fourth to jump backward so fast that the man tripped over his own boots.

Spinning, Bolan raced toward a mound of kegs. They were unlike any ammo storage containers he had ever seen, and it wasn't until he crouched behind the mound and read a label that he realized they were beer kegs.

Evidently, Garth had bought the brew to indulge his men. It would have been amusing if it weren't so pathetic. No military leader worthy of the name would do the same.

For all of Garth's undeniable brilliance and tactical ability, the man wasn't the George Washington of the insurgent fringe, as Garth liked to picture himself. Washington had tempered his men into iron warriors; Garth pampered his.

Then again, maybe Garth figured that there was no need to ride roughshod over the Minutemen. For what they lacked in military skill and discipline, they made up for in one very critical respect.

No one would deny that the Minutemen were supremely devoted to their cause. So much so, they could rightly be labeled fanatics. And as any student of history knew, fanaticism had successfully fueled the flames of many a revolution down through the centuries.

A rifle boomed twice. A keg above Bolan partially burst, showering beer onto his head and shoulders. Momentarily blinded, he backpedaled, wiping his face with his left sleeve.

Footsteps pounded on the concrete floor. The wily rifleman was rushing him.

Flattening, blinking furiously, the soldier fired in the direction of the sound. A startled yelp proved that he nearly scored. Reversing, the footsteps faded, allowing Bolan to clear his vision.

The beer had soaked his hair and parts of his blacksuit. He reeked of the stuff, but there was nothing he could do until after he eliminated the opposition.

Bolan crawled toward the west wall, winding among the ordnance and supplies. He was almost to a pallet laden with canned goods when a shot rang out and a slug dug a furrow in the floor near his elbow.

Twisting, he sought the shooter. But the remaining gunners had learned from their mistakes. He crawled on, going only a few feet when another blast reverberated off the corrugated metal walls.

This time the round missed by a hair. It spanged off into the canned goods, blowing a hole the size of a walnut in a box. Baked beans oozed out.

Flipping to the right, Bolan again tried to pinpoint the marksman. Wherever he was, the man had to have an unobstructed view of that section of the warehouse. Bolan scanned all the likely spots without spotting him.

Snaking to the foodstuffs, Bolan crouched. He rose just high enough to peer toward the flatbed trucks—and nearly lost his head when a bullet smashed into a box inches from his left eye.

Dropping low, Bolan noticed the sharp angle at which the slug had penetrated the carton. The only way that could have happened was if the shot came from somewhere high up, and there was only one place high enough to qualify.

The shooter was up among the girders.

Bolan searched long and hard. Shadows hugged the ceiling, effectively shrouding the sniper. He did spot metal rungs in the far wall, which explained how the man had reached his roost.

"Horatio? That's you, isn't it?"

The shout came from the vicinity of the empty barrels. Bolan recognized the voice of Mills, one of Garth's right-hand men. He didn't respond. To do so would tell the others exactly where he was.

"Listen, Fed," Mills yelled. "This won't get you anywhere. We have you outnumbered. Why not make it easy on yourself and throw out your hardware? I give you my word that you won't be harmed."

Easing onto his elbows and knees, Bolan crawled

to the wall and turned right. The whole time, he watched the steel beams overhead.

"What are you waiting for?" Mills called. "We know that you're alone. Pretty damn stupid, if you ask me. Did you think you could take us all on by your lonesome? Or did you know that the boss and most of the boys had already left to wipe out the three cities?"

So it was three, Bolan noted. Ahead the tailgate of the last truck appeared. He headed for the rear tires. Suddenly, the rifleman on high fired. Something plucked at Bolan's leg but didn't break the skin. Thunder rumbled, drowning out whatever Mills said next.

A few more feet, and Bolan was there. He rolled under the truck and swung toward the front end.

"This is your last chance!" Mills said. "Come out with your arms up and you get to live. What do you say?"

Was the man really that naive? Bolan wondered. He crawled to the front bumper and stopped. A four-yard gap separated the truck he was under from the next. He'd be cored before he got halfway. How was he to cross?

The man on the girders provided the answer. He hollered, "Pax! The Fed is under the truck nearest the double doors. Flank him, and we have him in the bag."

"Thanks, Martin," Mills replied.

Now Bolan knew that the rifleman was on the left side of the flatbed. The soldier edged far enough out to see the girders. A vague form moved at the junction of two cross beams. He sighted, but the form promptly disappeared.

Meanwhile, Mills and the others were converging. Bolan had to get out from under the truck quickly, or they would pin him down.

So far Bolan had resorted to the M-16, and that alone. He hadn't used the grenade launcher out of concern for the stockpiled ammunition scattered about. It wouldn't take much to set it off.

But there was no ammo up on the girders. The soldier slid out farther, glimpsed a figure scurrying along a wide beam and worked the M-203.

The grenade glistened as it looped toward the ceiling. At its apex, it was just under the wide beam. Bolan flung himself back under the flatbed at the moment of detonation.

A shriek punctuated the explosion, only to be smothered by the grinding tear of twisted metal and the crash of mangled girders.

Bolan was on the move before the echoes died. Rolling out from under the opposite side, he bolted to the nearest cover, a collection of fuel drums. He took it for granted that none of the Minutemen would be insane enough to risk igniting them, but one shooter had to prove just how fanatical he was by working the lever of a Winchester .30-30 like a madman.

The soldier bent and whirled, spotting the upper half of the gunner's body framed by a crate, and gave tit for tat. At the crackle of autofire, the Minuteman's features dissolved in pink froth and the man lurched to one side in a gory pantomime of the Frankenstein monster.

"Get the son of a bitch!" Mills raged.

Three fanatics were left, and they came at him all at once, shooting indiscriminately.

The only available cover consisted of several spare truck tires piled on top of one another. Taking a long stride, Bolan tucked and executed a shoulder roll that brought him up on one knee beside them. High-powered rounds smacked into the rubber with the cadence of boxing gloves striking a punching bag.

The Minutemen were in the open, rushing madly forward, counting on their combined firepower to overwhelm him. Mills was the only one armed with an SMG, a standard Uzi that spit 9 mm death in a sporadic stream.

Bolan didn't have time to aim. He snapped shots at one of the Minutemen and was rewarded by the sight of the shooter staggering backward. Pivoting, he went to do the same to Mills.

As fate would have it, the M-16 picked that moment to cycle dry.

CHAPTER FIFTEEN

Combat skills vary. Those of someone who played at being a soldier could never hope to rival those of someone who had devoted his entire adult life to soldiering.

Mack Bolan was the latter. In combat his reactions were second nature. He did what had to be done without pausing to rationalize what that should be.

This instant was a case in point. For where others might have fumbled for a new magazine while awkwardly ejecting the spent one, he performed the drill smoothly, fluidly, doing in the blink of an eye what would have taken most men five or ten precious seconds.

Hardly did the autorifle go empty than the soldier had reloaded. He fired at the same split second that Mills did. Of the two of them, his aim was better. Where Mills's burst ripped into the tires, his ripped into the Minuteman's torso.

Garth's lieutenant danced like a puppet on tangled strings, disjointed limbs jerking spasmodically, the Uzi falling from limp fingers.

That left one fanatic, a man armed with a Marlin .45-70. The big rifle thundered, but the Minuteman's aim wasn't all it should be. A trio of perfectly spaced rounds from the M-16 decided the issue.

Bolan straightened slowly. Wary of being duped by gunners playing possum, he double-checked each and every corpse. They were indeed dead.

All that remained of the sniper who had been up on the girders was a ravaged chest with a single arm and half a leg attached.

Unclipping the radio, Bolan put in a call to Brognola. The big Fed answered so quickly that Bolan knew he had been glued to the frequency. Succinctly, Bolan detailed his clash. He was about done when a commotion at the other end resulted in Brognola coming back on the line with a smile in his tone.

"One of us must have gotten up on the right side of the bed, Striker. Agent Jiminez has dug up the name of another dummy corporation owned by our millionaire friend. This one is called Vorter Air Freight Service."

Bolan saw the connection; "Vorter" was an anagram for "Trevor."

"They operate out of a small private airfield near Reno. Jiminez had a team check it out. We've just received word that three Augusta choppers are parked beside a hangar owned by Vorter Air. We have them, Striker! Garth thought that he could hide right under our noses, but he was wrong.''

So it seemed. But Bolan was learning not to take Garth lightly. Locating him and putting him out of operation were two different things.

"I'll have the Air Force chopper there to pick you up inside of fifteen minutes," Brognola stated. "I take it that you'd like to be in on the finish?"

"I wouldn't miss it for the world," Bolan said.

TREVOR GARTH WAS enjoying himself immensely. Why shouldn't he be? He had outwitted the Feds. His grand scheme was proceeding according to schedule, and by the same time tomorrow, he would be the most famous person in America.

Extra zest came from the fact that he was about to do what no foreign or civil power had ever been able to accomplish—namely, bring the federal government to its knees. The socialist, atheistic elite was about to get its due.

Garth wasn't deluding himself, though. It would be a long, hard fight. Months, if not years, would go by before enough people joined his cause to insure victory. But he had no doubt that victory would be his.

Once the American people understood how corrupt politicians controlled every aspect of their lives, once they saw that the Constitution they revered was being perverted by special interests, they would rise in rebellion just as their forefathers had done against the British generations past.

A new American Revolution was about to dawn, a bloody, glorious struggle that would rival the first in epic scope. When it was over, the American people would have reclaimed their rightful heritage.

Gone would be the days of Big Brother. Once again the United States government would be of the people, by the people and for the people. It would be as it had been back in the days of Garth's illustrious ancestors. And it would all be thanks to him.

Garth had spent many an idle moment dreaming of the accolades that would be heaped on him. In his more whimsical moments, he saw himself as the new leader of the country, guiding America to her rightful destiny as a shining beacon of true freedom to the world at large.

Silly? Perhaps. But Garth liked to flatter himself that it was his due. After all, he loved America more than anyone he knew. Hadn't he bankrolled the Minutemen at vast expense to himself? Hadn't he seized the moment when circumstance delivered the chemical weapons into his hands? And wasn't he now leading the first open assault on the forces of tyranny and corruption?

Just like George Washington, Garth was in the vanguard of the budding revolutionary movement.

In the years to come, schoolchildren would read about his life and times just as they now read about Washington's. He would be honored above all men for his role in the rewriting of history.

"Excuse me. Sir?"

Garth roused himself from his daydream and focused on Blanchard. "What is it now?" he asked testily. Sometimes it seemed as if his followers were little better than small children. They could do nothing right without his supervision.

"The tanks have been checked, just like you wanted. No leaks to report. Pressure levels are where they should be. It looks like everything is a go for tomorrow."

"Have you heard from Mr. Mills yet?"

"No, sir. We've tried a dozen times. He doesn't answer."

Garth rose and walked to a window that overlooked the property, yet another in a string of hideouts he had set up beforehand. Mills was supposed to report in every two hours. It could only mean one thing. "Evidently our warehouse in the desert has been compromised."

"But the mustard gas! And the chlorine canisters!" Blanchard said. "Not to mention the trucks and the arms we kept there."

"We have other trucks, other arms," Garth reassured him. "What puzzles me is how the Feds located it so soon. They must be a lot more intelligent than I gave them credit for being.''

"Or lucky," Blanchard said.

What were the odds, Garth mused, of the Feds finding their current sanctuary before the Minutemen left at dawn? The fate of the entire nation depended on their not being caught. Should he give the order to vacate now? Or should he trust in Providence to see them through?

"Any orders, boss?"

"Send in Mr. Starkey."

Before Blanchard could so much as turn, the Texan materialized at his side. Starting, Blanchard clutched his chest and snapped, "Dammit, Ren! I wish you wouldn't do that! You know it scares the hell out of people."

"Sorry, pard," Starkey said, but he didn't sound sorry.

Garth dismissed Blanchard, then motioned for the tall Texan to close the door. "You heard, I gather?"

Starkey nodded.

"I can't take it for granted that the Feds won't show up on our doorstep before we leave," Garth said. "A countermeasure is called for. A preemptive strike, if you will." He took out his wallet and flipped to a photograph taken when he was decades younger. "I wonder if the Feds know that I was a star quarterback during my high-school days. If they did, they would realize that I'm a master at misdirection, at making an adversary think I'm going one way when actually I'm going another.''

"What do you have in mind, Mr. Garth?"

"I need a distraction. Something to slow down the federal investigation. Something that will draw in a lot of their agents from the field. Something they would never expect.''

"And you want me to handle it?"

"I want you to pick two men, Mr. Starkey, and attack the FBI office here in Reno.''

The man in black didn't betray a hint of emotion. Where others would have ranted and raved that Garth must be insane, Starkey took the news as if he were being asked to run to the market for a quart of milk. "How do you want the job done? With dynamite, like at the mansion?''

"No. Something more exotic.'' Garth sat on the edge of the desk and steepled his fingers. "Why not give the Feds what they are hunting for?'' He pointed at a fire extinguisher on the east wall. "Empty that, then refill it with TL-14 and water. You will find the necessary equipment downstairs.''

Starkey's mouth tweaked upward. "Understood.''

As the Texan began to turn, Garth held up a restraining finger. "Not so fast, my friend. I don't want any of you to come to harm. Take the same precautions we'll take tomorrow. Issue gas masks and wear one yourself. And make certain that every square inch of skin is covered."

"Will do."

Garth chuckled, thinking of the confusion he would sow. The Feds wouldn't know what to expect next. They would be running around like a flock of beheaded chickens, unable to mount a concerted effort against him. Which was just what he wanted.

Another seven hours, and the Minutemen would be on their way.

Another seven hours, and the downfall of the federal government was assured.

He could hardly wait.

THIS TIME there were two USAF Sikorsky HH-60 Night Hawk helicopters. Turboshafts whining, they flashed in low from the northeast. Their pilots and copilots, wearing Gentex SPH-4 flying helmets, maintained radio silence.

Squatting behind the center communications console in the cockpit, Mack Bolan couldn't help but be impressed by the elaborate controls, with their full dual displays. From his position, he could glance down through the nose Plexiglas panels at the terrain sweeping by under them.

The captain glanced at the soldier and held up two fingers. Bolan nodded.

This time they were leaving nothing to chance. This time—the Feds hoped—they would catch the

Minutemen unaware, and put an end to the so-called revolution literally in one swoop.

The private airfield was northwest of Reno. It handled primarily small charter flights and weekend fliers who didn't want to contend with the heavy air traffic at the airports.

East of the runway, in a long row, sat fourteen hangars. Most were rented or owned outright by various local companies. Among them, third from an end, was the hangar belonging to Vorter Air Freight Service.

The FBI had done its homework. The hangars nearest Vorter Air's weren't occupied at that time of night. So the warrior need not worry about accidentally harming innocent civilians.

What Bolan did have uppermost on his mind was preventing the fanatics from using the TL-14. The FBI psych-profile people felt it would be right in keeping with Trevor Garth's character for Garth to unleash the chemical agent out of sheer spite if he saw his grand designs crumbling around him.

So not only did Bolan and the servicemen in the Night Hawks have to prevent the Augustas from getting airborne, but they had to keep Garth from using the TL-14 as a last resort.

Fortunately, the airstrip was separated by a highway and a field from the closest residential area. In addition, the prevailing winds would tend to blow the chemical agent out over the desert, not toward downtown Reno.

Bolan's backpack was in the chopper's bay. He wouldn't need it. This time he was going in fast and hard, mowing down the opposition as it presented itself, not pausing for a breather until Garth was no longer a threat and the TL-14 was safe and sound.

The captain held up a single finger, then flicked a switch that killed the Night Hawk's running lights. A button put the turboshafts in their stealth mode, muting their whine even more.

The Air Force crews had gone over the drill again and again before taking off. Thirty seconds out from the airstrip, they banked, the other Night Hawk veering north while the craft Bolan was in cut to the south. The chopper slowed and dipped, skimming so low that Bolan swore he could have poked a leg through the Plexiglas panel and tapped his toes on the ground.

Everything seemed to be unfolding according to plan. The airstrip lay quiet under a myriad of stars. Dozens of private planes were parked on the far side, Pipers, Cessnas, Cherokees and the like. Most of the hangars were metal, and gleamed dully in the moonlight.

The one owned by Trevor Garth stood out from all the rest not only because it was the biggest, but also because it was the hangar painted bright yellow, a touch Bolan attributed to Garth's vanity.

No lights appeared to be on inside. No activity was taking place outside. "Maybe we've caught them napping," he said softly.

But Bolan spoke too soon. A door swung open on the side, and half a dozen men spilled from the yellow building, sprinting madly toward the Augustas.

The captain had his orders. In the event that the mission was compromised before Bolan was set down, the Night Hawks were to take whatever steps were necessary to stop the Augustas from taking off. He swooped toward them, his fingers flying over the control console.

The Night Hawks were armed with Hellfire antiarmor missiles in addition to a pair of M-60 D machine guns. It was more than enough firepower to reduce the three Augusta helicopters to smoking ruins.

However, there was a hitch. The Feds didn't want the tanks containing the TL-14 touched. The Air Force crews were to disable the three Augustas, but to do so with a minimum of damage. It was easier planned than executed.

Bolan gripped the edge of the console as the chopper looped in between two hangars and soared out over the airstrip, then swung its nose toward the Augustas. The pilot gained altitude before firing so the angle would be just right.

The soldier saw several of the scampering figures

reach the Augustas. He also saw two men who had stopped halfway to the craft and were on their knees, doing something with an object he couldn't quite make out.

The copilot spotted them, too. "What the hell are those two doing?"

What *could* the Minutemen do against heavily armored Night Hawks? The fanatics didn't have any surface-to-air missiles. Rifle and small arms fire would be like trying to take out tanks by flinging spitballs. They were finished, but they were too pig-headed to admit it.

Then Bolan realized the pair was bent over a short cylinder supported by a bipod, and he stiffened. He recalled all too vividly his encounter with the Minutemen in the Spring Mountains, and the Libyan. "It's a mortar!" he warned, too late.

A round shot up out of the tube, vaulting high in the air. The two men using the mortar were hardly experts; their aim was atrocious. But they didn't need to be all that accurate when they were firing 70 mm frag rounds. All they had to do was get close to the Night Hawk and the chopper would be crippled, or worse.

Instantly, the pilot banked and shot to the south down the runway. He barked a warning into his headset to alert the other Sikorsky.

Behind them the sky briefly lit up. It revealed that

one of the Augustas was already rising, rotors straining for lift.

Bolan shifted to see better as the pilot brought the Night Hawk around.

The other Night Hawk was bearing down on the yellow hangar from the north. A Hellfire spurted from under one of its shoulder-mounted stub pylons. At that range, the missile was on the Augusta almost too quick for the eye to follow. It sheared into the tail assembly, detonating with brutal force, shredding the stabilizer supports, the tail rotor and the horizontal stabilizer.

The Augusta plummeted like a rock, smashing down thirty feet from its takeoff point. The undercarriage buckled, but the chopper stayed intact.

Bolan exhaled. The other captain had taken a terrible risk. If the tanks holding the TL-14 were to burst—

A second Augusta was rising, swifter than the first. The other Night Hawk moved in to disable it when there was a puff of smoke and flame under the Augusta's nose. A small rocket leaped the distance between the two aircraft, catching the Night Hawk full in the cockpit.

"No!" the pilot of Bolan's chopper cried as the nose of the other Night Hawk broiled outward in sheets of searing flame and blistered metal.

The stricken chopper tilted, nose down. Its rotors spun crazily, with one of them busted partway off.

Almost in slow motion, it dived, twisting to one side. The impact was tremendous, the Sikorsky folding in on itself like an ungainly accordion.

"Damn them!" Bolan's pilot raged. "Those were friends of mine!" He whipped the control stick and pumped the pedals, bringing the Night Hawk the rest of the way around. Like a vengeful bird of prey, it streaked toward the still rising Augusta, the pilot oblivious to the men with the mortar who were shifting position to bring the mortar to bear.

Bolan slapped the copilot and pointed. The lieutenant snapped commands into his headset. A second later one of the M-60 Ds opened up, the heavy thud of the powerful machine gun a counterpoint to the spewing geysers that erupted near the pair of mortarmen, then stitched a ragged line toward them.

The Minutemen saw their peril and attempted to flee. The first man took multiple rounds in the back as he rose, transforming him into a human sieve. The second Minuteman tripped as he stood, inadvertently saving himself. The rounds that would have cored his body cleaved empty space instead. On all fours he scrambled toward the yellow hangar, throwing himself through the doorway in the proverbial nick of time.

While all this was taking place, the M-60 D on the other side of the Night Hawk roared into operation, sending a 7.62 mm firestream into the tail of the third Augusta, which hadn't tried to lift off. Now it never would. In mere moments the M-60 D reduced the tail pylon to so much scrap metal.

The Augusta that had shot down the other Night Hawk was in full flight. It had shot off over the yellow hangar, gaining altitude rapidly, the pilot swerving wildly from side to side to make his craft harder to hit.

Captain Bennett zoomed in pursuit. Even when he cleared the hangars, he didn't let fire a Hellfire missile. Nor would he, Bolan knew, as long as there was any chance of having the Augusta explode and rain TL-14 on innocent citizens.

The soldier glanced back at the yellow hangar. By rights he should be in there already, mopping up, but Bennett could ill afford to drop him off and chance losing sight of the Augusta.

It bothered Bolan that only a handful of Minutemen had been present, and not one had resembled Garth. Were the rest of the fanatics and their demented leader still inside?

"Look!" the copilot declared. "We have a clear shot broadside."

The Augusta was swinging to the south instead of heading out over the desert. Scattered homes passed below it, along with a secondary highway heavily traveled.

"We can't knock it out of the air until it's safe to do so," Captain Bennett stressed.

"If he turns his nose around, we'll have no choice," the lieutenant said.

Bolan agreed. It was either that or share the grisly fate of the first Night Hawk. "Can you get close enough to use the M-60s?" he inquired, since there would be less danger of puncturing the TL-14's containers.

"I can try," Bennett said. "Just so they don't have any other nasty surprises up their sleeve."

The lieutenant pointed again. "What the hell is that guy up to?"

As they talked, the Augusta had continued to execute a wide loop and was now bearing due west.

"Sweet Jesus!" the captain exclaimed. "Don't you see? He's heading straight for Reno!"

"He's going to spray the downtown area, I bet!" the lieutenant said in outright horror.

At that juncture the Augusta banked and lanced lower, barely clearing power lines. It dropped until it was at rooftop level, directly over a road leading into the heart of the city, which it followed.

A brilliant evasive tactic, Bolan reflected. The Air Force crew was hamstrung. They couldn't fire for fear of hitting the cars and trucks under the Augusta. Yet they had to do something, and soon.

"Look there!" the lieutenant cried.

Reno's garish skyline loomed ahead, home to upward of one hundred and fifty thousand souls. Like an arrow whizzing toward the heart of its intended victim, the Augusta zoomed toward the heart of the unsuspecting city.

CHAPTER SIXTEEN

Normally, the FBI office on East Plum Street would have been closed long before midnight rolled around. The front doors would have been locked.

But with the greatest manhunt in the history of Nevada in full swing, agents were coming and going constantly. No one thought to lock the doors. No one considered posting a guard.

The receptionist was earning overtime working the phone. She had just placed a call to Washington, D.C., for the bigwig named Brognola and was punching a lit button to answer an incoming line when she noticed three men who were crossing the street in front of the building.

All three wore dark suits. She would have taken it for granted they were FBI agents if not for the wide-brimmed black hat and black cowboy boots worn by the tallest of the trio.

Now who could they be? Lisa Blount wondered. She answered the line, relayed the caller to an extension, then looked up to see if the three men had entered. To her amazement, they stood just outside the office with their backs to her. Each was bent over and appeared to be doing something that involved his face or his head.

What in the world?

She thought of buzzing her boss, but she convinced herself there had to be a logical explanation for whatever the trio was up to. Then they turned.

Blount laughed. She had seen a lot of foolish sights in her time, but this one took the cake. Grown men in business suits, wearing bizarre Halloween masks. Baggy affairs, they were, with big goggles where the eyes should be and nosepieces similar to the trunks of elephants. Even more ridiculous was the bright red fire extinguisher the man in the cowboy hat carried.

Shoving the doors wide, the trio entered.

"Hold on there, fellows," Blount said good-naturedly. "This is the FBI, not a costume party. You'd better leave before you get into trouble."

"We know what this is, ma'am," said the tall man in black, his words distorted by the heavy mask. With that, he pointed the fire extinguisher at her. For some reason, he wore gloves.

"What are you aiming to do, gentlemen?" she scoffed. "Ruin my perm?"

"I'm truly sorry," the man in the black hat said. His finger closed on the lever.

A green spray spurted onto Blount's face and neck.

A bitter taste filled her mouth. Shocked, she recoiled, saying, ''I don't know what kind of stunt you're trying to pull—'' That was as far as she got. An intense burning sensation choked off her breath. Her face and neck were on fire. Her throat was the worst of all. She had to gasp for breath.

Abruptly scared, Lisa clawed at the phone, but the man in the black hat pulled it beyond her reach. Only then did it dawn on her that the three men were there to cause harm, and she opened her mouth to scream. No sound came out.

REN STARKEY WATCHED the receptionist collapse, blood marring her dainty nostrils and rosy lips. He felt a twinge of guilt, but that was all. More than a few lives had to be taken before the federal government would be overthrown.

The receptionist was but one of the first in a long string. It had just been her bad luck to be in the wrong place at the wrong time.

The Texan turned to an elevator. Above the door, the indicator panel showed that the car was descending and would reach the ground floor next. Quickly, the Texan stepped closer, extending the fire extinguisher.

Four men were inside, FBI agents, judging by their suits and neatly trimmed hair. They were joking and laughing when the door slid open, the laughter dying on their lips the moment Starkey sprayed them at point-blank range.

"What the hell?" one blurted.

It was the last question any of them ever voiced. Two of them apparently realized what had happened and made stabs for their pistols, but they were dead on their feet before they could draw.

Starkey entered the car, shoving limbs aside with his boot. He nodded at Meekum, who was to hold the lobby while he went from floor to floor with Buscema. "Three minutes, no more," he said.

"The way will be clear," Meekum promised, taking an Auto-Ordnance Pit Bull from a shoulder holster and moving into a corner where he could cover the entrance without being seen.

With a loud ding, the elevator doors closed. Starkey hit the button for the second floor. To be safe, he adjusted the flaps of his jacket so he could get at the Remingtons in a hurry if he had to.

Another federal agent was waiting for the elevator. He was the next to fall, gagging and clutching his throat.

Starkey hurried, moving methodically from office to office. Most weren't occupied. In those that were, the Feds were busy on the phone or studying files or chatting with co-workers. In the few seconds it took them to realize what was happening, they weakened and fell.

Seven more agents died without a shot being fired.

Then the Texan pushed open the door to a council room occupied by three men and two women. One of the latter was ungodly fast. The moment she laid eyes on Starkey, she bawled, "Look out!" and went for her gun.

Ren Starkey swung the nozzle from right to left, spattering her and the others. But her SIG-Sauer kept on rising. She had him dead to rights when Buscema's Coonan .357 Magnum pistol boomed.

The five dropped like poisoned flies.

Without missing a beat, the Texan strode on. Under his gas mask, he wore a grim smile, for it pleased him to be striking a blow for freedom and justice.

As an ardent shootist, Starkey had seen his Second Amendment rights whittled away bit by bit by obnoxious liberal busybodies who felt they had the God-given right to deprive law-abiding Americans of their consitutional guarantees.

Well, enough was enough. Starkey, and many thousands like him, were sick to death of having politicians play at being petty dictators. It was high time the liberals learned that true Americans weren't going to stand for any more meddling with the order of things.

Resisting tyranny wasn't new to those who honored the Stars and Stripes. Patriots had stood firm at Yorktown, at New Orleans, at the Alamo and San Jacinto. Starkey could do no less, not when the Constitution itself was at stake.

An FBI agent came rushing around a corner, blundering into a shower of green spray. Dispassionately, Ren Starkey stood over the twitching figure and watched the man die.

The second American Revolution was under way in earnest.

And he was honored to be a part of it.

ONE FLOOR ABOVE, Hal Brognola raised his red eyes from a report he had been reading to tilt his head and listen. Was it his imagination, or were those gunshots he had heard? Setting down the manila folder, he rose and stepped to his door. As he opened it, another muted retort sounded somewhere below.

Brognola moved into the hallway. A commotion at the far end caught his eye. A slim brunette sped from an excited knot of agents, her weapon drawn, her features pallid. Agent Walters, if he remembered correctly.

"What the devil is going on?" he demanded, and was flabbergasted when she seized his wrist and hauled him toward a door farther down.

"Quickly, sir. We must get you off this floor. There's no time to lose."

Brognola dug in his heels, bringing her to a stop.

"What's going on? What is all the shooting about?"

At the far end of the hall, several agents had pushed through the stairwell door and rushed downstairs. Shots rang out, but only a few, and they were punctuated by a piercing, wavering scream such as no human throat should be able to produce, a cry so unearthly that it raised the short hairs at Brognola's nape.

"We're under attack, sir," Walters said, tugging hard to get him to move. "Please. Come with me before it's too late."

"Under attack by whom?" Brognola asked, refusing to budge. He was in charge. It was his duty to lead the others, not to slink off like a cowardly cur with his tail between his legs. What did this agent think she was doing?

"We believe it's the Minutemen, sir." Walters glanced anxiously at the stairwell. "And they're using that chemical toxin, TL-14, on our people."

"What?" The full scope of Trevor Garth's twisted, cold-blooded nature was borne home with all the jarring effect of a vicious slap to the cheek. "How can you be sure?"

"I was with Agent Spritz, sir. We were taking the stairs down, and he was a few steps below me when a tall man in an old-fashioned gambler's hat and a gas mask came through the door and sprayed Spritz point-blank. Larry never had a chance. The tall guy aimed at me, but I stumbled around a corner before he could nail me.''

"I need my gun," Brognola said, turning to return to his office. But she held on with surprising strength, digging in her own heels to stop him.

"Please, sir!" Walters pleaded. "We have no time to spare! Go back in there, and I can guarantee that we'll end up like the rest."

Brognola hesitated. The last of the agents had disappeared into the stairwell, but no sounds broke the unnatural stillness.

"I'm begging you!" Walters said. "You're too important to throw your life away needlessly. If they get you, who will coordinate our manhunt for Garth?"

Begrudgingly, Brognola had to admit that she had a point. Washington would have to send in someone else to replace him, and that would take hours. By the time the new head honcho had everything sorted out, the Minutemen would have struck. Come to think of it, maybe that was exactly what Garth intended. "Damn!" he rasped.

"Please," Walters pleaded. "Follow me. And hurry, before they spot us."

It rankled Brognola to turn and run. But he recalled all too well how he had erred at the Garth estate; he wouldn't err here, not with the consequences so dire.

Walters threw open the last door on the right. A

short flight of stairs brought them to another door. As she flung it open, a blast of cool air fanned Brognola's perspiring brow. They were on the roof.

"Is there another way down?" Brognola asked.

"No."

"Then we're trapped?"

"I'm afraid so."

Walters pushed him around the corner and planted herself between him and the door, clearly intending to sell her own life to safeguard his.

Brognola swelled with pride. A lot of criticism had been heaped on the Bureau of late. Thanks to the mistakes made in the past, many had branded the FBI as nothing more than a bloodthirsty pack of cold-blooded killers. But nothing could be further from the truth. Sure, there were incompetents, but most FBI agents were decent, hardworking Americans doing the jobs they were paid to do to the best of their ability.

The big Fed moved toward the woman to suggest that they retreat to a corner of the roof where they would have a clear field of fire. Just then Walters placed a finger to her lips and nodded at the doorway.

Faintly, from below, came voices. One spoke in a distinct Western drawl.

The big Fed crept to the jamb to listen.

"—reckon that's all of them. Let's light a shuck before more show up."

"What about those steps there, Ren? Shouldn't we check where they lead to?"

"No. I'm runnin' low on the stuff and we're runnin' low on time. We skedaddle, pronto."

"Whatever you say."

Brognola motioned to Walters. Together they dashed to the front of the building and crouched. They didn't have to wait long before the glass doors opened and three men in dark suits emerged. One wore a broad-brimmed black hat. Working swiftly, they shed gas masks, stuffing them into a plastic bag one of the men produced. Then, with a glance in both directions down the deserted street, they hurried toward a car parked at the curb half a block away.

"We can't let them get away, sir," Walters said.

Brognola remembered what Bolan had told him about the gunman in the hat. He went to warn the brunette but she stood erect and adopted a two-handed stance.

"FBI! Hold it right there! Put your hands in the air and turn slowly!"

The trio froze. Two of them started to comply, but the third, the Texan, glanced over his shoulder, saw Walters and grinned. "So we missed one of the nits, did we? Put down that gun, missy, and pretend you never saw us."

Walters firmed her grip on her pistol. "I'm warning you, mister!'' she responded. ''Do as I say or I'll put a bullet into you.''

''I reckon not, ma'am,'' the gunman said.

Brognola knew that the tall man in black was going to make a stab for those fancy six-shooters. He was expecting it. But since Walters had the Texan covered, her finger on the trigger of her cocked piece, the outcome was a foregone conclusion. Or so he assumed until the tall man moved.

Maybe *moved* was the wrong word to describe what happened next. For, in an ambidextrous draw so lightning fast it would have taken a stop-motion camera to record it, the gunman drew and fired. In less time than it took for Walters's brain to send a nerve impulse to her trigger finger to tighten around the SIG-Sauer's trigger, the tall Texan drew and squeezed off two shots of his own.

Few could rival his feat. Even Bolan, who possessed some of the quickest reflexes the big Fed had ever seen, would be hard-pressed to match it.

At the crack of the six-guns, Walters tottered backward and would have fallen had Brognola not caught her. She had been shot in both shoulders, nearer her arms than her chest. Brognola realized that the gunman had shot her there on purpose, rather than in the head or the heart. For some unfathomable reason, the Texan had spared her life.

Setting her down gently, Brognola snatched up the fallen SIG-Sauer and pivoted. Two of the Minutemen had reached the car, and one slid behind the wheel. The man in the black hat was ambling along as if he had all the time in the world, his pistols gleaming in his hands.

Brognola popped up to shoot. As he did, the Texan whirled. The Remingtons spit lead and thunder. Chips flew from the roof cresting, stinging Brognola's face as he threw himself onto his stomach. He heard the car's engine turn over and rose onto his elbows to peek down. Another shot nearly took out an eye.

Seconds later the car raced off into the darkness. Brognola rose to fire, but the speeding vehicle was already almost out of sure range. Besides, the street was lined with residences.

Walters had her arms clasped to her sides and was writhing in agony.

"Stay put. I'll have an ambulance here soon," Brognola promised, then ran toward the stairs. He thought of all the agents who had been in the building and had to have been wiped out by the TL-14. Raw rage coursed through him, a rage so powerful that it constricted his throat and made him clench his fists until the knuckles were white.

No matter what, he was going to bring the Minutemen down.

At the top of the stairs, Brognola paused. What if the toxin the killers had sprayed was still potent? The report sent from Washington had neglected to mention how long the TL-14 stayed active once dispensed.

A groan from Walters spurred Brognola into action. If he died, he died. He couldn't stay there mentally biting his nails while someone was suffering. Squaring his shoulders, he pushed on the lower door and stepped into the hall.

THE PILOT of the Augusta was as devious as they came. Whenever the Night Hawk began to close in, he swooped low over a car or truck on the road below.

The Air Force captain swore a blue streak, then glanced at Bolan. "We were told that you get to call the shots. So what will it be, Mr. Belasko? Do we let him reach the city? Or do we stop him here and now, with a minimal loss of life?"

Bolan shifted on the balls of his feet. It was the age-old dilemma of whether a few should be sacrificed so many more might live. Should they be? Or should he hold off and hope that the Minuteman pilot wouldn't carry out Trevor Garth's threat?

"What's he doing now?" the lieutenant said.

The Augusta had been hovering over a pickup. Suddenly, it zoomed forward to an intersection just as a city bus turned from a side street. The chopper paced the bus, which was half-filled.

"There's your answer," Bolan said. "If we take him down, we kill ten or eleven others."

"What's ten or eleven compared to thousands?" Bennett asked.

Reno's neon-lit center was less than two miles away. Whatever they were going to do, they had to move soon.

The soldier approached the pilot's door. "Slide your window open," he directed.

Bennett gave him a quizzical look. "What do you have in mind?"

Resting the M-16's muzzle on the lower frame, Bolan tucked the stock to his shoulder and lined up the front sight assembly with the rear sight. "I want you to fly parallel with the Augusta, about one hundred yards apart."

"You're going to take out the pilot with your rifle?" the copilot said skeptically.

"What if his cockpit is shielded?" Bennett asked. "If they went to all the trouble to fit their choppers with rocket launchers, they might have installed special glass, too."

Bolan was tracking the other helicopter. His feet were flat, his knees against the door. "It's not like we have a whole lot of options," he said. "If this doesn't work, we use the M-60s."

"And pray for the best," Bennett said. Under his expert manipulation, the chopper swerved wide to the right and took up the position Bolan had requested. The other pilot glanced repeatedly at them.

"He's nervous," Lieutenant Smith guessed. "He's wondering what we're up to."

Thanks to special tinting on the Night Hawk's cockpit, Bolan had little fear of the Minuteman spotting him. He fixed a bead and held it as steady as he could, what with the slight sway and dip of the Night Hawk.

The soldier didn't adjust either sight. There was no need. The M-16 had been preset, as were those used daily by troops in the field, for ideal battle sights. This meant the autorifle had been sighted in at the standard range of three hundred yards. Since the trajectory was relatively flat at that distance, a shooter could hit any target within that range by aiming right at it.

The big question was whether to try for a kill, or only to wound. Bolan decided on the latter. Wounded, the pilot could still land safely. Dead, that Augusta would drop like a five-ton boulder on top of the bus or whatever else was below it at the time.

Reno was getting closer by the second. Bolan saw the city bus stop to pick up another passenger. When it braked, the Minuteman brought the Augusta to a stop directly over it. Bennett hovered, as well. Neither chopper went on until the bus did.

The Minuteman thought he was being clever, but he had just given Bolan an idea. The soldier gazed up the highway and saw another bus-stop sign. Sure enough, when the bus stopped to let a passenger off, the Augusta stopped and waited until it went on.

"Look at him," Smith said. "He must think he's damn clever."

"Not clever enough," Bolan replied. "Be ready." He lowered his chin to the M-16 and locked the sights on the green shirt worn by the other pilot.

Almost as if they were conducting a military drill, the two choppers flew westward abreast of each other. The Minuteman watched the Air Force chopper closely, while Bolan kept his eyes peeled for the next bus stop. Soon one appeared.

The soldier had to time it just right. He placed his finger on the trigger, glancing out of one eye to gauge the distance remaining. When the bus was sixty feet from the sign and just beginning to slow, he steadied his aim, took a deep breath and held it.

Bolan had noticed that there was a lag time of two or three seconds between the time the bus pulled out from each stop and when the Augusta's pilot flew on to keep up with it. That was when he intended to fire. With any luck, the pilot would be so preoccupied by his wound that the bus would be able to pull several lengths ahead before the helicopter came down.

Then the unforeseen occurred. The bus driver picked that moment to realize he had an aerial shadow. Bending forward to peer up through the windshield, he did the last thing Bolan expected. The driver slammed on the brakes, bringing the bus to a halt dozens of feet from the stop.

CHAPTER SEVENTEEN

A good soldier is one who adapts as the situation
warrants. Going by the book isn't always possible
or even desirable.

No one knew that better than the Executioner.
Having honed his combat skills on the killing fields
of the world, he adapted automatically as circumstances required.

In this case, the moment that the bus braked, the
Augusta flew past it. The pilot was so intent on the
Night Hawk that he didn't notice his living shields
were no longer underneath his craft.

Bolan fired when the Augusta's fuselage cleared
the front of the bus. He triggered two crisp shots
and was rewarded by seeing the Minuteman
punched against the far cockpit door. Involuntarily,
the man clutched at his ribs, forgetting to hold on
to the stick.

Immediately, the Augusta tilted steeply and
dipped toward the road. At the last possible moment, the pilot pulled up, barely clearing a tree at

the roadway's edge. Flying erratically, he headed to the south.

"Now?" Bennett asked.

"Not yet," Bolan responded.

They were over tranquil suburbs. Neatly trimmed lawns bordered equally neat homes with their tidy flower gardens and shrubs.

The Augusta lost altitude, recovered, then lost it again. Clearly, the Minuteman was finding it difficult to stay aloft.

"Now?" Bennett repeated.

Bolan glanced down. A shopping center was below, a vast mall with its parking lot crammed with cars. A woman pushing a shopping cart was on her way to her car, a toddler in her other arm. "Not yet."

Rising steeply, the Augusta gained speed. It had no hope of outrunning the Night Hawk, but that didn't deter the pilot from trying.

"One missile is all it would take," Smith remarked.

"No Hellfires," Bolan stressed. A long, low building materialized, flanked by a large green rectangle bearing white stripes, with a goalpost at either end. A school and a football field.

"Now?" the captain asked for the third time, his tone hopeful.

At last Bolan granted permission. "Now," he said, and held on to the door as the Night Hawk banked steeply, then swooped toward the Augusta at top speed.

The port gunner opened up at the captain's command, stitching the aircraft's tail section. They saw the Augusta shudder to the multiple impacts, saw smoke gust from its tail rotor and bits and pieces of the stabilizer spinning away. The Minuteman fought to keep his chopper in the sky, but it was like a buzzard trying to stay up with one wing out of commission.

Gravity wouldn't be denied. The fuselage spun crazily, gaining momentum as it fell, until, with a rending crash, the Augusta smashed down on the forty-yard line and burst into flames.

"Take me down there," Bolan said. Billowing clouds of smoke poured from the crumpled undercarriage. It wouldn't be long before the entire chopper went up.

The pilot's door on the Augusta opened, and a man sprawled onto the field, one arm across his midsection. Awkwardly, he scuttled toward the school. The man had no hope of reaching safety before the chopper exploded.

"Drop me off and get out of here," Bolan said, slinging the M-16 over his shoulder.

"Are you nuts, Belasko?" Smith asked. "Why risk your skin for that bastard after what he did a short while ago to our boys back at the airstrip?"

"You'll never make it," Bennett added.

Gripping the door handle, Bolan said, "Level off at ten feet. I'll jump."

The Air Force officers swapped glances, and the lieutenant shook his head.

Dutifully, the Night Hawk was brought to a hover at the desired height. Bolan flung the door open, tucked his knees and leaped, careful to duck his head and shoulders below the sweep of the rotor blades. Landing hard but upright, he pumped his legs for all they were worth.

The football field was eerily lit by the flickering flames that ringed the bottom of the Augusta, flames that were growing higher and brighter every second.

The Minuteman was still desperately crawling away, but he had weakened to such an extent that his movements were as sluggish as a snail's. He collapsed, rose onto an elbow and tried again.

Bolan ran past the doomed chopper, holding a hand in front of his face to ward off the intense heat. Reaching the man, he hooked a hand under the guy's arm and propelled the pilot toward the sidelines. A rising crackle and hiss hinted that the blast was imminent.

Bending, Bolan shouted into the Minuteman's ear. "How much TL-14 was in your helicopter?"

"What?" the man bleated, his face the color of a sheet, blood drenching his shirt.

"How many gallons of TL-14 did you carry?"

The pilot looked up and laughed, a sneer in his

voice. "Is that what you Feds thought? Idiots! I wasn't carrying any of that stuff!"

They were twenty-five yards from the Augusta, which was nowhere near enough. Bolan gripped the man with both hands and picked up the pace, and they covered ten more yards. Fifteen.

The fuel tank ignited. Like a miniature volcano erupting, flames and smoke spewed upward and outward, searing the grass to a crisp. An invisible wall of force slammed into the soldier's back, lifting him off his feet and tumbling him as if he were made of straw.

Bolan struck the ground, was flipped another half-dozen feet and came to rest on his belly. He didn't rise. Throwing both arms over his head, he listened to the zing and whiz of flying shards of metal, scores and scores of them, some no bigger than a pencil point, some the size of his leg, and every one as deadly as shrapnel from a hand grenade.

Amid the din a deep grunt sounded close at hand, followed by a low, inarticulate cry and violent thrashing.

Not until the last echoes of the explosion had died and the air was empty of flying projectiles did Bolan lift his head and gaze around. The Augusta was a flaming mockery of its former aerodynamic grandeur. Dotting the football field were tiny patches of flames, blazing shards shed by the burst fuselage.

Something moved to his right. Drawing the Beretta, Bolan slowly rose.

The pistol wasn't necessary. Lying on his stomach, pinned to the earth by a charred spear of jagged metal over six feet in length, was the pilot. The tip had caught him between the shoulder blades and passed completely through his body.

Amazingly, the man was still alive. His lips moved despite the crimson froth that coated them and his jaw.

Bolan sank onto a knee. "Where is the TL-14?" he asked. "Is it back at the hangar?"

The Minuteman attempted to speak, but all that came out was more blood.

"The TL-14," Bolan repeated. "I need to know."

Sometimes, at the point of dying, a man who had lived a creed of selfish evil would have moments of lucid thought and moral clarity, moments when he saw his misspent life for what it was and tried to atone, however ineptly. This man wasn't one of them. As Bolan leaned lower, the pilot scrunched his mouth and spit on the warrior's cheek.

"Go to hell, Fed!"

Those were the last words the fanatic ever uttered. Letting out his breath in a ragged gasp, he expired, as bitter in death as he had to have been in life.

"You first," Bolan said, rising and wiping his cheek. Once again he had been stymied. But the battle was far from over.

The Night Hawk was setting down several yards distant. Bennett threw open his door and beckoned urgently, waving his headset.

Sirens blistered the night as Bolan jogged to the Sikorsky. The aircraft started to rise before he was all the way inside. Slipping the headset over his ears, he said, "Belasko here."

"Striker, this is Brognola."

In the many years they had known each other, Bolan couldn't recall his friend ever sounding so depressed, so stripped of confidence and vitality. "What's wrong?"

Miles away, Brognola stared glumly out the door of his office at a victim of the chemical toxin being put into a body bag. He'd had to call in a dozen field agents to assist the paramedics and police who responded to the emergency.

There was little anyone could do. Several dozen fine men and women had lost their lives, sacrifices on the altar of a madman's private revolution. They were but the first of many to come unless Brognola and Bolan managed to outwit an adversary who had outmaneuvered them at every turn so far.

"Are you all right?" Bolan wanted to know.

"I'm the only one who is," Brognola said, and told him, in vivid detail, of the unprecedented assault on the FBI office and the dire result.

It shook Bolan. He had witnessed more acts of unbridled savagery than anyone should ever have to. He had seen the handiwork of mobsters and murderers, of terrorists and tyrants. But this was especially disturbing because it elevated homegrown insurgency to a whole new level.

The Minutemen had dared to do what no one else had ever tried. They had attacked the FBI on the FBI's home ground, as it were, and they had gotten away unharmed. Their vile tactic had filled the Reno morgue, leaving widows and children to suffer in heartfelt sorrow for the rest of their lives, yet they escaped to be hailed by their twisted kind as heroes.

"No one survived except you?" the stunned soldier asked.

Brognola detailed Walters's fate. "She lost a lot of blood, but that Texan merely winged her. How he could shoot so accurately at that range, and in the dark, using those old-fashioned revolvers, is beyond me."

Bolan told about the Augustas. "I'm on my way back to the hangar. I doubt the Minutemen stuck around, but the TL-14 should still be there. They haven't had enough time to bring in a truck and haul it out."

"Let's hope you're right. I want this ended, Striker. Tonight."

"That makes two of us."

BOLAN WASN'T A MAN given to wild premonitions. He never let his imagination get the better of him, never allowed his intuition to supplant his reason.

Yet on this dark and somber night, as the Night Hawk cleaved the brisk air en route to the private airfield, the soldier had a gut feeling that he wouldn't like what he found when they got there.

Part of it had to do with Trevor Garth's track record. To date, the man had outfoxed them at every turn. Just when they thought they had the madman cornered, he pulled a figurative rabbit out of his hat and got away.

The attack on the FBI office had been a tactical stroke of genius. Even Brognola had admitted that it was slowing their investigation terribly, which was exactly what Garth wanted.

Trevor Garth was a rarity among evil men. He was truly brilliant. Bolan had met many like him who thought they were. Mafia Dons, drug lords, criminal kingpins, terrorist leaders and the like who strutted about like peacocks, convinced they were smarter than any enemy and would never, ever be caught. Most deluded themselves. Their inflated egos were bigger than their brains.

Not Trevor Garth. He was as competent as he

was evil, which made him doubly dangerous. Certainly, of all the foes Bolan had gone up against, Garth ranked as one of the deadliest. It gave him all the more reason to want to bring Garth's trail of bloodshed and mayhem to an end.

Most of the time, Bolan dispatched enemies with cold dispassion. It was just something that had to be done, and he was one of the few with the ability to do it.

But not this time. This time the eternal war was personal. It happened every so often, instances when he was moved body and soul to squash one of the many cockroaches who infested the human race, no matter what doing so entailed.

It would please Bolan greatly to eliminate Garth. For Brenda Mathews's sake, for the sake of the fine agents who had lost their lives at the mansion and on East Plum Street, and for the atrocities yet in the works, Garth could not be permitted to live a minute longer than it took Bolan to find him.

Some would say that was wrong, that Bolan was setting himself up as judge, jury and executioner. But if not Bolan, then who? If not now, when? After thousands had fallen victim to the TL-14?

There were times in the course of human events when drastic measures were called for. The government sanctioned Bolan for just that purpose. He was their living ''drastic measure,'' their recourse of last resort when conventional means of law enforcement would not or could not get the job done.

No sane person would deny that Trevor Garth had to be stopped at all costs.

"There's the airfield," Captain Bennett announced, the Night Hawk tilting so they could see the strip and the hangars clearly. He went in low and fast, standard procedure when flying into a hot zone and anticipating enemy fire.

None materialized, though. They flew between the yellow hangar and the next structure to the south, the gunners swiveling their M-60s right and left. No targets appeared.

The Night Hawk that had been blown out of the air was a mass of charred wreckage. Hungry fingers of flame ate at what was left.

Surprisingly, fire hadn't engulfed the Augusta that had been shot down, nor the one that had been blasted before it could lift off. Bolan did notice, however, where fuel had formed a wide pool around the first aircraft, and meandering rivulets had flowed toward the burning Night Hawk but hadn't quite reached it yet.

The captain also saw. "If the fuel reaches our downed bird, it might trigger a chain reaction and both Augustas could go up. Are you sure we should put you down?"

"We have to know what's inside that hangar," Bolan said. "Take me in, then dust off and put in a call to make sure the local fire department is on its way. Someone was bound to have spotted the explosions and contacted them.''

''You hope,'' the lieutenant commented.

Bennett worked the controls, bringing the Sikorsky down to within six inches of the asphalt, a dozen yards from the hangar door. ''Stay alert, Belasko. These wackos don't give up without a fight.''

Bolan patted the officer on the shoulder, then ran to the bay. The door had been flung wide by one of the crew. Without slowing, he jumped and hit the ground running. Weaving, he dashed to the side of Vorter Air Freight Service.

Rotor wash buffeted him as the Night Hawk rose to assume a monitoring position a hundred feet up. Bolan edged to the door, which was closed.

Stealth wasn't called for. Any Minutemen inside were bound to have heard the Night Hawk arrive. They would be expecting someone to enter, so the soldier went in low and quick, slamming the door wide and diving to the right.

A shot cracked. The slug spanged off the floor and into the wall. Bolan rolled several times, then snaked away from the yellow wall so his body wouldn't be silhouetted against it.

The interior of the hangar was murky. A small plane, a Piper, occupied the center. Beside it was the aircraft's engine, in the process of being overhauled.

No one had told Bolan that Vorter Air owned a plane. Odds were that the Feds weren't aware of it, not if Trevor Garth had purchased the aircraft through one of his many dummy corporations.

It raised a disturbing specter. What if Garth had other planes? What if the madman had intended all along to use them to disperse the TL-14, not the helicopters?

A faint rasping noise came from the far side of the hangar. Standard equipment and aviation supplies were scattered about, but for the most part the interior consisted of open floor space. The office was against the left wall. A large window showed that the office was dark and apparently empty, but Bolan kept one eye on it anyway.

He headed for the Piper on elbows and knees. Whoever was in there with him was also jockeying for position. Twice he heard rustling, once a low grunt. He figured that it was the mortar man who had escaped, but there might be more.

No shots rang out. Bolan gained the cover of the aircraft and crouched beside the Piper's front wheel. Warily moving to the wing, he climbed on top of it, then rose onto his knees to peer through the cockpit. The windows weren't tinted, so he could see the other half of the hangar. No movement betrayed the Minuteman.

Sirens wailed in the distance. Fire crews would

be on the scene within five minutes or less. So would sheriff's deputies.

Bolan scanned the far wall. The Minuteman would make his break soon. It made no sense that the man had lingered this long. Maybe a round from an M-60 had clipped him earlier.

Suddenly, the shadows in a corner shifted and congealed. A high whine sounded overhead. A second later the huge hangar door started to rumble upward on rollers recessed in metal tracks.

Bolan stood, bracing his arms on top of the plane. No sooner did he do so than an engine growled to life in the corner. Only this was a small engine with a high rpm. A motorcycle! he realized, just as a dirt bike darted out of the corner and shot toward the rising door like a greyhound out of the starting gate.

The bike gained speed rapidly. Bolan tracked it, firing a short burst that raised fireflies behind the cycle's rear tire. Swinging his elbows to the left, he zeroed in on the front tire, led it by a hair and triggered four tight rounds.

By then the motorcycle was almost in the clear. The dirt bike swerved wildly, nearly throwing the rider. It hurtled under the rising door, but he got no farther. Metal screeching, the bike crashed onto its side and slid dozens of feet. The Minuteman tumbled to the ground in a windmill of flying limbs.

Bolan sprinted to the door. The dirt bike's engine growled and sputtered. Nearby lay a revolver. To his left, a dark shape bounded toward the front of the yellow hangar, limping terribly with every frantic stride. Bolan automatically brought up the M-16, but changed his mind. Brognola needed the man for questioning.

"Stop!" the soldier shouted.

Naturally, the Minuteman didn't comply. Casting a vile look over a shoulder, he flipped his middle finger.

Bolan gave chase. He wasn't worried that the man would escape. Captain Bennett would see to that. Already the Night Hawk had swung around to the side of the hangar so the Air Force officers could observe what was transpiring.

A shout wafted down. Bennett's window was open, and he was yelling and pointing at the front corner of the building. Thanks to the thrum of the rotors and the rumble of the still rising hangar door, Bolan couldn't hear a word the pilot said. He shook his head to signify as much.

The Minuteman reached the corner and hopped off toward the downed helicopters.

Bolan poured on the speed to overtake his quarry. He was a few strides from the corner when he saw a rivulet of fuel reach the burning Night Hawk. Instantly, a sheet of flame shot toward the two Augustas.

The explosions that ensued lit up the airfield like the blazing midday sun.

CHAPTER EIGHTEEN

"How's your head?" Hal Brognola asked.

"Fine," Bolan lied. The truth was that it felt as if his skull had been stomped on by a berserk bull elephant. Shifting, he adjusted the damp cloth on his forehead. He lay on a small couch in a ground-floor office in a building two blocks from the one attacked.

"You're lucky to be alive, Striker."

"Don't I know it."

In his mind's eye, Bolan relived the blast. A massive billowing inferno had incinerated the Minuteman in midstride and would have done the same to him if not for the corner of the hangar, which partially shielded him. As it was, a hot invisible fist had slammed him flat. Dazed, he had seen the building seared, seen twisted, molten fragments rain all around.

Marshaling his will, Bolan had lurched upright and run, tottering like a drunk. A flaming piece of wall had struck him in the shoulder, burning his blacksuit and the skin underneath. He had snuffed the tiny flames with a few swats from his hand, then been knocked off balance when a secondary explosion rocked the airfield.

Falling to his knees, Bolan had started to turn when something hit him in the back of the head. It was a wonder his cranium hadn't been crushed. The world had spun, his vision blurring, his stomach churned by nausea. Dimly, he was aware of being hemmed in by sheets of burning fuel. He had tried to get up and run, but his legs wouldn't respond.

Then gusts of wind had buffeted him. Someone shouted. Strong fingers hooked under his armpits, and he was hauled into the air. The devastation receded under him as he was whisked into the sky.

Only later did he fully appreciate what Bennett had done. The courageous pilot had brought the Night Hawk down into the middle of the crackling flames and flying debris to snatch him from the jaws of death. He owed those Air Force boys his life, a debt he would never forget.

Now, listening to the bustle of activity in the corridor outside, Bolan couldn't help but wonder if it had all been for nothing.

After the fire department had the situation under control, the Feds had gone over what was left of the hangar and what was left of the choppers with a fine-tooth comb. The results were discouraging.

No trace of the TL-14 had been found. It hadn't

been in the hangar. It hadn't been on any of the Augusta helicopters. Vorter Air Freight Service had been a bust, a dead end. As Brognola succinctly put it, "We've wasted hours thinking we had the Minutemen dead to rights, and the whole time, Garth and the TL-14 have been somewhere else."

The phone rang. Brognola answered, spoke briefly, then hung up. "That was our man in charge of the mop-up operation at the warehouse out in the desert," he reported. "They've found truck tracks leading to the nearest road, about eighteen miles away." He tapped a pad with his pen. "Big trucks, judging by the tire size."

Bolan sat up. "Tanker trucks, possibly?"

Brognola nodded. "That would be my guess." He consulted his watch. Annoyed, he slapped his pen down. "It's almost seven. They could be anywhere by now."

"I doubt it," Bolan disagreed. "Garth knows that we're combing the state from end to end. He's too clever to risk them being spotted at night when traffic is so light. He'd lie low until daylight."

It made sense, Brognola reflected. So did something else. "Unless Garth owns other choppers or planes we don't know about, he never intended to disperse the TL-14 from the air. He's going to drive his tanker trucks into the heart of Reno or some other city and spray the people right there in the streets."

A shiver ran down the big Fed's spine. It would be the callous slaughter at the FBI office all over again, only on a much larger, infinitely more horrifying scale. He imagined hundreds of convulsing bodies on sidewalks and in doorways, vehicles piled in countless wrecks, the wails of the dying rising in a soul-shattering chorus.

Bolan had been doing some fast thinking. "Maybe Garth has finally made a mistake. Maybe the tankers are his Achilles' heel."

"How so?" Brognola asked.

"He hasn't had the TL-14 all that long. Unless he just happened to have some tanker trucks on hand, which I doubt, he must have obtained them within the past twenty-four hours or so."

Brognola snapped his fingers, then snatched the phone. "There can't be very many outfits offering tankers for sale or lease. I'll have my people get right on it."

The soldier lay back down. Finding the party who had supplied the tankers was important, but not nearly as important as learning where the tankers were at that very moment.

Were the Minutemen still in hiding, or had they launched their attack? Bolan gazed out the window at the golden orb perched on the eastern horizon. The new day had begun, and it didn't take a genius to know that time was running out.

TOM BLANCHARD CURSED at the sight of a traffic jam ahead. He downshifted, cursing again when he inadvertently mashed the gears. "I told Trevor to have someone else drive this rig, but would he listen? No!"

"Lighten up, will you?" Albert Stokes said. "You're doin' just fine."

"Like hell I am," Blanchard snapped. "I've never handled a truck this size. It's like operating a tank." He shifted again, his scowl deepening when the transmission gnashed its metallic teeth.

"We're on schedule. That's all that counts," the other Minuteman said.

Blanchard nodded at the snarl of cars and trucks blocking both lanes of Interstate 80. "We won't be for long. Traffic is backed up clear to the first Reno exit."

Stokes shrugged. A native of Arkansas, he had belonged to a small group of hard-core militia before being tapped by Trevor Garth to join the Minutemen. Everyone considered him a hillbilly because he dressed in bib overalls and flannel shirts. It didn't help matters that he seldom shaved and rarely bathed.

"So what?" Stokes said. "Reno ain't goin' nowhere, is it? The people will still be there, won't they?"

"Trevor will be upset if we don't stick to the schedule," Blanchard reminded him.

"The boss will be hundreds of miles away by the time we're in position. Let him throw a hissy fit if he's of a mind to. What's he goin' to do? Call us and chew us out?"

Blanchard didn't waste his breath arguing. Stokes was one of the most laid-back men he had ever met. Nothing ever ruffled the Arkansan's feathers. Applying the brakes, he brought the tanker truck to a lumbering stop and straightened to try to see the cause of the jam. Flashing lights sparked surging panic. "Cop cars! What if it's a roadblock? What if they're looking for us?"

"Tarnation, but you're a worrywart!" Stokes declared. "Use your head. The police have no way of knowin' about the trucks. Stay calm and everything will be all right."

Blanchard tried, but his companion had hit the nail on the head. Fretting was second nature to him. He worried about everything. His philosophy on life could be summed up by saying, "If anything can go wrong, it will."

So by the time the highway patrolman directing traffic appeared, Blanchard had worked himself into a nervous funk. His brow was caked with perspiration, and he couldn't sit still if his life depended on it.

Beyond the patrolman was the cause of the delay. A tractor-trailer rig and three cars had been involved in a pileup. Two of the cars were crushed, the third had been ripped open on the passenger's side, and the big rig itself had been heavily damaged.

Ambulance crews and fire personnel were everywhere. So were highway-patrol officers and deputies.

The inner lane was closed off. Traffic was being slowly funneled into the remaining one. The flow would have gone smoother if not for all the gawkers, who crawled along pointing and jabbering like chipmunks.

"Look at that!" Blanchard said in disgust when an elderly woman leaned out of her car for a better look at a shrouded victim being placed on a stretcher. "Some people have no respect!"

The burly patrolman directing traffic beckoned the tanker. Blanchard shifted from first to second. In his haste and anxiety, his foot slipped off the clutch. The truck jolted forward, making a noise like a garbage disposal with a rock stuck in it. He had to stamp on the brake, or he would have plowed into the Jeep in front of him.

The burly patrolman approached. "Are you awake there, buddy?" he asked.

Blanchard fought off a wave of fear. "Sorry, Officer," he blurted. "I guess my mind wandered. It's taking forever to get past the wrecks."

"We'll have the interstate cleared within the hour," the patrolman stated, his gaze straying to the side of the tanker. "Blestacon Lawn And Fertilizer," he read. "Never heard of it. Where are you guys out of? Reno?"

"Yes," Blanchard answered. But at the same moment, Larry Stokes chimed in, "No, we're out of Elko."

The patrolman studied the two of them. "Well, which is it? Reno or Elko?"

Blanchard glared at Stokes to insure the man did not make another grave blunder. "Actually, both," he said as calmly as he could. "We have branch offices in both cities, and we're opening another in Las Vegas before the year is out."

Just then, to Blanchard's immense relief, the traffic crawled forward again. The patrolman motioned. Blanchard pumped the shift, once more clashing the gears noisily. The truck rumbled into the passing lane. In the side mirror, he watched the patrolman, who was staring intently after them. "That nosy so-and-so suspects something is wrong," he said anxiously.

"Why? Because you can't drive worth beans?" Stokes chuckled. "I swear. It's a miracle you don't have an ulcer. That cop is too busy to pay us much mind. As soon as we're out of sight, he'll forget all about us."

"I hope to hell you're right."

LESS THAN HALF AN HOUR after Hal Bragnola issued a directive to have local law-enforcement agencies be on the lookout for tanker trucks, there were two big breaks in the case.

The directive didn't reveal exactly why the FBI was interested in the tankers. It implied that the Feds were investigating a smuggling operation, and it requested all tankers be stopped so the credentials of the drivers could be checked. Should any discrepancies exist, the drivers were to be taken into custody for questioning and the FBI was to be contacted.

Per instructions from the Oval Office, Brognola made no mention of the lethal chemical. The President had made it plain in the strongest terms that a statewide panic was to be avoided at all costs. Secrecy was essential. Only those with a need-to-know were to be given full details.

The first break came when the agents assigned to check how Trevor Garth obtained the trucks hit paydirt soon after they started to call around. A local business had sold three of its largest tankers to a Mr. C.T. Tharg the day before. Tharg had waltzed in off the street, as it were, and paid cash, up front. The owner had deemed it a little strange, but he hadn't pried. Not with that much money at stake.

The second break came at eight o'clock. Sergeant Pete Spence of the Nevada Highway Patrol contacted Brognola's task force. Earlier he had been called to assist at a traffic pileup on the interstate. While he was directing traffic, a tank truck had gone by.

Spence remembered it so well because the driver had been oddly nervous, as well as the worst truck driver Spence had ever run into.

Added to that was the peculiar name of the company. "Blestacon Lawn And Fertilizer," Brognola quoted the patrolman's report. "Another anagram, this time for Garth's middle name." He wagged the paper at Bolan. "Trevor Garth isn't as brilliant as he likes to believe. Does he really think his juvenile word games will fool us?"

Bolan thought so. In his experience, arrogance bred overconfidence. Garth saw himself as better and brighter than everyone else. So it would never occur to Garth that anyone would see through his asinine subterfuge.

"According to Sergeant Spence," Brognola continued, "the tanker was headed for Reno. Even allowing for the delay due to the accident, it must be in the city by now. I've ordered every city cop and county lawman to lend a hand searching."

"Let's hope that's enough," Bolan said. If it wasn't, by the end of the day the city of Reno, and the rest of the nation, would be in mourning. "What I'd like to learn is where the other two trucks got to. Are they still in hiding, or on their way somewhere else?"

"Your guess is as good as mine," Brognola answered. It inspired him to resort to the phone for the umpteenth time to request that planes be sent out to scour every major artery within seventy-five miles, and most of the secondary roads, as well.

"Maybe Garth has crossed into California or Utah," Bolan speculated.

"Doubtful. He'd be too easy to spot on back roads, and tankers on the interstate have to stop at ports of entry and weigh stations. Unless he has bogus papers for his cargo, he'd be in a world of hurt."

At that juncture an agent rushed breathless into the office. "Sir, you wanted to be notified the second we had word!"

Brognola gripped the edge of his desk. "Yes?"

"A tanker truck answering the description of the suspect vehicle is parked at a downtown lot. Two men are with it. Reno police have it under surveillance, as you ordered."

"Bingo!" Brognola said, elated that at last something had gone their way. "We have them now."

Bolan didn't say anything, but he did not share his friend's confidence. He was a realist at heart. Time and again, the Minutemen had foiled them. Time and again, Garth had slipped through their fingers. He'd reserve judgment until the fanatics were either in custody or six feet under.

WEARING A LIGHT BLUE windbreaker and casual tan slacks, Bolan made a circuit of the block, hiding his face behind a newspaper when he passed the public lot where the truck had stopped. He recognized Blanchard but not the guy in the bib overalls. They were in the front seat, eating food purchased at a hamburger joint across the street.

Brognola wanted this one played out with all due caution. Given Garth's fondness for booby traps, the Feds were worried that the truck was rigged to be blown up if a concerted rush was made. Brognola preferred that Bolan go in alone, catch the Minutemen off guard and deal with them by whatever means were necessary.

The locals had been pulled back and were only to intervene if things got out of hand.

Bolan couldn't help but remind himself that at any moment the TL-14 might explode, showering a two-or three-block area with deadly green drops. He had to make his move soon.

There were complications, though. Not the least of them was the heavy downtown traffic. Dozens of shoppers and other citizens used the parking lot each and every hour. Cars were constantly pulling in and out. Pedestrians were constantly passing by.

Approaching the lot from the rear, Bolan saw his chance when a group of women carrying sacks and bags walked toward a van parked several spaces from the tanker. Falling into step behind them, he ignored their curious stares, dogging their steps until they halted at the van. There, he angled to the left, striding briskly. He gained the rear of the tanker without the driver or the other man being the wiser.

Clambering onto the back step, he gripped one of the metal rungs that led to the top, and climbed. A twelve-inch-wide flat strip, sort of a metal catwalk, brought him to the center of the tank where a large cap and several valves were installed. Stepping over them, he crept toward the front.

He planned to leap onto the cab, shove the Beretta into the driver's face through the open window and have the Minutemen get out. Or else. It would have worked if not for one of the women near the van, who apparently thought she was doing the right thing by cupping a hand to her mouth and calling out, "Excuse me! You there in the truck! Did you know a man just climbed on top and seems to be sneaking up on you?"

Heads poked out both cab windows. Blanchard cursed and drew back. In a twinkling, the other man produced a pistol.

Bolan flung himself onto his belly as the Taurus boomed twice, lead buzzing like angry wasps above him. The women scattered, several screaming in panic.

The soldier crawled forward, unlimbering the Beretta. He saw the man holding the Taurus, but the man also saw him, and Bolan had to duck lower as the Taurus banged twice more.

It was then that the starter growled and the engine thundered to life. Bolan rose to fire, but the tanker lurched forward, throwing him onto his shoulder. He had to grip both sides of the flat strip in order to keep from being pitched off as the truck veered to the right, making for an exit.

Gears mashed loudly. Blanchard misjudged and clipped the tail end of a parked Volkswagen, the huge truck crumpling the fender as if it were so much paper.

Bolan had to stop them quickly. At any moment, the tank under him might go up. He rose onto his knees and fired at the roof of the cab, but the 9 mm slug spanged off the heavy-gauge steel. Lowering his sights a few inches, he started to fire again.

The tanker took the turn doing more than thirty miles per hour. Like an ungainly behemoth of old, it tilted to one side, the rear end fishtailing just enough to spill Bolan onto his stomach again and send him sliding toward the rim.

Desperately, the soldier clutched for support and snared the edge of the metal strip. It gouged into his fingers but he held on tightly, swinging like a pendulum as the tanker swerved from side to side.

INSIDE THE CAB, Blanchard tromped on the gas. Overwhelmed by panic, his sole thought was to get out of there before the law closed in. He knew the Fed on the tank wouldn't be alone.

"What are you doin'?" Stokes demanded. "Slow down and pull over! We'll use the poison!"

Blanchard paid no heed. To spray the TL-14, they had to unravel a big hose housed at the rear of the truck. They would be cut down before they reached it. "Just keep that damn Fed off of us until we reach the interstate," he rasped.

"Are you loco? We can't outrun the cops in this thing! It can't do much better than sixty!"

"Who said anything about outrunning them?" Blanchard responded. "This baby is built like a tank, isn't it? I'll just plow through anything that gets in our way!"

Stokes didn't think much of the idea, but there was a wild gleam in Blanchard's eyes that no amount of reasoning would extinguish. And the man was in charge of their operation. "Do whatever you think is best," he said, then patted his Taurus. "All I ask is that I get to take a bunch of stinkin' Feds with me when I cash in my chips."

Blanchard said nothing. If anyone had asked him the day before, he would have stated that he was ready and willing to throw down his life for Garth's glorious revolution. Now that his life was actually on the line, though, he was having second thoughts. Could he help it if he liked being alive?

UP ON THE TANK, Bolan dangled by his left arm. The truck hit a straight stretch, and he swiftly holstered the Beretta, surged higher and attempted to grasp the catwalk with his other hand also.

Tires squealing, the tanker careened into a turn. Bolan had no warning. He was thrown to the right, his left hand losing some of its purchase, the weight of his own body working against him. Gritting his teeth, he hung on.

Once around the turn, Bolan was pitched violently in the opposite direction. He was in very real danger of losing his grip and falling under the vehicle's enormous tires. That was, if he wasn't smashed against a vehicle or a building and reduced to so much broken pulp.

Bunching his shoulders, the soldier heaved himself upward. His clawed right hand closed on the strip, his scrabbling feet narrowly missing the side step.

Sirens howled behind the truck. A police car shot out of a side street to glue itself to the tanker's bumper. Elsewhere, other sirens wailed. The word was going out. Soon every officer in Reno would be in on the chase, and none realized the extreme risk they were taking. Only the chief and a captain knew about the TL-14. Bolan pulled himself up, inch by muscle-taxing inch. His cheek rested on the catwalk, and he paused to catch his breath while striving to find support for his legs.

The tanker abruptly took another turn. It keeled wildly, like a ship about to capsize. Bolan was catapulted toward the front with such force, his hands were torn from the strip. With nothing to hold on to, he plummeted toward his death.

CHAPTER NINETEEN

The side rail saved him. At the last instant Bolan's grasping fingers closed around it and held. His chest pounded against the side step. His legs fell lower, close to the truck's huge, grinding tires.

Something brushed against Bolan's left leg. Friction heat seared his flesh. He felt the fabric being pulled, felt his leg start to be tugged down under the tire.

Exerting every ounce of strength he possessed, the Executioner heaved upward, scrambling onto the side step, his body flush with the tank. His shoulders throbbed, his wrists hurt and his fingers were in agony.

IN THE CAB, the Minuteman from Arkansas glanced at the side mirror and cackled. "Lookee there!" he gloated. "That Fed is a sittin' duck if I ever saw one. In about three shakes of a lamb's tail, you won't need to worry about him no more."

Blanchard was too busy avoiding vehicles to

spare a look. There were three cop cars behind them now, and the city sounded as if an air raid were underway.

Under his breath, Blanchard cursed himself for being a fool. They should have sprayed the TL-14 as soon as they reached the city, not sat around waiting until noon as Garth had directed.

"Keep a straight course for a little bit longer," Stokes said, shifting to tuck his knees under him so he could lean out the window and adopt a two-handed grip on his Taurus. The notion of slaying the Fed made him giddy with glee.

The Fed was trying to rise but managed to reach under his jacket and come out holding the Beretta. He had to shoot while lying on his side with the tanker bouncing under him and the wind tearing at his face. It was enough to spoil anyone's aim, and his first shot missed.

So did Stokes's. The fanatic's pistol blasted twice, but the slugs struck the grille of one of the police cars behind them. Frowning, he steadied his arms just as the Fed loosed a second shot.

Blanchard heard the Arkansan grunt. He glanced over, his fury mounting at the new nostril his companion had sprouted. "Damn incompetent jack-ass!" he declared. Irate, he placed his right hand against Stokes's backside and shoved.

BOLAN HAD FORKED a knee onto the side step and was rising when the man in the overalls sailed from the cab and crashed onto a parked station wagon. The windshield shattered under the impact, leaving the lower half of the Minuteman's body jutting from the cavity, one leg poked into the air as if in macabre salute.

Replacing the Beretta, Bolan rose carefully. By sliding one foot forward at a time, he worked his way toward the cab. The shouts of people on the sidewalk barely registered. Overhead, a police helicopter had appeared and was pacing the tanker.

Unmarked cars had joined the police cruisers. The FBI, Bolan guessed. He measured the distance he had to cover, some twenty feet, and went on.

Bolan was concentrating on his footwork and he didn't see the garbage truck until the tanker veered sharply. The driver's strategy was self-evident; he hoped to dash Bolan to bits against the other truck.

In reflex, the soldier placed a foot on the side rail and levered upward, his arms thrust high, his fingers groping for anything substantial enough to bear his weight. His right hand found the catwalk, and he flipped upward.

Metal grated together under him. Steel sparked on steel. The side rail he had been holding on to moments earlier was reduced to scrap metal.

Winded, Bolan lay flat. That had been much too close. Blanchard had risked puncturing the tank in order to kill him. He crawled toward the cab, anxious to end the chase before innocent lives were lost.

When the cab was only a few feet away, Bolan gripped the edge of the tank and slid to the right. His next move had to be executed precisely, or he would end up dead.

There wasn't enough space between the cab and the tank for a man to slip between them. Bolan had to grab hold of the cab and swing onto the step below the passenger's door in one smooth motion. As fast as the tanker was going, it would be no mean feat. Bolan timed his move, then suddenly swung down from above and grabbed hold of the passenger's door.

"Son of a bitch!" Blanchard hollered, pumping the wheel hard to the right when he saw Bolan materialize.

Bolan was reaching for the Beretta when the truck pitched toward the curb. He was tossed like a leaf in a gale, his right foot nearly slipping off, his right hand all that stood between him and oblivion. A pickup truck loomed large. Thrusting himself against the door, he avoided being ripped from his perch.

Swearing lustily, Blanchard tried again. A utility pole was just what he needed.

The soldier yanked on the door handle. As the door opened, he ducked inside and lunged for the steering wheel. The Minuteman lashed an elbow at his face. He blocked the blow with a forearm and retaliated with a jab to the jaw that shook Blanchard but didn't force him to relinquish his hold.

They grappled, each gripping the steering wheel with one hand, each determined not to lose that grip. Bolan drove his shoulder into his adversary's chest, pushing him against the driver's door. Blanchard snapped a head butt at the soldier's face, but he wrenched aside.

They exchanged flying fists. In the cramped confines, they were hard-pressed to land a solid punch. Bolan succeeded twice as often as the Minuteman. In mounting fury, Blanchard let go of the wheel and clamped both hands around the soldier's neck.

The tanker careened down Sahara Avenue, swerving all over the road. Cars slanted to the right and left, scared motorists leaning on their horns.

Struggling fiercely, Bolan tried to step on the brake pedal, but Blanchard's leg blocked him. He kicked, pushed and speared his foot down. Missing, his foot became wedged between pedals. He couldn't take the time to free it because his adversary's fingers were choking off his air. Forced to release the wheel, he seized both of Blanchard's wrists and attempted to break the chokehold.

Blanchard hissed like a serpent. Teeth clenched, beet-red, he exerted all his might, his nails digging into Bolan's flesh. In the heat of the moment, he had forgotten that no one was driving the tanker.

Bolan remembered. He saw the curb sweep toward them and was jarred when they bounced up and over. Beyond the curb was a plaza of some kind. A building reared before them, and they shot toward it like a mobile battering ram.

Pedestrians scurried out of harm's way.

A collision with the building was inevitable unless something was done. Bolan willed himself to disregard the iron fingers digging steadily deeper into his neck. He had the wheel and he wrenched it even as he tore his foot free and stomped on the brake pedal. Since the tanker was still in gear, the truck kept going, charging forward yards at a time.

Bolan's lungs were near to bursting. His right fist caught his opponent under the chin, rocking him. A second blow caused Blanchard to let go of his neck. They traded more blows, brutally, savagely.

Somehow, in the jumbled confusion of the moment, the door handle was jarred. The door swung outward. With nothing to brace him, Blanchard fell from the cab. His right hand closed on Bolan's ankle, and with a superhuman effort he hauled the soldier out after him.

Twisting in midair, Bolan contrived to land on his side rather than his head. Still, it rattled him clear to the bone. A gigantic crash nearly deafened him as he struggled to rise before his adversary did.

The truck had slammed into a corner of the building, embedding itself in the masonry. Steam and smoke spewed from the engine, which chugged and coughed.

Blanchard stood. Police cars were pouring into the plaza. He made a grab for his pistol, but he had lost it somewhere along the line. As a last resort, he raced to the truck, grasped the end of the hose and turned like a jackal at bay. His frantic fingers hovered next to the lever that would release the TL-14 in a powerful pressurized torrent.

"Come and get it!" Blanchard roared fiercely. His gas mask was out of reach in the cab, but he figured that he would be all right if he held his breath and didn't get any of the goop on his skin.

Police cars and unmarked vehicles squealed to a halt. Uniformed and plainclothes men and women spilled out, brandishing weapons.

"You there!" an agent yelled. "Throw up your hands! This is the FBI! We are placing you under arrest!"

"Not in this life!" Blanchard chortled. They were converging from all sides. Laughing in defiance, he waited, letting them get closer so when he opened the valve they wouldn't be able to evade the spray.

"This is your last warning!" the agent shouted.

Blanchard swiveled the nozzle. "Go to hell!" he countered, and was all set to release the deadly toxin when he realized that the Fed he had grappled with in the cab was pointing a Desert Eagle at him. "Oh, sh—"

The boom of the big pistol echoed loudly in the plaza. Propelled by three hundred grains of powder, the .44 Magnum slug cored the Minuteman's brain at a velocity of over 1200 feet per second. It blew a hole as large as an orange in the back of Blanchard's head, splattering the tanker with gray matter and shredded bits of scalp and hair.

The nozzle fell from limp fingers.

Bolan rose slowly. He was torn and bruised and sore all over. Mechanically, he returned the Desert Eagle to the holster strapped at his hip.

A young officer scrutinized him intently, saying, "Who the hell are you, mister?"

The soldier stared at the tanker, at the hose that would have spelled doom for all of them if the Minuteman had flipped the release lever, and sighed. "I'm your guardian angel."

Hal Brognola strode from out of the press of authority. He clapped Bolan on the shoulder, then barked crisp orders. A cordon was thrown up around the truck. Reno police moved to clear the plaza. Others rushed to steer traffic from the area.

In under five minutes, the entire block was blocked off. In under fifteen, barricades had been erected.

An official press release informed the world at large that a tanker truck containing hazardous chemicals had been commandeered by a mentally unbalanced individual who was slain in the course of a high-speed pursuit.

A federal emergency-management team was onsite within half an hour, making arrangements for the TL-14 to be safely transported to a disposal facility.

Brognola didn't linger once the specialists arrived. One of the tanker trucks had been found, but two were unaccounted for. Until they were, he wouldn't enjoy a moment's rest or respite from worry. "All in all," he commented as an agent drove Bolan and him back to his command post at the FBI building, "it went pretty well."

Bolan rubbed his sore shoulder. He knew his friend was being upbeat for his benefit. The war was far from won.

"You must be hungry," Brognola commented. "I'll have sandwiches brought up once we get back. Anything else you'd like?"

"Peace on earth. Since that would take a miracle, I'll settle for a pot of black coffee."

"Consider it done." Brognola gazed at the passersby going about their daily routines in complete ignorance of the ghastly fate they had been spared. "Where do you suppose Trevor Garth is right about now?" he mused aloud.

"Your guess is as good as mine."

THE OBJECT of their mutual interest was pacing like an irate bear in front of a tanker truck parked on the shoulder of a road flanked by verdant forest. "How much longer?" he snarled.

"Another twenty minutes, no more," promised Dan Vincent, the best mechanic in the Minutemen. "It's not unusual for a rig this size to overheat at this altitude."

"It's these damn back roads, Mr. Garth," added Billy Klein, who had been following the tanker in a Ford two-door with Vincent. "All the twists and grades."

Garth didn't care what was to blame. The important thing was that he had fallen half an hour behind schedule because a radiator had overheated. Clasping and unclasping his fingers, he stared out over the sprawling vista of majestic mountain ranges and deep, lush valleys to the west.

It had been his idea to take the back way, to use roads seldom used by trucks that size. Naturally, he'd had Vincent go over the engine before they pulled out that morning. All the fluid levels had been checked, the tires inflated to their proper pressure, the fuel topped off. It was just dumb luck that the radiator hadn't been up to the strain.

Garth looked at his watch again. The delay rankled, but it wasn't critical. As long as they reached their destination by eight that night, everything would be fine. He walked to the cab and glanced up at Ren Starkey, who was listening to the radio. "Anything yet?"

The Texan shook his head.

"Strange," Garth said. He didn't understand it. By now there should be word of Blanchard's chemical attack on Reno. If his lieutenant had failed, and survived, Garth would see to it that Blanchard paid dearly for the lapse.

His master plan called for a one-two-three punch that would leave the federal government reeling and awaken the American people to the despotism that reigned in the hallowed halls of Congress and the White House.

First, Reno. Then, at four, the second target city would be hit. Finally, he would personally strike, slaying more witless dupes than Blanchard and Collins combined.

Garth had staggered the times on purpose. By doing so, he counted on keeping the Feds off balance. They would be so busy mopping up after the first two attacks that they would have scant manpower and resources to devote to tracking him down.

Garth's reverie was cut short by the sight of Dan Vincent and Billy Klein heading down the slope again. Each man carried an empty plastic two-liter pop container.

"This should be our last trip," Vincent said.

"The radiator will be full and we can go," Klein added.

Nodding absently, Garth glanced at the blue ribbon of a stream hundreds of yards below. For all his careful preparation, he hadn't thought to bring extra coolant. If not for the stream, they would have been stranded for as long as it took them to drive the car to the nearest town and purchase some.

"Mr. Garth!" Ren Starkey called, then cranked the volume on the radio so that the hourly news he was listening to blared loud enough for Garth to hear.

"In Reno, Nevada, today, thirty-four-year-old Tom Blanchard was killed by police after he reportedly tried to ram a truck loaded with hazardous chemicals into the White Sands Casino. There is no word on a possible motive, although authorities have indicated that Blanchard was mentally unstable." The man paused. "In other news, a Sacramento woman was found murdered in her home this morning—"

The Texan turned down the radio. "There's no mention of Stokes. The Feds are coverin' up the truth, I reckon."

"I wonder," Garth said. "If Blanchard and Stokes had used the TL-14, hundreds of people would be dead. There would be no covering up a slaughter of that magnitude." He scratched his chin, deep in thought. "No, I'm afraid that our brothers have let us down. They were killed before they could disperse the chemical." Garth smacked a fist into his palm, a habit of his when he was mad. "Damn! Can't anything go right today?"

As if in answer, the sound of a car engine purring up the mountain brought him around the cab, closer to the road. It was only the second vehicle to go by since their radiator overheated.

Garth idly watched the nearest bend. He anticipated no trouble, since the Feds had no way of knowing where he was headed. So he was all the more startled when a California Highway Patrol car wheeled around the bend. He moved closer to the tanker and spoke out of the side of his mouth.

"Mr. Starkey, we have company. It's the law. Would you be so kind as to have that little item under the seat ready to use when I give the word?" Garth plastered a smile on his face for the benefit of the approaching trooper.

"No problem."

The patrolman had slowed and was slanting toward the shoulder. Garth waved, casually taking several long strides that put him a healthy distance from the cab door.

Stopping, the patrolman climbed out. He was a big man, his uniform neat and clean, his attitude friendly but vaguely suspicious.

"Greetings, officer," Garth said.

"What's going on here?" the patrolman inquired, hooking his right thumb in his belt close to his gun.

Garth motioned at the tanker. "Nothing much. I saw this truck had pulled over and the hood was up, so I stopped to see if I could be of assistance. Apparently, their radiator overheated. A little while and they should be on their way."

The patrolman glanced at the cab, where Starkey sat framed in the window. "I take it you're the driver, cowboy?"

Garth answered before the Texan could. "No, he's not. The driver is off collecting water to fill the radiator. He should be back shortly."

"Is that so?" the patrolman said. He moved to the right a couple of paces so he could watch both Garth and Starkey at the same time. "I want to see the papers on this rig," he told the Texan.

Starkey glanced at Garth, who gave a barely perceptible bob of his chin and said to distract the cop, "I'm on my way home after a business trip to Carson City, myself. Ever been there?"

The patrolman's eyes flicked at Garth. "Plenty of times," he answered. When he flicked them back at the cab, Ren Starkey held a small fire extinguisher. "What in the world?" he said, and was sprayed full in the face with a short burst of TL-14.

Even as it happened, Garth backpedaled a dozen feet. He stood with arms folded, wearing a mocking smile, while the patrolman clutched at his throat and sputtered and gagged.

Valiantly, the patrolman managed to draw his weapon, but the toxin overcame him before he could fire. He flopped about like a fish out of water, blood gushing from his mouth and nose, and died in a state of utter shock.

"It doesn't always pay to be too diligent in one's duty," Garth addressed the corpse.

To Starkey, he said, "Drag this pathetic cretin into the bushes. We leave as soon as Vincent and Klein return. You drive the truck. I have to put the finishing touches on the manifesto I'm mailing to the *Times* before we strike."

A stiff breeze gusted against Garth's back and he turned into it, savoring the chill. The delay hadn't been a total waste. Killing the patrolman was an enjoyable diversion, a prelude to the much greater slaughter soon to come.

Trevor Garth could hardly wait.

CHAPTER TWENTY

The Night Hawk was a glittering knife, slashing the crisp air above the Sierra Nevadas. It whirred in low over Monitor Pass and bore to the southwest, paralleling Highway 4.

"Another five minutes, Mr. Brognola," Captain Bennett dutifully reported.

The officer's voice sounded tinny in the big Fed's headset. "Acknowledged," he responded. Below them stretched a magnificent vista of forest and peaks.

Brognola was riveted to the cabin window as if he were a typical tourist who couldn't get enough of the scenic beauty. So hectic was his job that he had to make the best of rare moments like this. Snug military webbing held him in his seat, as it did the grim figure in combat fatigues beside him. "You haven't said much since we left Reno, Striker. Cat got your tongue?"

Bolan looked up. He had been thinking about the confrontation to come. Prior to that, he had dwelled on the lives already lost and the many more that would be if they didn't catch the devious madman, and soon. At times like these, the full weight of his responsibility bore heavily on his broad shoulders.

"Cheer up," Brognola said. "Two down, one to go, and this whole nightmare will be over with."

Bolan cradled his M-16, remembering.

It had been three hours ago that Brognola received word from the Air Force. A second tanker truck, identical to the first, had been discovered speeding down U.S. Highway 95, the artery that linked Reno to Las Vegas. It had just passed Tonopah when it was spotted.

Compared to the ordeal in Reno, stopping the second truck had proved to be child's play. Five helicopters from Nellis Air Force Base had brought it to bay shy of Stonewall Flat.

Caught in open country, the two Minutemen had nowhere to run, nowhere to hide. They had climbed out and opened fire on the gunships with Winchesters, of all things. Their resistance melted when one of the warbirds let fly with a Hellfire that blew a crater close to the road, showering the Minutemen with dirt and dust.

Wisely, the pair surrendered.

Brognola had been ecstatic until it became clear that the pair knew nothing of their leader's whereabouts. Garth hadn't confided to anyone where the third tanker would strike.

So the Feds were back to square one. That was, until forty-five minutes earlier when word came down the wire that a California Highway Patrol officer had been found dead under mysterious circumstances.

With his usual foresight, Brognola had sent word to all appropriate federal agencies and other law-enforcement bodies to report any unusual deaths the day before. It had been a common-sense precaution, in case the Minutemen used the TL-14.

So now Bolan and his friend were deep in the heart of the Sierra Nevadas, having left shimmering Lake Tahoe far behind. An unbroken carpet of green unfolded under them, the Night Hawk's shadow rippling across the treetops as if imbued with a life of its own.

"That must be the spot," Bennett announced.

Four highway-patrol vehicles, a county sheriff, an ambulance and two unmarked cars were parked on a ridge that crested the highway. Everyone peered skyward as the Sikorsky touched down in the cleared space across the road.

They settled as gently as a feather. A crewman threw the door wide, and Bolan followed Brognola out, squinting in the bright sunshine.

A husky patrolman awaited them. "Mr. Brognola? I'm Captain Palmer," he said, offering his callused hand. "We've done exactly as you requested."

"I appreciate the cooperation," Brognola said. "If the men we're after are responsible, you've done your country an invaluable service."

"That's nice to know, sir, but I'd much rather that Patrolman Kent was still alive." Palmer, frowning, nodded at a shrouded form on a stretcher resting near the ambulance. "That's him there."

Brognola strode over and with the utmost care lifted the corner of the sheet. "What do you think?" he asked Bolan.

There could be no doubt. The soldier had seen the effects of the lethal chemical close up. Dried clots of blood under Palmer's nose, at the corners of his mouth and on both ears were dead giveaways. "TL-14," he confirmed.

Brognola faced Captain Palmer and jabbed a thumb at the road. "Where does Highway 4 lead? To any big cities?"

"It comes out of the mountains down at Angels Camp, then crosses the valley to Stockton." The patrolman pondered. "From there, your suspects could go north to Sacramento, west to San Francisco or south to Los Angeles."

The big Fed rumbled deep in his chest, like a confounded bear.

Bolan knew why. The sun was low in the western sky. They didn't have many hours of daylight left. Unless they guessed correctly, there was a very real likelihood that Garth would elude the federal dragnet, and the next day's headlines would blare the worst civilian slaughter in U.S. history.

Brognola tried to put himself in Trevor Garth's shoes. Sacramento was the state capital, but it wasn't half the size of San Francisco or L.A. Since Garth wanted to rack up as many deaths as possible, one of the larger cities made a better target. Which, though?

San Francisco was closer to Stockton. Logically, that should be where the sociopath would unleash the toxin. But San Francisco also had hills galore, and steady breezes off the bay weren't uncommon. Both would dilute the potency of the TL-14.

Los Angeles, on the other hand, wasn't nearly as windy and not nearly as hilly, and it had the added plus of being one of the most populous cities in the country. Downtown L.A. was packed with people from dawn until midnight. In terms of a kill ratio, in terms of the number of innocents who could be slain in the shortest span, Los Angeles was ideal.

"They're heading for L.A.," Brognola declared, calculating the distance and time factors involved. "How long ago would you say Patrolman Kent was slain?" he asked Palmer.

The captain nodded at one of the medics. "Sawyer here would be better able to answer that."

The ambulance crewman had been waiting to load the stretcher. He hesitated, nervous about abruptly being the center of attention.

"Well, son?" Brognola prompted.

"It's hard to say," Sawyer said. "My best guess would be no more than three or four hours, but I'm not the coroner. It could have been longer."

"No," Palmer said. "Three is about right. The last time Kent reported in was three and a half hours ago, at Markleeville."

Brognola stared to the southwest. "How far could a tanker truck travel in that amount of time?"

"It's an hour's drive from here to Angels Camp," the patrol officer revealed. "But that's by car. Bearing in mind the steep grades and all the switchbacks, I'd say a big truck would take an hour and a half, minimum. From there it would depend on which route they took."

"Put in a call to your headquarters," Brognola said. "Have them issue an alert for a large tanker with Nevada plates. Also ask them to shunt as many cars and troopers as they can to the southern half of the state. It's crucial that we find this tanker as soon as possible."

"Consider it done."

Brognola gestured, then led Bolan at a trot to the helicopter. "We're at the five-yard line and we're a TD behind. If we don't score now, we never will." A crewman helped him in, and the first thing he did after the Sikorsky was airborne was don his headset and direct Captain Bennett to put him in touch with the FBI offices in Los Angeles, San

Francisco and Sacramento, as well as the California attorney general and McClellan Air Force Base.

By the time Brognola was done, he had thrown into motion a massive ground and air search.

In the meantime, the Night Hawk sped down the west slope of the Sierra Nevadas. Bolan kept busy scanning Highway 4. He saw only one truck, a pickup.

It took the chopper twenty minutes to reach the base of the range. At Angels Camp they headed southeast, hugging the foothills. Bolan was of the opinion that Garth would stick to the high country for as long as he could, and Brognola agreed.

They flew over the sparkling expanse of Melones Reservoir, skirted Chinese Camp and followed Don Pedro Reservoir down to Highway 132. By then the sun rimmed the western horizon, painting the sky with vivid red-and-orange bands.

Past Coulterville lay Lake McClure. They were paralleling Highway 49, a few miles out of Mount Bullion, when twilight descended.

"Damn it all," Brognola groused. "Another half hour and it will be too dark for us to see a thing. We'll have to head for L.A. and hope the highway patrol or the agents I've sent out locate the tanker before morning."

Bolan's lips pinched together. Given the vastness of the California wilderness, it was like looking for the age-old needle, only in a near limitless green and rocky haystack. The odds were all in Trevor Garth's favor.

THE MINUTEMAN LEADER would have disagreed.

At that moment Garth and Ren Starkey were speeding south from Mount Bullion in the two-door sedan to catch up with the tanker. Vincent and Klein were minding the truck at a scenic pullover a mile or so out of Mariposa.

Yet another delay had occurred, and this time Garth had no one to blame but himself.

Earlier they had stopped in Mount Bullion for gas and a quick bite to eat. Garth had carried his manifesto inside and made a few changes in the text while waiting for their food. When it came, he had placed the manifesto in his briefcase and the briefcase beside his chair.

Probably the stress was to blame. Or maybe not sleeping more than four hours the past two nights had caught up with him. Whichever, Garth left the briefcase behind when they pulled out and didn't realize his mistake until they were two miles down the road.

Rather than try to turn the tanker around on the narrow mountain road, Garth and the Texan had switched vehicles with Vincent and Klein and raced to Mount Bullion.

During the whole ride, Garth feared that someone had stumbled onto the briefcase and opened it. The first few paragraphs talked about the chemical warfare the Minutemen were instigating. Any dunce would conclude that it was something the cops should see, and he dreaded that it had been turned over to the local law.

To his immense relief, their waitress had found the briefcase, remembered Garth having one and set it behind the counter in case he came back.

Garth was so pleased, he left her speechless, gaping at a fifty-dollar reward.

Now, zipping along at seventy miles per hour, Garth hugged the briefcase as if it were a dearly loved child, vowing never to let it out of his sight again.

One more night, the revolutionary told himself. That was all he needed. By morning they would be in Los Angeles, ready to start spraying the TL-14 during the height of the early rush hour when the streets and sidewalks would be thronged.

It was all up to them. Blanchard had failed. So, apparently, had Collins. Not one word had been mentioned on any radio station about the attack that was to have taken place at four in Las Vegas. Therefore, Garth reflected, it hadn't happened. Somehow, the Feds had thwarted him again.

Garth supposed it was fitting that the destiny of the nation now rested on his shoulders, and his alone. He was the one who had founded the Minutemen. His money had financed them. What could be

more appropriate than he pers
death stroke that would topple the
in the new?

"There are the boys, sir," Re

Dan Vincent and Billy Klein w
legs, Vincent puffing on a cigar.
tanker as the Texan brought the

"You found it?" Klein said.

Since Garth held the briefcas
the question was too ridiculous
Stalking to the cab, he opened th
"Are you going to stand aroun
tlemen, or can we get this show

They had heard him use that t
and Klein were in the sedan and
Starkey started the truck.

Garth settled back, willing h
relax. Despite the setbacks, the
City of the Angels by 1:00 a.m
allowed plenty of time to find a
town.

Starkey handled the big rig
been raised on a farm and tau
and farm trucks by his twelft
nearly as skilled a driver as he
he wheeled onto the highway,
mirror to verify no cars were
them.

The tall Texan's eyes narrow

ination, or was there a dark speck far off in the sky, a speck too large to be a bird? He looked closer. The twilight made it hard to see, but the longer he stared, the more convinced he grew that it was an aircraft. Then it veered off over the forest, out of sight.

Starkey debated whether to say anything. When Garth was in a foul mood, even he would rate a tongue-lashing if he was to cry wolf.

Garth was admiring the broad sweep of the San Joaquin Valley. Lights sprinkled the lowland like a horde of twinkling fireflies, more flaring bright each minute. It gave him the illusion that he was astride the crown of the world, looking down on those who would one day look up to him as their political savior.

A turn appeared. Starkey downshifted, tapped the brakes and glued the inner tires to the center line. He had ridden in mountains before.

"You know, my friend," Garth said. "It's a rare man who can pinpoint the defining moment of his life. But I know as surely as I live and breathe that this is mine. Tomorrow I will commit the deed I was born to commit. I will strike a blow against tyranny that will ring down through the ages." He chuckled. "To be, or not to be, eh?"

There were times, and this was one, when Ren Starkey had no notion of what the millionaire was talking about. Grunting as if he agreed, he completed the turn and promptly stiffened in alarm, as if a sidewinder had reared to strike.

Only in this case a reptile wasn't to blame. For hovering squarely in the middle of the road seventy yards away was an Air Force helicopter.

CHAPTER TWENTY-ONE

The Night Hawk had just banked to the southwest to head for Los Angeles when the eagle eyes of the Executioner spied a big rig ahead, on Highway 49. He reported it to Captain Bennett, who promptly swung around and shadowed the truck just long enough to confirm that it was a tanker.

Electric excitement tingled through Hal Brognola. At long last they could bring Trevor Garth's trail of carnage and mayhem to an end. Wary of being spotted, Brognola said urgently, "Captain, I want you to get around in front of them without Garth and his friends catching on."

"No problem," Bennett said. "Just hang on to your safety restraints."

The Night Hawk dipped, its rotors whining as it spurted off across the treetops like a dragonfly zeroing in for the kill. "Do you want us to use our missiles?" the captain asked.

"When I give the word," Brognola said, eager to do so. He would do whatever was necessary, use whatever force was called for, to put the tanker out of commission. No more innocents were going to die if he could help it.

Bolan loosened his harness, just in case he had to engage the Minutemen in a firefight. The rapidly darkening twilight limited visibility drastically. Where before he could at least make out the shapes of the trees below, now the pines blended into an inky mass of vegetation.

The Night Hawk looped wide, soared in over the highway and rotated broadside.

Headlights played over a bend screened by tall trees. Moments later the tanker came into view, lumbering out of the night like a prehistoric beast with glowing orbs for eyes. Almost immediately it braked.

"Now, sir?" Bennett urged. "At this range we can't miss."

Brognola opened his mouth, then had second thoughts. He would rather capture the truck intact, if at all possible. Granted, no bystanders were around this time. But he had no idea whether the blast would vaporize the TL-14 or disperse it over a wide area. Should that be the case, the cleanup would be a monumental chore at a staggering cost to taxpayers.

They couldn't simply let the stuff lie on the ground until it was washed into the soil. For one thing, the widely scattered drops would still be lethal on physical contact. For another, no one could say with any certainty how long the TL-14 remained chemically active.

In the fleeing seconds it took Brognola to decide, an unforeseen element was brought into play. A car passed the tanker, then stopped in the middle of the road.

"Don't fire!" Brognola commanded, appalled that more civilians might lose their lives.

"Where the hell did that come from?" Smith wondered.

Bolan saw the driver of the sedan poke his head out the window and say something to a passenger. They were probably shocked witless by the chopper. Then the passenger leaned out his window, and in his hands was something long and metallic that glinted dully as he pointed it at the Sikorsky.

"They're Minutemen!" Bolan warned, a shade too late. Autofire crackled in a deep, staccato bass. Rounds pinged off the bay door, smashed into the cabin window and drifted upward. "Evasive action!" he yelled.

The Air Force crew was already doing just that. The Night Hawk tilted and rose steeply, but not steeply enough. Bolan heard heavy-caliber rounds thudding into the fuselage, heard a loud crump, then, in mere seconds, detected the telltale acrid scent of smoke.

The chopper pitched, recovered and pitched

again. Bennett bawled, "We're hit! We're hit! I think it's the hydraulic pump! We're going down!"

Suddenly, the helicopter spun with breathtaking speed in a complete revolution and went on spinning, the centrifugal force slamming Bolan against the back of his seat. As it spun, it dropped like a meteorite and he braced for impact.

"Hang on!" Bennett shouted.

They hit hard, to the sound of grinding metal and creaking frame supports and joints. Bolan's teeth crunched together. The back of his head smacked against the bulkhead. One of the crewmen who hadn't had time to slip into a web harness was slammed onto the floor, his wrist snapping like dry kindling.

The cabin door slid ajar. Through the opening, Bolan glimpsed the road. The chopper had come down near the shoulder, partially barring one lane.

Headlights flashed. The sedan was racing toward them, the whole upper half of the Minuteman's body protruding from the window as he brought his weapon to bear.

One of the Night Hawk's M-60s opened fire. The Minuteman answered, a shriek testifying to the man's accuracy.

A glance assured Bolan that Brognola was unhurt. He released the catch on his harness and sprang to the door. It was stuck, and he had to exert all the power in his biceps to open it wide enough for his body to squeeze through.

As the soldier leaped to the ground, the Minuteman's weapon thundered. The deep hammering wasn't that of an ordinary SMG. High-powered slugs gouged into the Night Hawk above Bolan, then chewed up the turf at his feet as he darted to the left, toward the tail.

It took a moment for Bolan to recognize the distinct pounding of a BAR, a Browning automatic rifle. Widely used in World War II and Korea, the M-1918 A-2 had a cyclic rate of five to six hundred rounds per minute. That was slow by modern standards. But it more than made up for the slow rate by being chambered to handle .30-06 caliber rounds.

Anyone who knew anything about firearms, and rifles in particular, knew that the .30-06 was one of the most powerful all-around cartridges ever devised. It had proved itself on the battlefield time and again. And sportsmen knew that it could bring down any species of big game.

Small wonder. Boasting velocities of well over three thousand feet per second, the .30-06 could shred metal and flesh with equal ease.

Bolan was all too aware of this as he ducked under the chopper with rounds blistering the soil below and the tail assembly above. He snapped a short burst at the Minuteman as the car came abreast of the Night Hawk.

The man jerked as if slapped. He cried out, which caused the driver to slow down and reach for him to pull him back into the vehicle.

Shoving out from under the helicopter, Bolan sprinted toward the sedan. Down the road, the tanker had catapulted forward, gaining speed swiftly.

The soldier had the M-16 tucked against his side when he reached the car. The BAR had slid onto the floor and the driver was trying to straighten the young gunner, who had slumped against the steering wheel. Suddenly, the driver glimpsed Bolan and whipped a hand under his jacket, producing a Ruger.

Bolan cut loose. The driver flapped and howled, dying with a snarl of defiance twisting his lips. As the Executioner reached for the door handle, the roar of the onrushing tanker alerted him to new peril.

Ren Starkey sat at the wheel, his harsh features cast in iron. It was plain that the Texan had no intention of stopping or going around. He was going to ram the sedan in order to slay Bolan.

Spinning, the soldier flung himself toward the shoulder. A gargantuan crash rent the night. Something rammed into his back and he was tossed through the air, missing the Night Hawk by only a few feet. The M-16 went flying. Grass cushioned his fall, though not enough to prevent searing pain from lancing his frame.

A second crash rumbled off the slopes. The tanker had shoved the car into the Night Hawk, ripping a jagged hole in the fuselage and tearing off the cambered fin. The chopper wouldn't be taking to the air anytime soon.

Gears meshed smoothly as Starkey veered onto the highway and barreled southward. The sneering image of Trevor Garth was framed in the passenger's window.

They were getting away! That was all Bolan could think about as he rose and sprinted to the sedan. The trunk had been pancaked, and the rear fender resembled a pretzel. The passenger's side had been smashed in and the passenger's door buckled, but the engine was still running.

Bolan ran to the other side. Yanking the driver's door open, he hauled the driver out and dumped his partner on top of him. Jumping in, he gunned the engine and sped off.

The car wobbled and groaned, but the speedometer steadily climbed. Bolan could barely hear himself think thanks to a ruptured exhaust pipe. It sounded as if he were driving a racing car with a souped-up engine.

The tanker's taillights vanished around the next turn.

Not this time, Bolan vowed. He took the same turn doing twenty miles per hour above the speed limit. The vehicle shimmied and shook and seemed on the verge of falling apart.

A sharp slope lay ahead.

IN THE TANKER, Starkey slowed. He dared only go so fast or they were sure to run into trouble at the bottom. The tanker handled poorly.

Garth glanced at the mirror on his side of the cab. "I don't believe it!" he fumed. "That damn Fed is still after us! Doesn't he know enough to quit while he can? What does it take to stop him?"

For the first time, uncertainty tainted Garth's confidence. It had stunned him to see the chopper. Here he had outwitted the Feds at every turn, yet they kept popping up, the proverbial bad pennies. How they had found him this time was beyond him.

"We have to dispose of this pest once and for all," Garth said.

A sign warned of a steep switchback at the base of the grade. The Texan downshifted, watching the Ford as it overtook them. The car had more speed, but the truck had more bulk. Starkey now used that bulk to his advantage by slanting to the left as the sedan came alongside.

The bottom loomed. Tires screaming, Starkey took the turn. For harrowing heartbeats, the big rig canted, and Starkey half expected them to go over.

"No!" Garth roared, the veins in his temples standing out in bold relief. He refused to be foiled, not when they were so close to fulfilling his destiny. He flattered himself that it was his sheer force of will that righted the rig.

The sedan had lost ground, but regained it quickly. The car clawed into the first switchback, shimmying madly.

"He's still with us, damn him!" Garth said bitterly. "Give me one of your pistols."

Starkey made no move to comply. It was a personal rule of his that no one else, absolutely no one at all, ever touched the Remingtons. They were his pride and joy, given to him by his father when he was only sixteen.

"Didn't you hear me?" Garth said, gesturing. "Hand me one of those ivory-handled beauties of yours, and I'll try to deter our friend."

"No."

"What?" Garth said, convinced he hadn't heard correctly. In the four years the Texan had been in his employ, Starkey had always done exactly as he was told. The gunman was the most dependable person Garth had ever met.

"You take the wheel and I'll stop him," Starkey proposed. To justify his request, he added, "I'm a better shot than you are. I have a much better chance of nailin' the bastard."

"True," Garth said. "But we can't hardly switch places now, can we?"

"Why not? It's the last thing the Fed would expect."

ANOTHER TURN SWEPT OUT of the darkness to meet the two vehicles. Bolan, trying his best to overtake the tanker again, had to drastically cut his speed when the truck veered into his path, nearly crushing the sedan's front end. He braked, churned the steering wheel and gave the engine gas.

Strangely, the tanker slowed briefly while swerving from side to side as if about to run off the highway. Stumped as to why, Bolan held back to avoid a collision. When the truck straightened, he shot forward, next to the tank.

Again the big rig slowed, this time to negotiate a hairpin turn. A face poked from the window, sneering hatred and triumph.

It was Trevor Garth, yet Bolan clearly remembered Garth being on the passenger's side just a short while ago. The madman and the Texan had switched places. There could only be one reason.

The soldier bent to peer up at the top of the tanker. Flame spurted at him, and lead bored through the windshield inches from his head. He cut his speed from fifty to thirty, then pulled forward until the sedan was directly behind the truck.

Drawing the Desert Eagle, Bolan looked for sign

of the gunman, but Starkey's black clothes made him invisible against the backdrop of black sky.

A Remington glinted dully above the metal rungs at the rear of the tank. It was all the warning Bolan had. He reduced speed just as the windshield was laced by pebbled fractures. The shots thumped into the seat beside him, so close that they sliced through the flap of his jacket.

Bolan had seen some exceptional marksmen in his time, yet it amazed him that anyone could shoot so accurately while atop a swaying truck in the dead of night. He veered to the left, then back to the right.

A shadow glided down the metal rungs to the back step. Bolan raised the Desert Eagle, banging off two shots that destroyed his own windshield. The howling wind whipped the razor-sharp glass against him, and he threw an arm over his eyes to protect them.

A Remington boomed. A lead slug snatched at his shoulder, plucking his jacket and shirt but not breaking the skin.

The soldier extended the big pistol, but his quick bead was hampered by a sudden lurch of the tanker. Trevor Garth wasn't half the driver the Texan was. The tanker pitched into the next turn at the wrong angle, and Garth nearly lost it going around.

A slug tore into the car's dashboard. Another clipped the top of the steering wheel and was deflected into the roof with a metallic clunk. Bolan hunched as low as he could and answered with a single shot that spanged off the tanker close to the Texan's elbow.

Yet another curve loomed ahead, foiling Bolan, who held his fire when the tanker went into a skid. He saw the Texan's look of surprise, saw the tall man clutch at the rungs.

The skid worsened. Garth had slid onto the gravel bordering the shoulder, and the tires on the passenger's side lost traction. Garth struggled to compensate, but the steering linkage was locked tight as the big rig left the roadway.

Trees slashed at the cab as the tanker plowed through a stand of saplings. Limbs shattered on the hood. Branches flailed the windshield. The truck bounced mightily. There was a jarring lurch and the tanker finally halted, the front end pointed at the highway.

Bolan had brought the car to a rocking stop at the edge of the road. Sliding out, he was fixing his sights on Starkey, who had been torn from his roost by a sturdy sapling. The Texan straightened, drawing his second pistol too swiftly for the eye to follow, pivoting as the barrel cleared his belt.

Bolan bent at the knees none too soon. The Remington cracked twice, the slugs whining off the sedan's hood.

Adopting a combat stance, Bolan took aim. Only

there was no one to aim at. Starkey had magically disappeared, while Trevor Garth had yet to show himself.

The soldier bent and sidestepped to the rear fender. He intently scoured the vegetation, then plunged into it half a stride ahead of a shot that whizzed through the space he had just occupied.

High weeds offered a temporary haven. Ears cocked, Desert Eagle molded to his palm, Bolan stood stock-still. Now it was a waiting game, a matter of which one of them made the first mistake.

Complicating matters was a stiff wind out of the northwest. Trees shook; brush bent; leaves constantly rustled. It was impossible to say which was the wind and which was caused by stealthy human movement.

A twig snapped on Bolan's right. He shifted, and was rewarded by twin blasts spaced so close together the sound rolled off across the Sierras as if they were one shot.

Throwing himself to the left, Bolan crawled to a log. From there he moved like a panther to a sequoia. The trunk was immense. Silently, he worked his way around it, facing the tree, the Desert Eagle in his right hand low at his side.

Something—a sixth sense perhaps—made Bolan wheel to the left. There had been no sound, no hint of stealthy movement, yet Ren Starkey stood eight feet away. The Texan had been gliding around the other side of the sequoia.

They saw each other at the same instant. Both held their weapons in the same position. For tense seconds they locked eyes and wills, and then two arms rose with lightning speed, two hands flashed up and out and the Desert Eagle and the Remington spoke.

The Desert Eagle fired first, its .44 Magnum slug smashing the gunfighter backward. Starkey's own shot kicked into the earth between them. Gamely, he tried to raise the six-shooter again.

Bolan centered on the man's sun-bronzed face, a pale swatch against the inky tapestry of darkness, and fired. Blood spurted as the Texan's feet left the ground. Starkey nearly did an ungainly somersault, thudding onto his side, the ivory-handled gun clamped in a viselike fingers that would never open again of their own accord.

"Mr. Starkey? Are you all right?"

Bolan didn't answer Trevor Garth's hail. Propping his back against the sequoia, he replaced the magazine. A peculiar whine fluttered eerily over the woodland.

Raindrops spattered the plant growth around him. Bolan began to move to the left when it occurred to him that the rain was strangely selective. The drops fell in his general vicinity but nowhere else.

"Here I am, Horatio! Come and get me!"

The taunt chilled Bolan to the core. It wasn't rain. It was TL-14 being sprayed by the man responsible for all the suffering and death. Automatically, Bolan held his breath. Thanks to the sequoia none of the chemical toxin landed very close to him, but all it would take was a vagrant drop borne by the gusting breeze, and he would be a lifeless husk in under ten seconds.

"WHERE ARE YOU, FED?" Trevor Garth yelled. "Afraid to show yourself?"

The Minuteman leader whirled to the left, certain he had glimpsed a moving figure. He pumped the lever, releasing a torrent of green that bathed trees and bushes and left them dripping wet.

Garth laughed. So what if he used a couple of hundred gallons? The tanker held thousands. He had plenty to spare for L.A. Losing a little would be worth it if he could finally dispose of the Fed.

The man had been a thorn in Garth's side since they'd first clashed. He had made a rare mistake in not killing the meddler when he had the chance.

Moving to the rear of the truck, Garth probed the shadows. Being shot didn't worry him. The Fed was bound to step into the open to do it, and the moment that happened, Garth would spray him.

No, shooting from ambush wasn't how the Feds did things. They had too much honor for dirty deeds like that. The thought jarred him. For someone to have a sense of honor, they had to be honorable. That meant he might be wrong about some of them, he might be—

"I'm over here."

Garth spun. The Fed stood near the car, holding the BAR. The autorifle thundered until the magazine went empty, but to Garth's astonishment all the shots were high. They struck the tanker, not him. Grinning, he went to throw the lever but froze when cool liquid drenched his hair and spilled over his face.

Sputtering, bewildered, Garth looked up. The BAR had torn a hole in the tank high up near the top, and TL-14 was spouting from the rent metal. He opened his mouth to scream, but the green watery mucus gushed down his throat.

The Executioner stepped back, watching as the toxic fountain tapered and died. Under it writhed the man who had plotted a second American Revolution, the mastermind who for all his brilliance had overlooked a very basic fact.

Despite her flaws, America was still the land of the free and the home of the brave. As long as her citizens had the right to vote, they could steer her course as they saw fit. The United States government truly was a government of the people, by the people and for the people.

Mack Bolan wouldn't have it any other way.

An old enemy poses a new threat....

JAMES AXLER
DEATH LANDS®
Gaia's Demise

Ryan Cawdor's old nemesis, Dr. Silas Jamaisvous, is behind a deadly new weapon that uses electromagnetic pulses to control the weather and the gateways, and even disrupts human thinking processes.

As these waves doom psi-sensitive Krysty, Ryan challenges Jamaisvous to a daring showdown for America's survival....

Book 2 in the Baronies Trilogy, three books that chronicle the strange attempts to unify the East Coast baronies—a bid for power in the midst of anarchy....

James Axler

OUTLANDERS™

ARMAGEDDON AXIS

What was supposed to be the seat of power after the nuclear holocaust, a vast installation inside Mount Rushmore—is a new powerbase of destruction. Kane and his fellow exiles venture to the hot spot, where they face an old enemy conspiring to start the second wave of Armageddon.